REVENGE

KERRY KAYA

Boldwood

First published in Great Britain in 2023 by Boldwood Books Ltd.

Copyright © Kerry Kaya, 2023

Cover Design by Colin Thomas

Cover Photography: iStock

Every effort has been made to obtain the necessary permissions with reference to copyright material, both illustrative and quoted. We apologise for any omissions in this respect and will be pleased to make the appropriate acknowledgements in any future edition.

A CIP catalogue record for this book is available from the British Library.

Paperback ISBN 978-1-80162-951-5

Large Print ISBN 978-1-80162-952-2

Hardback ISBN 978-1-80162-950-8

Ebook ISBN 978-1-80162-953-9

Kindle ISBN 978-1-80162-954-6

Audio CD ISBN 978-1-80162-945-4

MP3 CD ISBN 978-1-80162-946-1

Digital audio download ISBN 978-1-80162-948-5

Boldwood Books Ltd
23 Bowerdean Street
London SW6 3TN
www.boldwoodbooks.com

For Ella

1

It was the heat that Max Hardcastle registered first. A burning, blistering heat that left him with no other choice than to retreat several paces back. And then the smoke, so thick, black and acrid, that he could actually taste the charred debris in the back of his throat.

His chest wheezed; his lungs screamed out for oxygen, and slamming his hand over his mouth and nose, Max turned his face away from not only the searing heat but from what had also once been his car showroom.

Everything was gone: the cars, the office, his livelihood. Even the iron railings surrounding the property were blackened and buckled. In the distance he could hear the familiar wail of sirens, and he hurriedly took out his mobile phone.

Locating the messaging service, he pressed play and brought the device up to his ear. He hadn't recognised the caller's voice, nor did he know how the culprit responsible for burning down his business had gained access to his personal telephone number.

Max listened to the recorded message again. A part of him had believed the threat to be nothing other than idle, until he'd seen the billowing smoke high above the rooftops as he'd sped towards the showroom. It was in that instant he'd known his business was gone, and that just as the assailant had warned, there wouldn't be an inch of the forecourt left unscathed.

Anger began to build inside of him and, as two fire engines screeched to a halt just feet away from where he was standing, there were only two questions on Max's mind. Who was responsible and what could he have possibly done to make himself a target?

* * *

At her home in Dagenham, Essex, Tracey Tempest climbed out of the bath, and wrapping a large white, fluffy towel around herself, she padded out of the bathroom and into her bedroom. Hanging on the outside of the wardrobe door was one of her favourite outfits. A cream, linen shift dress that she would accessorise with a leopard print, chiffon scarf draped loosely around her slender neck. She had a particular penchant for leopard print and to finish off the outfit she had placed her trademark leopard print heels on the floor beside the wardrobe.

Despite the excitement that coursed through her veins for the briefest of moments, Tracey faltered. Had she done the right thing by agreeing to a fourth date with Max Hardcastle?

Not so long ago, Tracey would have baulked at the notion of even looking at another man, let alone actually enjoying dates with someone other than her husband, and yet here she was doing just that. Her husband Terry was gone, murdered by his business partner Kenny Kempton, and she was in the throes of a budding romance with one of Terry's oldest and closest friends, Max Hardcastle. For months Tracey had classed Max as a friend, a good friend – they got on well and enjoyed spending time in one another's company, and in the grand scheme of things that was all that mattered, wasn't it? At the end of the day, Max made her feel happy, an emotion she could never have envisaged for herself after Terry had been brutally gunned down at his own birthday party. Still to this day she could hear her screams, they had been animal-istic, so raw was her grief. In the aftermath of the shooting, her desperate attempts to keep her husband's heart beating had proven to be futile, and as Terry had taken his last breaths, Tracey had cradled him in her arms, begging him not to leave her. The injury he'd sustained had been too great, and the bullet had torn through his upper back, obliterating flesh, muscle and vital organs in its wake.

Her mind wandered to her two sons, Ricky and Jamie. Would they be happy for her, she wondered, or could her and Max's rela-tionship potentially tear her family apart? And more to the point, was she prepared to take the risk? Her sons meant the world to her, and even though they were adults now she would still lay her life on the line for them, as any good mother would.

It wasn't as though she had actively sought Max out and her sons were bound to understand this. They knew her well enough to know that she had been devoted to their father. Her boys also knew that when she had first met Max she had despised him on sight and that she had even accused him of having a hand in her husband's murder. But she couldn't have been more wrong and the false accusations she'd made still caused her cheeks to flush with shame. Max had only ever been a true friend to Terry and he had been there without question for both her and her sons after Terry's murder. And no matter how much she had tried to resist Max's charms, she couldn't help but feel drawn to him. He had a certain something about him. Not only was Max a handsome man, but he also had high morals; it was just one of the many traits that they shared. He was strong yet fair and he didn't take fools gladly.

Above all else, Tracey felt safe around him, and more importantly, she trusted him too, and after being married to a man who had lied to her throughout their entire marriage, Tracey was determined that going forward she wouldn't settle for anything less than honesty.

And perhaps that was where the problem lay. As much as her boys liked, trusted, and respected Max, they had adored their father. Growing up, both Ricky and Jamie had looked up to Terry, and after his death they were still finding it difficult to come to terms with the fact that their dad hadn't been the man he'd portrayed himself to be. No, in reality her husband had been a liar, a cheat, a bully, and even worse than that he had forced women into prostitution, something she and her boys could never forgive him for.

An hour later, Tracey had applied her make up, dried her hair, sprayed just the right amount of perfume behind her ears and across her wrists, then dressed. Slipping on her heels, she took a quick glance at her watch. It was almost time to leave and the familiar sense of butterflies began to flutter within her tummy. As much as she chastised herself, Tracey couldn't help but laugh out loud. She should know better at her age; after all, she was a grown woman fast approaching her fiftieth birthday, not a school girl longing after her first crush.

Collecting her handbag, Tracey paused. Terry's car key still hung on a brass hook beside the front door. It wasn't often that she drove her late husband's car, yet there was something about the Audi that she loved. It was the power she supposed, not to mention there was no denying that it was a beautiful car, the gun metal grey paintwork sleek and shiny. It was the kind of car that was guaranteed to turn heads, something that had once embarrassed Tracey, but now she embraced the car's elegance and luxurious interior and didn't blame those who gave the car a second glance.

A smile drifted across Tracey's face, and snatching the car key off the hook, she clasped it tight in her fist. Bugger it, she decided. Terry had no need for the Audi; it wasn't as though he was going to miraculously rise from the dead, was it? So she may as well make full use of the car. Where was the point in leaving something so beautiful to rot and turn to rust on the drive?

Tracey stepped outside the house and as she made her way towards the car her mobile phone began to ring. On seeing Max's name flash up on the screen, Tracey beamed. But as Max spoke, Tracey's grin froze and with the phone cradled between her ear and shoulder she unlocked the car. 'I'm on my way,' she told him before ending the call and flinging both her handbag and mobile phone onto the passenger seat.

As she drove towards Southend-on-Sea, concern was at the forefront of Tracey's mind. Had the burning of the car showroom simply been an accident or was there something more sinister at hand? As soon as the thought popped into her mind her forehead furrowed and she shook her head. Why on earth would someone have deliberately set the car dealership alight? The very notion seemed ludicrous to her. Admittedly Max was no angel. After all, he'd served two prison sentences, the first for murder, and the second for ABH, but he'd put the past behind him, and in recent years had turned his life around. Fair enough, one or two of the cars that he'd sold on to private buyers in the past may not have exactly been kosher, as her sons so eloquently put it, but as of now the cars on the forecourt were legitimate, or at least this was what Max and the boys had reassured her whenever she had enquired as to where the cars had come from.

A heavy sense of foreboding slid though Tracey's veins and pushing her foot down on the accelerator, she could only hope and pray that the damage to the car showroom wasn't as bad as Max had first indicated and even more than that, she hoped that there was an innocent explanation for the fire – perhaps faulty wiring or maybe even a kids prank gone wrong. The alternative was too much for her to even think about, and the last thing any of them needed was to be embroiled in yet another active feud, one that could potentially put everyone she cared about at risk.

2

By the time Tracey pulled up outside the car showroom forty minutes later, the fire had all but been contained. Only the deep orange glow from small, dotted burning heaps remained as wisps of white smoke drifted up from both the charred remains of the burnt out cars and what had once been the office.

Tracey climbed out of the Audi, and slamming her hand over her mouth, she took a sharp intake of breath, her eyes wide and horror stricken. The damage was so much worse than she could have ever imagined, and from where she was standing it was more than obvious that there was nothing salvageable, at least nothing of any value anyway. Even the portable cabin that served as an office had burnt down to its foundations. As far as she could tell, everything that Max had worked so hard to build had been destroyed.

Her gaze searched him out. Broad shouldered and standing at over six feet, he wasn't exactly hard to miss. With his back turned away from her she took a moment to study him. The car showroom had been Max's pride and joy, and despite owning a number of bookmakers, he spent most of his day at the car lot, preferring to leave the running of the betting shops to her sons. As if sensing her presence Max turned around and, making eye contact, he gave a helpless shrug.

The look on Max's face was almost enough to break Tracey's heart, and as she walked into his arms, she held him to her, tight.

'I don't understand,' she choked out. 'How could this have happened?'

Max gave a second shrug, and stalling for time, he turned back to look at the damage. 'I don't know, darling,' he finally answered. He shot a surreptitious glance towards the attending fire crew and police officers and raised his voice slightly. 'Maybe one of the cars had a fault. I mean, you do hear about these things happening, don't you? A car spontaneously bursting into flames, or even the manufacturer recalling a series of cars; it happens all the time.'

Tracey narrowed her eyes. She may have been green around the edges but she was no fool and as such wouldn't be treated like one. Fair enough, she was no expert but even she could see that the fire hadn't been started by a problem with one of the cars; the damage was too extensive for a start. She opened her mouth to answer when out of the corner of her eye she spotted her eldest son's car approaching, which not only forced her to snap her lips closed but also to reluctantly step out of Max's arms.

'Fuck me,' Jamie Tempest exclaimed as he jumped out of his elder brother's car and brought his hands up to his head. 'How did this happen?'

Max shook his head, and slipping his mobile phone back into his pocket, he crossed his arms over his chest. 'Like I was just saying to your mum,' he said, nodding towards Tracey. 'There must have been a fault with one of the cars.'

Tracey's eldest son Ricky narrowed his eyes and turned to look at his mother, a puzzled expression sweeping over his face. 'Mum,' he asked, 'what are you doing here?'

A sliver of fear ran down the length of Tracey's spine. This wasn't exactly how she'd intended for her sons to find out about her relationship with Max. No, if she and Max had any kind of future together then she wanted to sit her boys down and then break the news to them as gently as she could. 'What do you think I'm doing here?' she snapped back. 'Max called me about the fire and I came over straight away.' Tracey's cheeks were flushed pink; she was sure that her son would see straight through her lies.

Satisfied with his mother's answer, Ricky turned back to assess the damage, oblivious to the knowing look that Tracey and Max shared.

'And you reckon all of this was caused by a fault with one of the cars?' As he jerked his head towards the forecourt, Jamie's voice held a note of suspicion.

Max raised his eyebrows and indicated to the fire crew and in particular the police officers. 'What other explanation could there be?'

Taking the hint on board, Jamie nodded. He was astute enough to know when to keep schtum and seeing as the old bill were crawling all over the place, now was as good a time as any to keep his mouth firmly shut.

'Well.' Inhaling a deep breath, Tracey gave a stilted smile and gestured towards the damage. 'It's a small consolation, I know, but at least everything is insured.'

An awkward silence fell. She looked between her two sons and Max and her heart sank down to the pit of her stomach. 'Please tell me that there is insurance?'

Max lifted his eyebrows and sighed. 'Some,' he mumbled with a glance towards where the office had once been situated.

Following his gaze, Tracey closed her eyes in distress. 'What do you mean by some?' she asked through gritted teeth.

'The office, and a few of the cars,' Max admitted.

'A few.' Tracey's eyes flew open and she placed her hand upon her chest. 'How many cars exactly are we talking about?'

'Does it matter, Mum?' Jamie implored. 'It's not going to change anything, is it?'

'Of course it matters,' Tracey spat. 'How many cars are insured?'

Max averted his gaze. 'Ten.' He swallowed deeply then gave a small shrug. 'Maybe eight, I can't remember the exact number.'

Tracey's jaw dropped. 'Eight,' she cried. 'But' – she turned to look at the burnt out wreckages, disbelief etched across her face – 'there must have been at least fifteen cars here.'

Glancing towards Ricky and Jamie, Max rubbed at the nape of his neck. The action wasn't lost on Tracey; if anything, all it served to do was prove that he was guilty of lying to her, that the cars weren't being sold legally.

'Oh, I see,' Tracey retorted. 'I should have seen this coming, considering your track record,' she spat. 'The rest weren't legal were they?'

'Keep your voice down,' Max hissed, indicating to a uniformed police officer standing just several feet away from them.

Incensed, Tracey motioned towards what was left of the car lot. 'And I suppose you expect me to believe that all of this was caused by a fault, that it was an accident? Do I actually look that stupid,' she growled. 'What is this, some kind of insurance scam?'

Jamie rolled his eyes. 'The cars would have had to have been insured in the first place for it to be scam, Mum,' he mumbled.

Snapping her gaze towards her youngest son, Tracey glowered. 'Well come on,' she demanded. 'Fill me in on all the gory details.'

Digging his hand into his pocket, Max pulled out the keys to his apartment. 'We'll talk about this later,' he said, his voice low as he slipped a spare key off the keyring then held out the bunch of keys. 'Just go to my place and wait for me there, all of you,' he added as an afterthought as he turned to look at the two brothers.

'You can bet your life we will talk about this.' Tracey bristled as she snatched the keys out of Max's hand. 'And believe me,' she said over her shoulder as she stormed back towards the Audi. 'You've got some explaining to do, and that includes the both of you too,' she said, glaring at her sons.

* * *

To say that Tracey was livid would be an understatement and as she stalked the length of Max's lounge she pursed her lips together. So much for honesty, she thought to herself. Her and Max were only four dates into their relationship and already he'd been lying to her.

'Did you know about the cars being stolen?' she demanded of her sons.

'The cars weren't stolen,' Jamie sighed. 'They just weren't put through the books.'

'Oh, so that makes it all right then,' Tracey cried, throwing her arms up into the air. 'Knocking the tax man is just as illegal, you know.'

Ricky rubbed at his temples. 'It's not a big deal, Mum,' he said, giving a nonchalant shrug. 'Everyone does it.'

'Not a big deal.' Tracey rounded on her eldest son. 'This was meant to be a fresh start for us.' She swallowed deeply as memories of her husband's betrayal sprang to her mind. Terry had dealt with stolen goods before moving on to pimping out innocent women. Was that the road Max and her sons were headed down? Was history about to repeat itself? She gave an involuntary shiver.

Over her dead body would she allow her boys to take the same path that their father had walked; it was bad enough they were carbon copies of her husband. Every time she looked at her sons' handsome faces it was as if she were looking at Terry himself, as though he were mocking her naivety and her stupidness from beyond the grave. And she had been naive when it came to her husband. Terry could have told her the sky was pink and purple and she would have believed him. Perhaps she should have seen it coming; after all, Ricky and Jamie were Tempests through and through and they had more of their father in them than she cared to admit. And as for Max, it was no secret that he'd once served time for killing someone. Handed down a life sentence as a teenager, he was still on licence and could be recalled back to prison the very moment he put a foot wrong. The burning question was: would he drag her sons down with him?

'Mum, for fuck's sake,' Jamie remarked. 'Will you just chill out? It's like Ricky said, it's not a big deal. Dad was selling stolen cars for years and it never did him any harm did it, the old bill were clueless, and it's not like the cars were even knocked off, Max just didn't declare them, that's all. It's no biggie, and it's hardly something the filth would be interested in.'

Tracey's heart began to pump faster. 'Don't,' she warned, pointing a stiff finger towards her youngest son, 'try to treat me like I'm a bloody fool. And as for your father...' She snapped her lips closed, not wanting to say the words out loud. Terry's deceit and subsequent death was still too raw for both her and her sons to even think about, let alone comprehend.

'As for Dad, what?' Jamie growled, his back instantly up at the mention of his father.

Coming to a halt, Tracey glanced anxiously at her watch. 'Where the hell is Max?' she asked in an attempt to change the subject. Three hours they had been waiting for the man in question to return home. A cold chill crept down her spine. Could the police have had their suspicions that the cars hadn't been declared and hauled him into the police station for questioning? Maybe he'd been charged with trying to evade the tax man and was already on his way back to prison?

'Answer the question, Mum,' Jamie said, a steely glint in his blue eyes.

Tracey turned to look at her youngest son, and seeing the hurt spread across his face, she sighed. 'Nothing, it doesn't matter.'

Jamie was about to protest when Ricky gave a slight shake of his head. 'Leave it, bruv,' he said.

'Yeah but...'

'I said leave it,' Ricky growled. He took out his mobile phone and noted the time. 'Mum's right, Max should have been back hours ago.'

Tracey opened her mouth to agree when the sound of a key turning in a lock followed by the front door gently closing made all three of them turn expectantly towards the lounge door. Moments later, Max strode into the room, his strides long and his face set like thunder.

Not only did a layer of dark stubble cover Max's clenched jaw but he also looked tired, Tracey noted, if the subtle hint of dark shadows underneath his eyes was anything to go by. Not that she felt much sympathy for him at this precise moment in time. No, she was so angry with both him and her sons that she could practically taste her fury.

Getting up from the sofa, Ricky spread open his arms. 'What the fuck is going on? You know as well as I do that that fire was no accident. Someone torched the gaff, and did a pretty good job of it while they were at it. There's fuck all left, at least nothing that can be saved.'

Without saying a word, Max threw the spare key onto the

coffee table then took out his mobile phone. Pressing play on the recorded message, he stared down at the device as though the answers he so desperately craved would suddenly become clear to him, as though the more he listened to the recording, the sooner the identity of the caller would become apparent.

Tracey, Ricky, and Jamie inched closer and, as the caller began to speak, they craned their necks to listen.

'What is this?' Tracey gasped once the recording had finished playing.

'Play it again,' Ricky interrupted.

Max pressed play a second time and once again the caller's voice filtered into the air. The threat was clear for them all to hear, despite the fact the culprit had gone to great lengths to disguise his voice.

'Does anyone recognise the bastard?' Max asked.

All three of them shook their heads.

'It's too muffled,' Jamie remarked as he rubbed at his chin.

Sighing, Max nodded in defeat.

'Why would someone have done this?' Tracey's anger was quickly replaced by fear. The caller hadn't only made a threat but he had actually followed through and decimated the car lot.

'This isn't a lone wolf,' Ricky said with a shake of his head. 'To have done that much damage to the showroom, there must have been more than one culprit. My guess is Dixon,' Ricky said, turning to look at Max. 'You're his closest competition and knowing that sly fucker, he'd do anything to wipe out the business. It makes sense. With you out of the equation, there isn't another car dealership around here for miles.'

Max's face contorted with anger. From the very moment he'd received the threat, Dickie Dixon had been one of the first names conjured up in his mind, too. They'd had more than one run-in over the years, and some of those run-ins had turned pretty ugly, not that Max considered his business to be an actual threat to Dixon considering Dickie only dealt with what Max would class as second-hand runarounds, the majority of which would be better off in a scrap yard rather than on the road.

Tracey's eyes widened, and placing a hand on her chest, she nodded towards the mobile phone. 'He didn't just specify the car lot. He said that he plans to destroy you and everything you hold dear.'

Max looked down at the phone again, his forehead furrowing.

'Oh fuck,' Ricky exclaimed. 'You know what that means, don't you?'

'No,' Tracey answered with a bewildered shake of her head.

'The bookies. Think about it,' he said, pointing to his temple. 'He's going to go after the betting shops next.'

His expression hardening, Max snatched back the spare key from the coffee table then headed for the front door with Tracey, Ricky and Jamie hot on his heels. 'I'm going to kill him,' he roared. 'And believe me, when I get my hands on the no-good bastard, I will destroy him over this.'

* * *

Ten minutes later, Max brought his car to a skidding halt outside the larger of the bookmakers he owned in Leigh-on-Sea, Essex, just a short, five-minute drive away from the car lot.

Throwing open the car door, Max jumped out. He let out a breath and dragged a hand across his clammy forehead. Much to his relief there was no tell-tale smoke billowing from the metal grills that secured the premises, nor any visible signs of a break-in.

He glanced towards the pub on the corner of the street. The throng of patrons spilling out on to the pavement was somewhat comforting. Surely no one would be stupid enough to attempt to burn the property down when they could be clearly seen, and perhaps even identified?

'I'll check around the back,' Ricky volunteered.

'Yeah, I'll come with you,' Jamie said as he shoved his hands into his pockets and made after his brother.

Max watched them go, his steely gaze travelling the length of the parade of shops, on the lookout for anything out of the ordinary. Were they being watched? Were the culprits getting a kick out of seeing his panic first-hand? He ran his tongue over his teeth, more than aware that they had played right into the bastards' hands and were giving them exactly what they wanted. But what was the alternative? Max mused. To sit back and wait for everything he owned to be destroyed? No, Max wasn't made that way; he'd never been in the habit of allowing someone to get the better of him in the past and he sure as hell didn't intend to start now.

Moments later, the two brothers returned.

'Well?' Max called out to them. 'Did you find anything?'

'Nah nothing.' Ricky shrugged. 'And from what I can make out, it doesn't look as though anything has been tampered with either.'

Chewing on the inside of his cheek, Max nodded. It was exactly as he'd suspected. The caller had chosen his words carefully and as a result, sent them on a wild goose chase, or at least this was what Max hoped, anyway.

'So what do we do now?' Tracey asked as she looked between her sons and Max.

Taking one final look around him, Max nodded towards where they had parked the cars. 'Go back to my place,' he said, pulling out his car keys. 'I'll be back soon.'

'What do you mean?' Tracey asked, her eyes widening. 'Where are you going?'

'It doesn't matter,' Max answered as he ushered Tracey towards her car. 'Like I said, I won't be long.'

'Do you want us to come with you?' Ricky said, jerking his head towards Jamie.

Max looked the brothers over. He had to admit the added muscle could come in handy, especially if he had a welcoming committee waiting for him, not that he actually needed them or anyone else for that matter to fight his battles, he was more than capable of taking care of himself, a fact that they were all well aware of. 'Yeah.' He nodded. 'You might as well come along for the ride.'

'No,' Tracey gasped, her skin turning ashen as she watched helplessly as her sons climbed into Max's car. 'You're going after Dixon, aren't you?' she cried.

Without answering the question, Max bundled Tracey into the Audi. 'Just go back to my place and wait for us there.'

About to protest, Tracey made to climb out of the car before Max pushed her gently back inside. 'Tracey,' he said, his voice brooking no arguments. 'For once in your life, will you just do as you are told without arguing? Go back to my place and wait for us. Like I said, we won't be long.'

'But...'

'No but's,' Max growled over his shoulder as he stormed back to his car. 'And make sure that you lock the front door behind you.'

* * *

By the time Max pulled into the car park of The Jolly Cricketers pub situated on the A127, near Basildon, Essex, his anger was so tangible that he was all but ready to commit murder.

'How do you even know that Dixon was behind the arson attack?' Jamie asked as he looked up from his mobile phone to peer out of the car windscreen. 'It could have been just about anyone.'

'There's no one else it could be,' Max answered as he surveyed Dickie Dixon's red Jaguar that was parked just feet away from them. 'From day one this bastard has done nothing but cause me grief. He would have got a kick out of this; he's warped in the head.'

Jamie didn't look so sure and as his forehead furrowed, he glanced towards his brother. 'Yeah but...'

Ricky rolled his eyes. 'Keep up bruv,' he said, gesturing towards the mobile phone that as of late appeared to be glued to his brother's hand. 'Dixon owns a car dealership just up the road from Max's.'

'Yeah, and?' Jamie frowned even further. Fair enough, he could see where Ricky and Max were coming from; it was no secret that Dickie Dixon was a major pain in the arse, the type of man who was more often than not tolerated rather than well-liked and respected. But despite his flaws he was still a face in his own right, albeit on a lower level than say Max for example. It would also be fair to say that Dickie went out of his way to cause ructions, and one of his favourite pastimes was to belittle those around him, but to commit arson, nah, Jamie just couldn't see it. For a start, Dixon wouldn't have the bottle; he was all mouth and no trousers, everyone knew that, and that went for his two sons as well. Barry and Marc Dixon might walk around as though they owned the town, but their arseholes soon started flapping the minute someone stood up to them and Jamie knew that for a fact. Just a few months earlier, he and Ricky had got into an altercation with the Dixon brothers and the Dixons had soon back tracked on their threats once they had realised exactly who they were dealing with.

'Who is Dixon's main competitor?' Ricky continued, fast on his way to losing patience with his younger brother. He waited a few moments for his question to sink in then jerked his head towards Max. 'With Max out of the way,' he said, spreading open his arms,

'Dixon's shitty little car lot is the only car dealership around here for... I dunno.' He shrugged and looked across to Max for confirmation. 'It's got to be at least two or three miles hasn't it?'

'Three,' Max confirmed.

'There you go, three miles. So it stands to reason that Dixon would be high up on the list of suspects; he's got the most to gain from Max being out of business.'

'Yeah I suppose so,' Jamie conceded, still somewhat unconvinced as they climbed out of the car and made their way towards the pub.

Before they had even stepped two feet inside the public bar, the sound of Dickie Dixon's laughter filled the air. It was a distinctive laugh resembling that of a hyena, the kind of laugh that grated heavily on Max's nerves and was more than a good enough reason for him to smash his fist into Dixon's face, not that he actually needed a valid excuse; there was enough bad blood between the two men to warrant a kicking of sorts.

As they followed the sound, soon enough the man himself came into view. Surrounded by his cronies, Dickie Dixon was standing at the bar. He was in his late fifties and had a slim build and ferret-like features, his once dark blond hair that was peppered with grey was stained with nicotine, giving it more of a dirty yellow appearance and his cheeks and hooked nose were riddled with tiny red, thread veins that brought further testament to the fact that he was a creature of habit and that he liked to prop up the bar on a nightly basis. He was decked out in grey trousers that had been washed and pressed so often they looked greasy and a white cotton shirt, a heavy gold signet ring glistened on his pinkie finger as he lifted an ever present cigarette up to his thin lips.

Max charged forward and before Dickie could even comprehend what was about to go down, Max had slammed him into a wooden pillar with so much force that the cigarette Dickie had been holding slipped from his fingers, scattering burning embers and ash across the front of his shirt.

'You no-good, snidey cunt,' Max roared, one hand wrapped around Dickie's throat, the other clenched into a tight fist. 'My business,' he spat into Dickie's face, spraying him in spittle as he did so. 'Everything is gone, the whole fucking shebang wiped out, all because of you.'

Dickie blinked rapidly, a mixture of both confusion and shock etched across his face. 'What business?' he managed to splutter out, his cheeks turning even redder as his startled gaze darted around him in the hope for some backup, preferably in the form of his two sons. 'I don't know anything about your business, you mad fucker. Why the fuck would I?' A craftiness settled in his eyes. To see Hardcastle looking so rattled was the equivalent of all of his Christmases coming at once. 'More's the fucking pity because there is nothing I would love more than to see you brought down.'

It was the exact answer Max had been anticipating. For all his faults, even Dickie wasn't foolish enough to admit to having first-hand knowledge regarding the arson attack. Pulling back his fist, Max threw the first in a series of punches and as blood exploded from the older man's nose, Dickie gave a loud whelp and brought his hands up to his face.

'My nose,' he shrieked, spitting out the blood that trickled into his mouth. 'You've broke my fucking nose.'

Anger creased Max's face. Once he'd finished with him, a broken nose would be the least of Dickie's problems. 'I'm going to destroy you over this,' he seethed. 'And believe me, this day has been a long time coming. You and that big trap of yours have finally gone too far.' Beginning to throw punch after punch, he was oblivious to the startled screams around him. 'I know it was you,' he spat between each ferocious jab. 'You did this.'

Underneath the blows that rained down upon him, Dickie dropped unceremoniously to the floor, and curling himself into a foetal position, he placed his arms protectively over his head. His face was bloody and already beginning to swell from the brutal assault.

Max lifted his foot ready to deliver a sickening kick to Dickie's head when Ricky pulled back on Max's arm, forcing him to a halt.

'It wasn't him mate.' He gestured down at Dickie's semi-conscious form then leaned in closer to speak privately in Max's ear. 'If it was him, he would have at least smirked or done something to give the game away. You know what a slimy little fucker he is; he would have got a kick out of this.' He shook his head, his eyes silently warning Max to step away before he could cause any more damage or maybe even go that one step further and kill Dixon in a pub full of witnesses.

Breathing heavily, Max narrowed his eyes, his foot still suspended in mid-air. It had to be Dickie; everything pointed to him, didn't it? It wasn't the first time they had almost come to blows, their businesses or rather the proximity of the businesses the main cause of their conflict. That and Dixon's big mouth that he had a nasty habit of running off at every available opportunity.

'Ricky's right,' Jamie added. 'He didn't have a clue what you were talking about; it's not him.'

As he looked around the pub at the stunned faces staring back at him, Max placed his foot back on the floor and wiped his hand over his jaw. Smeared across his knuckles was Dickie's blood, and as the iron scent filled Max's nostrils, he hastily wiped the back of his hands down his blood splattered jeans in an attempt to rid himself of not only the sticky substance but also the evidence of the brutal assault he'd carried out. Backing away slightly, he looked towards the bar staff. 'No need to call in the old bill,' he said in a warning, his menacing stare going back to patrons. 'We're leaving.'

Outside in the car park, Max blew out his cheeks, the muscles across his shoulder blades still rigid, and as his breath streamed out ahead of him, he was barely conscious of the bitter cold wind that blew around them. He wanted to kick himself for wading in without getting his facts straight first; it was a rookie move, one that he'd warned Ricky and Jamie about time after time until he was blue in the face, not that they ever listened to a word he said, that much was evident considering the number of scraps they got into on a weekly basis. He turned his head to look back at the pub. Still, the burning question remained: if it wasn't Dickie, then who else could have that much of a problem with him that they would resort to burning down the showroom?

'So what do we do now then?' Ricky asked as he looked between his brother and Max.

Met with silence, Ricky nudged Jamie in the ribs. Not only was his younger brother preoccupied with his phone yet again but the sickening, soppy grin plastered across Jamie's face was beginning to royally get right on Ricky's tits. 'Are you actually with us tonight?' he barked out as he craned his neck to get a better view of the phone screen in an attempt to see what it was his brother was so fascinated by.

'What?' Looking up, Jamie ever so slightly leaned back before slipping the device into his pocket, out of his brother's view.

Ricky narrowed his eyes and, giving Jamie a hard glare, he crossed his arms over his chest and shook his head. 'What the fuck is with you lately? You're acting weird.'

Before they could start bickering like a couple of kids, Max held up his hand to quieten them down. 'We go home,' he sighed, beginning to wearily make his way to the car.

'Yeah, but...' Ricky turned to look back at the pub. 'What about

Dixon? You did him over like a fucking kipper; that's not something you're going to be able to brush under the carpet. And you know as well as I do what he's like; he's got a big trap on him and once he starts giving it all the mouth, this is going to cause us untold grief.'

Max sighed. He didn't need Ricky to tell him that his actions were going to bring him a shit load of trouble, he'd already worked that much out for himself. Not that Dickie Dixon or his sons were worth him losing any sleep over. 'I need to think the situation through.' In the circumstances, what else could he do? He had a nasty feeling that the real culprits weren't done with him yet, not by a long chalk. The arson attack on the car lot was just the beginning, a taster of what was to come, he could feel it in his bones.

'But what if they call in the old bill?' Jamie asked. 'There's bound to be CCTV; you'll be carted off to nick again.'

'They won't,' Max answered with an air of confidence.

Jamie lifted his eyebrows and, giving a shake of his head, he caught his brother's eyes. 'The boozer was packed solid; someone's bound to open their trap, you know they are.'

'Trust me, no one will call the filth.'. Unlocking the car, Max pulled open the door and took a seat behind the wheel all the while keeping his gaze firmly focused on the entrance to the pub. 'They wouldn't fucking dare.'

Barry Dixon was the image of his father Dickie. The hooked nose and premature greying hair more than a clear indicator that he was a Dixon. It would be fair to say that he wasn't a handsome man, not that this had ever held Barry back when it came to the ladies. His name alone was enough to guarantee that women fell at his feet, a fact that he had used to his advantage more than once over the years.

As he and his younger brother Marc charged into the pub, a hushed silence fell over the bar, the patrons all keen to see how Dickie's offspring were going to react to the pounding he'd received.

'Who did this?' On locating his father at the far end of the pub, spittle gathered at the corners of Barry's snarled lips, his hard stare boring into Dickie's skull.

Dickie waved the question away. He'd always considered himself to be a tough man and the fact Max Hardcastle had pretty much knocked him off his feet with one punch wasn't something he wanted broadcasted to the world. Not only was his pride severely dented, but his reputation was also hanging precariously in the balance. He'd underestimated Hardcastle, had wrongly assumed that the fact he himself was widely known as a hard fucker would have been enough to make Max retreat. The last thing he had ever expected was for Max to actually lay into him. After all, word out on the street was that Max had gone soft, that after his second stint inside he'd come out a changed man, and even more than that, Dickie hadn't expected his legs to give way nor subsequently find himself laid out on the floor, his nose pissing out blood and his jaw smarting from the right hooks he'd received. He took a sip of whisky, making sure to keep his hand from shaking as he picked up the glass.

'Dad,' Dickie's youngest son Marc barked out. 'Answer the question. Who did this to you?'

Holding up his hand, Dickie had never felt more ashamed. 'It was nothing,' he answered dismissively, his cheeks turning a bright shade of red. 'Just drop it.'

'No Dad,' Marc hissed as he looked his father over. His old man had always been a strong man but looking at him now as he sipped at a whisky, Marc couldn't help but notice how his father had seemingly aged overnight. The truth was, Dickie was no longer a spring chicken, his lined face a dead giveaway to the fact that he wasn't far off from collecting his free bus pass, not that Dickie would actually be seen dead using public transport, especially seeing as his usual mode of transport was a Jag. 'Give me a name Dad.'

Dickie looked up, a familiar craftiness settling in his eyes. He had been wronged after all; why should Hardcastle get off scot-free for humiliating him in front of the entire boozer. 'It was Max Hardcastle.' He screwed up his face, the anger he felt clear for them all to see. 'The bastard made a beeline for me the minute he walked through the door and before I knew what was happening, he'd lamped me one.' Making a point of touching his swollen jaw, Dickie dipped his head. 'I just can't get my head around it,' he cried. 'There was me, minding my own business, looking forward to an evening out with my pals and then bang.' He clenched his fist and mimicked throwing a punch. 'The next thing I knew, I was on the deck and the fucker was still swinging for me. I think the cunt got a couple of kicks in too, and as for the other two little bastards, the Tempest brothers, I think they landed one or two punches as well. How could I fight back? It was three against one.' He shifted his weight and grimaced as pain tore through his rib cage, all the while hoping that his little act was enough for his sons to believe he'd been outnumbered.

'I should have known those muppets would be involved,' Barry growled, sharing a knowing glance with his brother.

'Well don't you worry Dad.' Marc gripped his father by the shoulder, his voice loud enough for the entire pub to hear. 'We'll make sure that they pay for this. No one whacks my old man and gets away with it.'

It took all of Dickie's effort not to smirk and, puffing his chest out with a sense of pride, he sipped at his drink. Of course his boys would take care of business; in all reality, he hadn't expected anything different from them, and good luck to Hardcastle and the Tempest brothers because with his sons on the warpath they were going to need all the luck they could get.

3

Early the next morning, Max wearily climbed out of bed. After tossing and turning through the night, he'd barely had a wink of sleep, and he had a sneaking suspicion that the only reason he was still able to function or think coherently was because of the adrenalin that ran through his veins.

In the kitchen he flicked the switch for the kettle to boil, then, leaning against the granite worktop, he wearily looked down at his grazed knuckles before closing his eyes and exhaling through his nose. He'd been so sure that Dixon had been the one responsible; everything had pointed to him, hadn't it? Not that he could say he was sorry for the mistake he'd made, Dickie had been asking for a pounding for months, years even, and as far as Max was concerned, the beating had been warranted. His only mistake was taking his fists to Dickie in a public place. Instead, he should have dragged the bastard out of the pub, bundled him into the boot of the car and then driven him out to the woods or somewhere else secluded before laying into him.

Once the kettle had reached boiling point, he heaped a large spoonful of coffee into a mug, added the hot water and a dash of milk then took a seat at the chrome and glass dining table. As he sipped on his coffee, he glanced in the direction of the bedroom where Tracey was sleeping. Despite them talking, or rather arguing, into the early hours of the morning, she was still angry with him. Not that he entirely blamed her; she had every right to be furious, he had lied to her after all, or as he liked to think of it, he hadn't exactly been truthful. Not that Tracey was able to differentiate between the two; as far as she was concerned he'd been deceitful, and he had been, he supposed. Only in his defence, it was more of a little white lie, rather than some great big whopper of a story that he'd concocted. Regardless of its origins though, it was still a lie nonetheless, one that he'd thought he would never be caught out on, and he wouldn't have been if the fire hadn't forced him to come clean and admit that some of the cars he sold weren't strictly legitimate.

But at the end of the day he'd never professed to being squeaky clean and Tracey knew him well enough to know that he didn't hold down a nine-to-five job. He was hardly going to stroll out of prison and find work in a bank, was he? No, he was better suited to robbing banks rather than sitting behind a desk counting out a customer's money. It was who he was; he couldn't change his mindset even if he wanted to. As for the car lot, the majority of the vehicles that passed through his hands would never even make it on to the forecourt. A few he would sell on to private buyers who knew exactly what they were buying and the rest he sold to chop shops. In other words, the cars would be stripped down and the parts would then be sold on. It was a lucrative business, one that over the years had earned him a great deal of money.

Wrapping his hands around the mug, he relaxed back on the chair. Over and over again he'd replayed the recorded message, and still he was no nearer to discovering the identity of the bastards who'd burnt down his business. Jamie was right; the recording was too muffled. The only sure thing he'd been able to determine was that the caller was definitely male, not that this fact was of any real help to him.

For most of the night, Max had been racking his brain for a reason as to why he'd been targeted, and no matter which way he looked at the situation, nothing made sense to him. Why would someone want to destroy him? He may have been what was considered a face in the criminal underworld, and it would even be fair to say that he had a reputation that was highly warranted, but to his knowledge he didn't have any active enemies, at least, none that he was aware of anyway. Well perhaps there was one, his former pal, and he used that term loosely seeing as he and Kenny Kempton had never been what he would call close mates to begin with. Even as kids they'd had a turbulent relationship, and it was only because of Kenny's persistent goading that Max had finally snapped and battered to death the man his mother had lived with, the same man who had put his mother on the game and forced her to sell her body down at the docks.

And Kenny certainly did have a motive seeing as it had been Max, with the help of Tracey and her sons, who'd brought down the prostitution ring that Kenny, Terry Tempest, and the Murphy family had been running. But even so, it was impossible. Kenny was banged up. How on earth would he have been able to orchestrate the arson attack from inside Belmarsh Prison? It wasn't as though Kenny had many allies; his business partners were either dead or were also serving lengthy custodial sentences, and he couldn't see the Murphy family lifting a finger to help Kenny out anytime soon; by all accounts, they despised Kenny almost as much as Max himself did.

'I take it you couldn't sleep either?' As she leant against the kitchen door frame, Tracey's arms were crossed over her chest.

Max looked up; he'd been so deep in thought that he hadn't heard her get out of bed. 'No, not really, how about you?' As soon as the question left his mouth Max inwardly groaned. He hated the fact that they were tiptoeing around one another. It wasn't as though they were strangers any more. Long before he'd developed any romantic feelings towards her, they had been friends, close friends. That wasn't to say that he hadn't recognised Tracey as being a beautiful woman from the very first moment he'd clapped eyes on her because he had, but she'd also been grieving at the time, not that his childhood friend had ever deserved her tears. No, Terry Tempest had cheated on her throughout their entire marriage; he'd shagged anything that moved and had often joked that the only stipulation he had was that the woman had a pulse and her own teeth. It was only by some miracle that Tracey herself had never cottoned on to her husband's womanising ways.

'Coffee?' he asked. 'The kettle hasn't long boiled.'

For the briefest of moments Tracey faltered and, sensing her hesitation, Max pulled out the chair beside him. 'Come on darling,' he said, his voice gentle. 'Enough of the silent treatment. You're pissed off and I get it; I wasn't entirely truthful about the cars and I should have been. At least I'm man enough to hold my hands up and admit I was in the wrong. I'm sorry, okay.'

Tracey lifted her eyebrows and let out a bitter laugh. 'You've got some bloody front if you think that some half arsed apology is going to cut it with me. I'm not some blonde bimbo, you know, and I'm certainly not going to fall at your feet and blindly believe every word that comes out of your mouth. That might be the type of woman you're used to,' she said, referring to Max's past relationships. 'But I've got more self-respect than that.' Her breathing became heavy as she poked herself in her chest to drive her point home. 'And what about my boys, eh? Isn't it enough that I've lost my husband to your immoral world, now you want my sons to carry on in their father's footsteps and become involved in illegal activity as well.'

'Give over darling,' Max answered with a half laugh. 'Terry had your boys running around for him long before I came on the scene. They're Tempests,' he added. 'It's in their blood. Did you honestly think that Terry would have missed out on the opportunity of grooming those boys, that he wouldn't have them do his bidding, his dirty work? And when I say dirty work I'm talking about breaking an arm or two or maybe even taking a sledge hammer to some poor bastard's knees, all because he couldn't pay back a debt on time.'

Screwing up her face, Tracey's expression was one of pure disgust. 'Enough,' she cried. 'My boys would never—'

'No.' Max sat up a little straighter, his grey eyes hard, and his expression serious. 'You were the one who wanted this conversation, so you'll hear me out. If you want to point fingers darling, then point them in your husband's direction. It was Terry who put them to work as enforcers, not me, and from my understanding they were good at their job. Just ask around,' he said, pointing towards the front door. 'Go on, ask anyone about your sons' reputations, because I can tell you now you won't like what you hear. So don't you dare stand there looking down your nose at me. I already know who and what I am. It's about time you took a good, long, hard look in the mirror at yourself, because you were the one who married a villain sweetheart, not me.'

Tracey's mouth dropped open and as the first sting of tears filled her eyes, she stumbled for an answer. There and then, Max wanted to kick himself. He hadn't intended to upset her; he'd only wanted her to hear some home truths and to stop viewing her sons through rose tinted glasses; they weren't children any more, they were grown men, and from what he knew of them they were also dangerous men. Both Ricky and Jamie had too much of their father inside of them to be any different and he knew from experience that they weren't choir boys, nor had they ever pretended to be. They were hard little bastards and they could have a ruck when they needed to, and he knew for a fact that as soon as they were old enough to walk and talk, Terry would have begun moulding them into what he wanted from his sons.

'I'm sorry,' Max said, holding up his hands. 'I was out of line.' He nodded to the empty seat beside him. 'Come on,' he coaxed, his voice becoming gentle again. 'Enough of this now, darling. Haven't I got enough on my plate without you and me being at each other's throats?'

Reluctantly, Tracey nodded and, taking a deep breath to hastily compose herself, she joined him at the table. Once seated she rested her elbows on the polished glass and steepled her fingers together. 'What a mess, eh?'

Max nodded. She could say that again. This certainly wasn't what he'd intended for their fourth date; they were meant to have spent the evening enjoying a candlelit meal for two in a fancy restaurant followed by what he'd hoped would be a romantic stroll along the promenade. Instead, they had found themselves watching the car showroom burn down and then had spent the rest of the night racing across town to check that the betting shops hadn't been dealt the same fate and all of this had taken place before he'd ended the night beating Dickie Dixon to a bloody pulp. He ran a hand through his light brown hair and sighed. Despite showering, he could still smell the acrid smoke; it stained his skin and hair and served as a lingering reminder that everything he'd worked so hard for was gone. The mere thought was enough to make him feel depressed.

Turning in her seat, Tracey glanced down at Max's grazed

knuckles. 'If it wasn't Dickie Dixon then who do you think could have been behind the arson attack?'

'I don't know,' Max answered. And it was the truth; he really didn't know. With Dickie ruled out, other than Kenny or maybe even the Murphy family, there was no one else who would want to see him brought down, or at least no one that he could think of anyway. He reached out to gently tuck a lock of dark hair behind her ear. 'Blonde bimbo, eh.' He grinned. 'Where the fuck did that come from?'

As Tracey's cheeks flushed pink, she playfully slapped his hand away. 'I don't know.' She shrugged. 'I just thought... well, everyone has a type don't they, and...'

Max shook his head and, taking her hand in his, he rubbed his thumb over the soft flesh of her palm. 'Trust me darling, I'm not interested in any blonde bimbos. All I'm interested in is you and me.'

For a few moments they both sat quietly, and clearing her throat, Tracey squeezed his hand. 'You don't think this could have something to do with Kenny...?' she began.

Max shook his head, cutting her off. 'Not a chance,' he quickly answered. Although it didn't escape either of their notice that his words came across as too rehearsed, as though he was trying to convince not only Tracey, but also himself that Kenny couldn't have been involved. The only thing he knew for a certainty was that someone wanted him brought down; the burning question was, who?

Just a few miles up the road in Southend-on-Sea, Jamie Tempest made his way across the shop floor of one of the larger betting shops Max owned. Out of habit he glanced up at the large flat screen television attached to the wall, not that he had any real interest in the race being shown, and other than perhaps the occasional flutter on the Grand National, Jamie steered clear of any other form of betting and actually likened gambling to a mug's game. It was a well-known fact that the punters would never beat the bookies, hence why they had a safe full of money whereas the customers would more often than not leave the premises with their pockets empty.

Catching Ricky's attention through the glass partition that sectioned off the shop from the office, Jamie jerked his head towards the door and motioned to be let through.

'Where the fuck have you been?' Ricky asked as he glanced at his watch. 'You're late. That's the fourth time this week and believe me I'm not carrying you.'

Jamie gave an agitated sigh. 'Are you my boss now? Only the last time I checked I thought Max was the one who told me what to do, not you.'

Ricky gave his brother a hard stare, not willing to drop the subject. 'So where have you been? You turn up late for work, then disappear for hours on end and no one can get hold of you. What's going on bruv?'

'What's it to you?' Jamie retorted. Dropping onto the chair his brother had vacated, he kicked his legs out in front of him. 'What's the latest, anyway?' he asked, avoiding the question. 'Any idea yet who these bastards are?'

As he leaned back against the wall, Ricky cast his gaze over the shop, scrutinising each of the customers in turn before blowing out his cheeks. 'You're not the only one who's late. I was expecting Max to have been here by now.' He glanced back down at his watch. 'He's bound to know that there'll be comebacks after the kicking he gave Dixon last night.'

Jamie shrugged. Like his brother, he'd fully expected Max to have already been at the shop before his arrival and had been fully prepared for Max to lay into him for being late. Considering one of his businesses been already targeted and that he'd also battered Dickie Dixon half to death, he would have thought Max's top priority would have been to at least show his face and check up on his remaining business interests.

From behind the desk in the office, Jamie glanced up to look out of the window. The screech of tyres skidding to a halt on the road directly outside the shop followed by the sight of two hulking figures jumping out of a silver Mercedes made his forehead furrow. 'We've got company,' he groaned with a roll of his eyes as he turned to look at his brother.

Moments later, Barry Dixon, followed by his brother Marc, burst through the office door. 'Where is he?' Barry roared. 'Where's Hardcastle?'

Lounging casually back on the chair, Jamie nodded towards the door. 'Have you ever heard of knocking?'

Barry's face contorted with rage and ignoring the question, he looked around the office, his hard stare falling upon Ricky. 'I asked you a question,' he growled. 'Where the fuck is he? And I'm warning you now, don't even think about trying to protect him. I'm going to kill the bastard with my bare hands for what he's done, for what he's caused. My old man,' he yelled, turning his attention back to Jamie, 'is black and blue because of that cunt. He battered him half to death. The poor bastard didn't stand a chance; three against one is hardly a fair fucking fight is it.'

In that instant, Jamie sat up a little straighter and, giving his brother a sidelong glance, he narrowed his eyes. It was no secret that he'd never been a big fan of the Dixons; their mere presence grated heavily on his nerves. But as far as he was aware, and he should know seeing as he'd been there, it had been a fair fight.

Dickie had had every opportunity to not only defend himself but to also give back as good as he'd received.

'Max isn't here,' Jamie said, holding up his hands and sounding bored. 'So why don't you try coming back later?' he added with a grin. 'Because I can tell you now, your beef isn't with us. Am I making myself clear?'

His face turning a bright shade of red, steam was practically coming out of Barry's ears. 'Not your beef,' he shouted. 'You and that muppet over there,' he said, jerking his head in Ricky's direction, 'had a hand in this and my old man is no liar. If he said that you gave him a dig then that's good enough for me, and I'm going to have the two of you over this as well as that cunt Hardcastle, am I making myself fucking clear?'

Jamie cast a second glance in his brother's direction. They'd expected a comeback of sorts and were more than ready for whatever the Dixons threw their way, not that he or Ricky had actually laid a hand on Dickie; more's the pity considering they were being accused of doing just that.

'Well come on,' Barry screamed. 'Where the fuck is he?'

Jamie shrugged and, lounging back on the chair, he rolled his eyes again, the action coming across exactly as it was intended, nonchalant. 'Like I've already said, this is nothing to do with us, so if you don't mind' – he nodded towards the shop floor – 'You can close the door on your way out.'

As soon as the words had left Jamie's mouth, Barry charged forward, his fists clenched into tight balls. 'Don't,' he warned, thumping his fists down on the desk that separated them, 'try to treat me like I'm some kind of mug. My old man said it was the two of you and Hardcastle who attacked him, so give me an address for the no-good cunt before I end up losing my rag and taking the lot of you out.'

With the threat hanging heavy in the air, Jamie jumped to his feet, with Ricky hastily following suit. 'Well come on then,' Jamie growled. 'Take a shot because believe me, I've been waiting a long time for an excuse to put you on your arse and trust me when I say this, nothing would give me greater pleasure than to take you down.'

Not having the foresight to bring backup with them, Marc Dixon was more than aware that he and his brother wouldn't stand a chance against the Tempest brothers, no matter how much they might pretend they were equally matched. 'Why don't we all cool down a bit, eh?' he said with a raise of his eyebrows towards his brother in a silent warning for him to keep his temper in check. 'Coming to blows isn't going to change the facts, is it? Our old man has been battered to within an inch of his life and if you were in our shoes, you would do the exact same thing; you would want to string the fuckers up by their bollocks for what they've caused.'

Tearing his hard stare away from Barry, Jamie sighed. In a roundabout way he could see Marc's point. If it had been one of his own family members who'd been attacked and left to bleed out on a dirty pub floor, he would have moved heaven and earth to hunt the culprit down, so what made Barry or Marc Dixon any different? Only, in Dickie's case, he knew without a doubt the pounding had been warranted, that he'd been antagonising Max for years, not that he was about to voice his opinion out loud; as it was, tempers were already beginning to flare without him adding fuel to the fire.

'We'll tell Max that you came by looking for him,' Ricky volunteered, his fists still curled into tight balls. 'We can't be any fairer than that.'

Satisfied, Marc nodded before manoeuvring his brother towards the door.

'You've got twenty-four hours,' Barry snarled in a final warning as he stabbed his forefinger in Jamie's direction. 'I want that fucker

Hardcastle on his knees in front of me grovelling for our forgiveness, because believe me, you've not heard the last of this. I will
have you over this, all of you, if it's the last thing I ever do.'

Jamie raised his eyebrows. Dixon had to be living in a fantasy
land if he thought that was ever going to happen. The muscles
across his shoulder blades tensed, but as he opened his mouth to
answer, the sharp look from his elder brother was enough to make
him snap his lips closed again. No matter how much he might
want to retaliate, there was a more pressing issue at hand: the
arson attack, or, to be more precise, who had been behind it.

Once the Dixon brothers had left, Jamie's expression was set
like thunder. 'Who the fuck do they think they are?' he barked out.
'They couldn't punch their way out of a paper bag and they've got
the audacity to come in here shouting the odds.' Sinking back
down on to the chair, Jamie leaned his forearms on the desk and
toyed with his mobile phone. 'You should have let me swing for
them,' he said, looking up at his brother, his lips set into a thin line.
'I could have taken them out and not even broken out in a sweat
and you know it.'

Ricky sighed. 'You swinging for them is hardly going to help
the situation is it.' He looked into the distance, a smile making its
way across his face. 'Although I've got to admit, it would have made
my day to see that big-mouthed bastard on the floor with claret
pouring out of his mouth.'

Jamie laughed out loud and, eyeing his brother's pocket, he
grinned even wider. 'I'll let you do the honours and inform Max
that Bill and Ben out there,' he said, nodding towards the street,
'want a word with him.'

Rolling his eyes, Ricky dug out his mobile phone and as he
scrolled through his contact list, he shook his head. If he knew
Max as well as he thought he did then he knew for a fact it wasn't
going to go down well. Not that Max would be overly concerned. If

Barry and Marc's threats had had any kind of weight behind them they would have started throwing punches the moment they had stepped inside the shop, instead of throwing a hissy fit like a pair of women. 'Nah, I've got a better idea,' he said, tossing his mobile phone across the desk to his brother. 'Seeing as you like being on your phone so much, you ring him.'

4

In Belmarsh Prison, Kenny Kempton lay back on his bunk, one hand behind his head, his free hand clasping a sheet of paper. A wicked grin was spread across his face as he re-read the contents of a letter. Good old Patricia; she may have been Terry Tempest's mother, but she had stood by him even when the jury had found him guilty of her son's murder. For want of a better word, Pat was as gullible as they came and he had well and truly pulled the wool over her eyes. She wholeheartedly believed his protests of innocence and, at the end of the day, why wouldn't she? He and Terry had known one another from childhood and had been the best of mates long before they had gone into business together; they had even been each other's best men when they had taken their wedding vows. It stood to reason that Patricia would find the notion that one could kill the other incomprehensible.

Sitting up, he swung his legs over the side of the bunk and planted his feet firmly on the floor. As luck would have it, he hadn't found prison life too difficult; he had his own cell, a television, a phone, and more importantly, he had respect from the other inmates. All in all, he couldn't fathom out why his former pal Max Hardcastle had complained so bitterly about life inside. In his mind it was a doddle, you could even say that it was a cushy little number. He had three meals a day; fair enough, the food left a lot to be desired, and half the time he had no idea what it was he was actually shovelling into his mouth, but on the upside he had managed to shift some weight; there was even a gym complete with several punching bags that he could take out any built up anger and frustration on.

He clenched his fists into tight balls, his lips curling into a snarl. He had only one source of anger – no, it was more than anger, it was a hatred – Max Hardcastle. He should have killed the bastard when he'd had the chance. Better still, he should have slaughtered the no-good cunt alongside his former business partner Terry Tempest.

It was all because of Hardcastle that he'd been banged up for murder and human trafficking. Less than a year into a life sentence, Kenny conveniently chose to ignore the fact that he was indeed guilty of forcing women into prostitution and, as for murdering Terry, well he was guilty of that too, or to be more precise, he was guilty of orchestrating the murder, seeing as it had been Kenny's son Shaun who had actually been the one coerced into pulling the trigger and blasting Terry to death. And as far as Kenny was concerned, good riddance to him. In the months leading up to his murder, Terry had become the equivalent of an albatross hanging around Kenny's neck. Not only had he wanted to call the shots on their business dealings, but he had also been dipping his hand into the profits, and as Kenny had repeatedly told his son, and anyone else who would listen for that matter, he was no mug and, as such, wouldn't be treated like one.

Ever so carefully, Kenny folded the sheet of paper and placed it inside the metal cubbyhole beside his bunk. Yes, as far as he was concerned, everything was fitting into place nicely. If it was the last thing that Kenny ever did then it would be to make sure that he brought Hardcastle down, and more importantly that he made the bastard suffer. Kenny was only sorry that he wouldn't be there in person to see Max Hardcastle's fall from grace; Kenny was only sorry that he wouldn't be there in person to see Max Hardcastle's fall from grace; that really would have been the icing on the cake.

Even from inside, Kenny had been able to pull some strings, with a little help from Patricia of course, and a rather surprising source, one that he was fully prepared to use to his full advantage, and one that he knew would rattle not only Hardcastle but also Tracey and her two sons. The mere thought of what was to come was enough to make Kenny chuckle out loud. But that was Kenny all over; he was a nasty piece of work, always had been, and the people in his life were only of a use to him while he was benefitting from them in some way. Take Shaun for example, he'd never given his only son a second's thought, despite the fact that Shaun too was spending a considerable length of his life imprisoned for the crime that his father had forced him to partake in. Talk about out of sight, out of mind. As far as Kenny was concerned, Shaun had served his purpose, and may as well not exist for how much Kenny cared about his own flesh and blood. The truth was, as much as Kenny hated to admit it, he had always been jealous of Terry, jealous that Terry's boys were handy with their fists, and that they could hold their own, whereas he'd been saddled with a son who was scared of his own shadow, who was weak and pitiful, and who took after his mother rather than his father.

Getting to his feet, Kenny ran his hand through his greying hair. It would be fair to say that he wasn't a handsome man. Before his imprisonment, he'd had a stocky build that ran to fat all thanks to the booze he'd guzzled in abundance and the cocaine that he'd snorted by the bucketload. The only good thing to come out of his stint inside was that he'd managed to get himself clean, not that he'd actually had a choice in the matter; prisons could be funny like that and for some strange reason they didn't want the prisoners to spend their days and nights as high as a kite.

Despite being locked up, all in all Kenny felt good about himself. His body was strong and even his mind was much more alert these days, which in Kenny's eyes was a necessity. He needed to be able to keep his wits about him and above all else he needed to remain on his guard especially since he was a category A prisoner and was being housed with some of the country's most dangerous men, who wouldn't think twice about killing their own family members if they got in the way of what they wanted.

'You all right Kenny?'

Kenny looked up and smiled. Cain Daly was one of the biggest men he'd ever seen. With dark brown skin and shoulders as wide as a barn door, it would also be fair to say that Cain was a hard fucker. Sentenced to ten years in prison for his part in an armed robbery, Cain was no stranger to prison life. And the fact that he stood respectfully at the threshold to Kenny's cell was enough to tell him and anyone else in the near vicinity, that Kenny had a lot of clout, and that regardless of his circumstances, he was still a man who demanded respect.

'Course I'm all right.' Kenny winked. 'I've got a visit this morning.'

Cain gave a deep, hearty chuckle. A visit from a loved one was always a sure way of putting a spring back into a man's step. Not only did it bring a welcome break from the monotonous routine that was prison life, but it was also a good way to catch up on life on the outside, especially for those who had left families and in particular, children, behind. 'Your missus coming in to see you then, is she?'

Kenny screwed up his face, and his eyes became hard slits. 'Who? That miserable old bitch? Fuck me, the thought of seeing her boat race is enough to put me off my breakfast. Nah.' He smoothed down his hair and leant in towards Cain, his voice becoming hushed, almost as though they were fellow conspirators. 'This is a welcome visit, very welcome if you get my drift. Let me put it this way,' he said, clasping Cain's shoulder. 'Shit's about to hit the fan Cain my old son. It's just a pity that I won't be there to see that fucker pay for his wrong doings.'

Stepping out onto the landing, Kenny whistled a cheerful tune, even though the view was what could only be described as bleak. On either side of his cell was a row of even more cells, the thick metal doors a constant, stark reminder that he and men just like him were being kept locked up like animals, that their liberty and human rights had all but been taken away from them. It was the price they had to pay he supposed, their punishment for the crimes they had partaken in.

As he leant against the metal railing that ran the length of the upper corridor, Kenny's gaze drifted down to the safety net below. Just days earlier, there had been a jumper. Of course, the safety net had caught his fall; more's the pity as far as Kenny was concerned. The man in question had run up a debt, and as of yet Kenny was still waiting for that debt to be repaid back to him.

'When is he due back on the wing?' Kenny asked as he jerked his head towards the net.

Cain took a quick glance around him before joining Kenny. Mirroring the older man's stance, he casually leant his forearms on the railing and looked down at the net. He knew Kenny was referring to the jumper, or more accurately, the man who was pushed, seeing as it had been Kenny who'd actually sent the man descending to what should have been his death. 'Should be soon.'

Cain shrugged. 'Other than sustaining a few bruises, the screw reckons that no real harm was done.'

Kenny grinned. One or two bruises was an understatement. He'd personally smashed the man's head repeatedly off the iron railing and knew for a fact that he had been left with a severe case of concussion and a broken nose, if the crunch of bone splintering followed by the gush of blood from the man's nostrils was anything to go by.

'Make sure he has a welcome home committee waiting for him.' Kenny straightened up and lifted his eyebrows at the hidden meaning behind his words. 'I want what I'm owed,' he stated over his shoulder as he sauntered off towards the shower block. 'And as you know,' he said, smirking. 'I'm a patient man but believe me when I say this, when it comes to that ponce, my patience is beginning to wear thin, very thin indeed.'

As he watched Kenny go, Cain sighed. He'd met his fair share of hard men over the years, but in his mind Kenny was in a league all of his own. Not only was he a sadistic bully, but he also relished in the misfortune of others. He glanced once again at the safety net. The man who'd taken a tumble seemed like a good bloke; he'd kept himself to himself and if anything, he came across as timid, and certainly not cut out for prison life. Wearily, Cain pushed himself away from the railing and with his hard gaze remaining on Kenny's retreating back, he made his way to his own cell, not for the first time wishing that he'd never become mixed up with the likes of Kenny Kempton.

Patricia Tempest loved nothing better than to be the centre of attention and as she queued up outside Belmarsh Prison she was almost giddy with excitement. The source of her happiness was the young man standing beside her, who also just so happened to be her grandson, and he was a good looking bugger too, a real chip off the old block if ever she'd seen one.

What a shock it had been for her when out of the blue Raymond had knocked on her front door. For a moment she'd actually thought she was looking at her son's ghost, that her Terry had risen from the grave, but no, the young man on her doorstep had quickly introduced himself as her grandson. Not that he'd actually needed an introduction, she could see with own two eyes that Raymond was Terry's son; the similarities were too strong for him not to be. Her only regret in life was that she hadn't met Raymond sooner, when he'd still been an infant. Why her son had felt the need to hide Raymond away she would never understand; it was almost as though he were ashamed of his infidelity, and she would have believed that to be the case if it hadn't been for the fact Terry had never been the kind of man to feel remorse for his actions.

All along she'd known that her only son had had strong genes, and as she looked up into Raymond's handsome face it was as if she were looking up at Terry himself, the same build, same face, and even the same shade of dark brown hair. Unlike the offspring her daughter-in-law Tracey had tried to palm off as Terry's sons. No, she could see it for herself now, Jamie looked nothing like Terry; no wonder her son had questioned the boy's parentage. She was only thankful that Kenny had filled her in on her daughter-in-law's wicked deceit.

'You all right, Nan?'

Patricia grinned. 'Of course I am,' she said as she patted her peroxide blonde beehive into place. 'I've got you with me and I can't ask for any more than that sweetheart.'

The only fly in the ointment as far as Patricia was concerned was Raymond's surname. Rather than using the name Tempest, as was his birth right, Raymond went by his mother's surname, Cole. She pursed her lips together. Terry should have seen to it that the boy was given his rightful name; it wasn't as though he hadn't known about Raymond's existence. Even Kenny had been aware of the fact that Terry had sired a child out of wedlock, and by all accounts Kenny and Raymond were well acquainted. Raymond even affectionately called Kenny, Uncle Kenny, which was a lot more than Ricky or Jamie had ever done.

A spiteful grin spread across Patricia's face. She was actually looking forward to showing Raymond off, especially as Terry and Tracey would have already been married around the time Raymond had been conceived. Not that she condoned adultery, mind, because she didn't, but her Terry must have had his reasons to stray, and if she was being entirely honest she didn't blame her boy, not one iota. In her mind Tracey had always been a difficult woman, and she would even go as far as to say that they had taken an instant dislike to one another. Over the years their arguments had become legendary on the Dagenham council estate where they lived, so was it any wonder that Terry had sought comfort in the arms of another woman?

Thirty minutes later, they were through security, and what a rigmarole that had been. Not once but five times they'd needed to have their identification clarified, and that was before they had even been patted down and searched. Anyone would think that she was a criminal herself the way the screws were carrying on, not that Patricia believed Kenny should be banged up in the first place. It was all lies; Kenny would never have harmed a single hair on Terry's head, they had been close friends for Christ's sake, and as for sex trafficking, it sickened her to her stomach to think that Terry and Kenny could have been accused of something so heinous.

How the jury had believed the lies was beyond her. Oh, but she knew the truth all right, and if anyone had been up to no good then it would have been the Murphy family. They were the real villains and it was common knowledge that they couldn't be trusted, that they were all liars and thieves; she'd even heard one or two rumours that they participated in incest.

And as for Max Hardcastle, well he was a barefaced liar an' all, and to see him in court giving evidence against Kenny as though butter wouldn't melt in his mouth had boiled her blood. She'd wanted to kill the smug bastard stone dead, and she would have done too if she'd thought she would have been able to get away with smuggling a weapon into The Old Bailey. If anyone was a murderer then it was Hardcastle. He'd even served time in prison for slaughtering his stepfather. The injuries that the poor man had sustained had been so horrific that the only way he could be identified was by his dental records. And as if that wasn't bad enough, deep down in her heart Patricia knew that Hardcastle was responsible for Terry's death; she could feel it in her gut and nothing and no one would be able to convince her otherwise.

Right from the get-go she'd known that Max Hardcastle was a wrong'un, that he was trouble with a capital T. Don't get her wrong, her Terry hadn't been an angel. In fact, it would be fair to say that as a child he'd been a right little scallywag, but at least Terry had never harmed anyone. Her son may have ducked and dived for a living, at one point he'd even sold knocked off goods from the back of a lorry, but that was the extent of his wrong doings, and at the end of the day, all Terry had been trying to do was support his family. What other choice did he have when he had a wife and two small kiddies to feed? Most businesses had insurance anyway so no one was actually out of pocket; it was a win-win situation for everyone involved.

Over the years, Patricia had lost count of how many times she had warned Terry that his friendship with Hardcastle would end in tears and she had been right to worry, only it was her tears that had been shed, not Terry's.

The death of her only child had devastated Patricia. It just wasn't right, was it? No mother should ever have to bury a child. As far as Patricia was concerned there was no justice in the world, and that right there was the truth of the matter. How were the likes of Hardcastle allowed to swan around without a care in the world, while poor Kenny, who was innocent of the crimes he'd been accused of, was forced to spend the remainder of his life locked up like a common criminal?

As they made their way to their allocated seats, Patricia held her head up high. From her perspective she was above the riffraff, as she liked to call the other visitors. Not that this stopped her from taking a good, long look around her. No, she loved nothing better than to have a good old gossip, and some of the sights she witnessed when she visited Kenny were more than enough to keep both her and her friends entertained for weeks. It took all sorts, she supposed, and the women who came to visit their husbands or partners could be put into one of two categories: those who looked as if they were in need of a good wash and hair brush, and then those who looked and acted like trollops. She'd even caught one or two of the tarts fluttering their false eyelashes at her Raymond! They clearly had no shame, and as the old saying went, while the cat's away the mice will play, only they wouldn't be playing anywhere near her grandson, not if she had anything to say on the matter. And as for their outfits, tracksuit bottoms and tight T-shirts, teamed with stilettos, appeared to be the uniform. In Patricia's mind the world had gone stark, raving mad. Back in her day women dressed like ladies; they made themselves look presentable for their men and wouldn't be seen dead walking out the house without combing their hair first or smoothing some red rouge across their cheeks.

Today women were pumped so full of Botox that they actually looked as if they were made from plastic, so much so that Patricia feared they would melt if they came into contact with any form of heat.

'Here he comes,' Raymond announced.

Dragging her gaze away from the visitors, Patricia watched as the prisoners made their way into the room. Dressed in their normal attire, the only accessory to distinguish those locked up from their friends and loved ones was a thick yellow arm band they wore.

As usual, whenever she visited Kenny, tears sprang to Patricia's eyes. It broke her heart to see him surrounded by the scum of the earth. He'd lost a lot of weight too. Gone was the larger than life character she was so used to, and in his place was a shadow of a man she would never have recognised if he were to walk past her in the street. 'How are you doing, darling?'

Kenny pulled Patricia into his arms. 'I'm doing okay,' he said with a mock sad grin. 'As well as can be expected I suppose. But you know me, Pat, I'll bounce back, I always do.' Releasing Patricia, he went on to shake Raymond's hand then took a seat.

'How about a cup of tea? And I'll see if they have your favourite: a beef and mustard sandwich.'

'Sounds smashing.' Kenny beamed. 'I've been looking forward to this,' he said, rubbing a hand across his stomach. 'It certainly beats the muck they serve up in here.'

'In that case I'll get you two. And how about you sweetheart?' she asked, turning to look up at her grandson.

'Just a tea for me, Nan.' Raymond smiled.

Once Patricia was out of earshot and making her way towards the canteen, the smile slipped from Kenny's face as he turned to look at his late business partner's son.

'Well?' he asked with a raise of his eyebrows. 'Is it done?'

Raymond cracked his knuckles and, lounging back on the chair, he threw a woman sitting two tables away a salacious wink.

'Hey,' Kenny growled. 'Pack that in. What are you trying to do, start a riot?'

'As if I give a fuck.' Raymond laughed. 'Come on, you should know me better than that, Uncle Kenny,' he said, enunciating the address. 'I'd go toe to toe with any of these fuckers in here and not even break out in a sweat.' Gone was the friendly façade Raymond put on for his grandmother's benefit; in its place was a cockiness that bordered on arrogance. 'As for your question about the car dealership, I can confirm that it has been destroyed.' He mimicked the action of striking a match. 'You would have loved it,' he laughed. 'The place went up like a fucking bonfire.'

A slow smile crept across Kenny's face. Right from the off he'd known that Raymond was like the spit out of his old man's mouth and not just in the looks department either. Even when Raymond had been a child, Kenny had sensed that Terry's son had an edge about him, and that as an adult he would prove to be a handful, much the same as Terry himself had been at the same age.

'And what about this mate of yours?' Kenny asked. 'Can he be trusted to keep his mouth shut? Because I'm warning you now, if he opens his trap and starts blurting out my business there will be hell to pay.'

'Of course he can be trusted,' Raymond barked out. 'He's my pal, not some stranger who I pulled off the street.' He lifted his eyebrows, his expression becoming suddenly menacing. 'Are you questioning my judgement? Do I look like I'm stupid, that I would purposely do something to fuck up the plan?'

Kenny swallowed deeply, his cheeks burning a deep shade of pink. At the best of times, Raymond could be unpredictable, and as much as Kenny didn't want to show his fear, he couldn't help but inwardly shudder. There was something dangerous about

Raymond, something sinister that Kenny wasn't afraid to admit made him feel uneasy. Raymond was more than just a little bit unstable; he reminded Kenny of a ticking time bomb waiting to explode and God help anyone within his vicinity when he finally erupted. 'Of course I don't think you're stupid,' Kenny answered with a light laugh. 'You've got too much of your old man in you.' He winked.

The words were more than enough to appease Raymond, and as his shoulders relaxed, he lounged back on the chair. 'You don't need to worry about my mate. He knows the score, and let's just say, he's well connected.'

Kenny's eyebrows knotted together as he stared at his visitor. 'How well connected?'

Raymond sniggered. 'His family are well known in the area. You might even know them.' He lifted his eyebrows, his expression smug. 'Ever heard of the Winters family?'

As he laughed out loud, Kenny shook his head in wonder. To have the Winters family as an ally was like music to his ears. He'd never expected Eddie Winters to go up against Hardcastle; he'd always been under the impression that the two men were on good terms. 'Of course I know Eddie. That fucker has had his eye on the manor for years. He's a good bloke, and he's got a rep not to be messed around with.'

Raymond shrugged. 'Well me and his younger brother Alfie are like this.' He crossed two fingers to emphasise his point. 'So take my word for it when I say that you can trust my pal.'

Impressed, Kenny nodded.

'Oh, and you were right about one thing,' Raymond continued. 'We had Hardcastle running around like a headless chicken. He even looked as though he was going to burst into tears at one point.'

Sinking back into his seat, Kenny narrowed his eyes. 'What do you mean?' he asked. 'How the fuck would you know what Hard-castle was doing. Were you there, watching him?'

As his lips curled into a smirk, Raymond gave a nonchalant shrug. 'Maybe.'

'That wasn't part of the plan,' Kenny said, his voice rising. 'What if you'd been seen? Hardcastle may be a cunt but he's no fool. All it would take is one glance in your direction and he would recognise you as being Terry's son. You're his double, and it wouldn't take much for Hardcastle to put two and two together, come up with five, and suss out who was behind the arson attack.'

'No one saw me,' Raymond snarled. 'I enlisted the help of two muppets to burn down the showroom. I didn't even have to get my hands dirty and Hardcastle had no idea that he was being watched.'

Kenny's eyes bulged. 'You did fucking what?' he snarled. 'Have you lost the plot? I said no witnesses. What the fuck is wrong with you?' He brought his hands up to his head. 'Which part of this don't you understand? Witnesses talk, and before we know it we'll have the old bill breathing down our necks, let alone Hardcastle.'

Raymond chuckled. 'What do you take me for? Do you really think that I'll let them live long enough to talk? Nah.' He cracked his knuckles. 'Don't worry, I'll make sure they keep quiet. Besides, I didn't want to miss out on the opportunity of witnessing Hardcas-tle's world collapse around him. That bastard killed my old man and he's going to pay for what he did. I'm going to do more than just destroy him, I'm going to tear him apart piece by bloody piece until there is nothing left of him. I want that bastard on his hands and knees begging me not to end his sorry excuse of a life.' He paused for breath and sat forward in the seat, his hard gaze boring into Kenny's skull. 'But do you know what I really want more than that, more than anything else?'

'What's that?' A coward through and through, it took every

ounce of Kenny's strength to keep the tremor from his voice. He should have known better than to embroil Raymond into his sadistic plan for revenge. After all, if Terry struggled to control the boy then what hope did he have? It had been hard enough keeping Raymond away from his father's funeral, and it had only been the promise of seeking revenge on the culprit responsible for Terry's death that had finally swayed Raymond's mind to stay away.

'I want Hardcastle obliterated off the face of the earth and then when the bastard is dead,' he said, sinking back on to the chair, a familiar smirk creasing his face. 'I'll piss on the wanker's body and laugh while I do it.'

A cold chill crept down the length of Kenny's spine. The quicker they were away from the subject of Terry's death, the better, seeing as he was the one who had actually orchestrated the murder, not Hardcastle. He jerked his head in the direction of the canteen, desperate for a change of conversation. 'Has she introduced you to your brothers yet?'

'Nah, not yet.' Turning to look at his grandmother, Raymond shook his head, his forehead furrowing. 'I dunno what the old bat is waiting for. All she keeps harping on about is how much I look like my old man, and how proud he would have been of me. She's starting to get right on my tits and that's an understatement.'

Kenny raised his eyebrows, not that he was overly surprised by Raymond's comments. Over the years, Terry had said exactly the same thing about his mother. 'Well,' he said as he spotted Patricia begin to make her way back to where they were sitting. 'Keep on at her. Tell her that you want to get acquainted with your family, and while you're at it, find out what's happened to my money. Those little bastards, Ricky and Jamie, had no right to sell the business. Half of that scrap yard belonged to me; maybe not on paper, seeing as everything was in your dad's name. But I still ploughed my hard-earned dough into buying that yard and I want what I'm owed.'

'Oh, I will do,' Raymond answered as he flashed Patricia a heart-stopping grin that was so like his father's. 'After all, I'm entitled to a stake of that money seeing as Terry was my old man too. And believe me,' he said, rubbing his hands together. 'I'm looking forward to being formally introduced to my brothers; it's just a pity they won't feel the same way about me,' he laughed, 'or at least they won't by the time I've finished with them, anyway.'

5

The next day, Ricky Tempest lounged on the sofa and absentmindedly chewed on his thumbnail, a sure sign that something was bothering him. Like his younger brother Jamie, Ricky was a handsome man with dark hair, blue eyes, and a tall, solid physique. Having worked as an enforcer for his father since the age of sixteen, Ricky was no stranger when it came to the dangers associated with the criminal underworld, and the fact that he and Jamie were Terry Tempest's sons meant that they may as well have had targets pinned to their backs, if the amount of aggro that had come their way over the years was anything to go by. It went with the territory, he supposed, and no matter where they went there was always someone, somewhere, who wanted to be able to brag that they had brought down a Tempest. One of the first things Terry had instilled in his sons was the need to be able to take care of both themselves and each other, and thankfully they could. Not only were they handy with their fists, but they were also astute – they took note of their surroundings and quietly observed those around them, and they could also sense trouble brewing a mile off, a particular knack of theirs that had come in useful more than once in their lifetime.

It was this knack that caused a sense of unease to ripple through Ricky's veins. The arson attack on the car showroom hadn't come about because of a disgruntled customer; he highly doubted it was even anything to do with someone who may have had a grudge to bear. No, the arson attack went deeper than that, beyond revenge. Whoever had started the blaze wasn't playing a game; they had set out to destroy Max, and by turning the show-room into a blazing inferno they were sending out a message, one that had been received loud and clear. Not that Ricky was concerned for his own safety, nor was he worried about the safety of his younger brother. Ricky knew that Jamie could hold his own, and that he had a quick temper that was both explosive and fero-cious in equal measures. It was the safety of his mother, Tracey, which concerned him the most.

Throughout his marriage, Terry Tempest had purposely kept his wife in the dark. Tracey had been oblivious to the full extent of her husband's criminal activities and to learn the truth of Terry's deceit had broken her heart. Not only had Ricky's father been a prominent figure in the criminal underworld, but the violent crimes Terry had participated in had shocked Tracey to the core. Instead of the lovable rogue she had whole heartedly believed her husband to be, Terry had in actual fact been a very dangerous individual, one who had no qualms about wiping out an entire firm if they so much as dared dip a toe into what he considered to be his turf. And even worse than that, Terry had been actively involved in the running of a prostitution ring. Discovering that she had lived off her husband's immoral earnings had almost been enough to send Tracey over the edge, so much so that for months she had point blank refused to even step foot inside the house they had once shared together.

Even now, almost two years after the discovery of the brothel, Ricky could barely comprehend that his dad had been involved in something so evil. The plight of those women who had been trafficked into the country then forced to sell their bodies against their will, had laid heavily on Ricky's mind. The problem Ricky had was that he couldn't help but blame himself; he should have seen the red flags or at least sensed that something was amiss, that his dad had been keeping dark secrets from his family. Terry had even had the front to ask Jamie to drive him to the house where he'd kept the women on the pretence that he was collecting something from a mate. What kind of father would even contemplate such a thing, let alone see it through? Was it any wonder that they had all been fooled by him?

A tiny part of Ricky wondered whether Terry had ever looked at his own wife inappropriately. Had he sized Ricky's wife Kayla up with the intention of wanting to pimp her out too, or had he had improper thoughts about her? Perhaps he'd even fantasised about her? Kayla was a beautiful woman after all, and not only did she turn heads wherever she went, but she also had a touch of class about her. She looked after herself, her hair and makeup were always faultless, and she dressed well too, not that there was anything flashy about Kayla, because there wasn't. She had a heart of gold and would give away her last penny if she could. As far as Ricky was concerned, his wife was a stunner; everyone loved her, even his mum adored her, and treated her as though she were the daughter she'd never had.

His thoughts wandered to his mum now. She had loved their dad, given him two sons and had devoted her life to him, and what had she been given in return? Sweet fuck all, that's what. Oh, Terry may have provided his wife with a home that was fit for a king, and a lifestyle that could be envied by her friends and neighbours, but emotionally he had never been there for her, she had even admitted once to Kayla that there were times when she'd felt lonely, an emotion that, as far as Ricky was concerned, no married woman should ever be made to feel.

Ricky screwed up his face as an image of Bianca Murphy sprang to his mind. Shortly before she was arrested for her part in the prostitution ring, Bianca, the youngest of the Murphy family, had claimed that she was pregnant with Terry's child. The mere thought that his father could have given a Murphy the time of day let alone anything else forced acrid bile to rise up in his throat. Swallowing quickly, Ricky pressed the back of his hand to his lips and squeezed his eyes shut tight in an attempt to block out the sickening images that had been conjured up in his mind. For want of a better word, Bianca Murphy was what could only be described as a tramp. Unlike Kayla, Bianca had favoured thick makeup that was at least three shades too dark for her complexion. She'd also walked around in skimpy outfits that were both revealing and unflattering for her figure, not that anyone would have been brave enough to tell her to her face that she looked a state. And as for the way she spoke, she was so foul mouthed that she wouldn't have been out of place working on a building site.

There was nothing classy about Bianca and, as far as he could tell, there wasn't even anything likeable about her, so why his dad had felt the need to impregnate her, for the life of him Ricky couldn't understand. Surely to God, his dad couldn't have been that hard up that he'd been prepared to be saddled with Bianca on a permanent basis? It was a hard push to spend even five minutes in her company without wanting to pull back a fist and fell her to the floor. And it was no secret that the Murphys were all crazy. Take Bianca's elder brother Kevin for example; he'd been in and out of psychiatric hospitals more times than Ricky had had hot dinners and he also had a particular penchant for slicing people up; by all accounts, he was notorious for it. So just what had Terry been trying to prove by becoming involved with the family? He certainly hadn't needed their reputations to bolster his own notoriety, that was for sure.

As for Bianca Murphy, whilst in prison, she had given birth to the baby that she had claimed was his father's. Whether Bianca's claims were true or not Ricky had no idea, but if there was some truth to her allegation then it was his father's blood that ran through the infant's veins, the very same blood that ran through his veins too. Not that Ricky would ever accept the child into his family; he wanted no part in his half sibling's life; he didn't even know where the child was, and he didn't want to know either. Whether that was because he felt hatred towards the Murphy family or repulsion for his father's actions, he didn't know. Perhaps it was because he felt a great sense of loyalty towards his mother and couldn't bear the thought of hurting her any more than she'd already been hurt. The only thing he knew for certain was that his mother had been devastated when she had discovered just how deep her husband's betrayal had run, and that was something that Ricky would never forgive or forget in a hurry.

No matter how strong his mother had been in the weeks and months leading up to the court case concerning both her husband's murder and the sex trafficking charges, Ricky had seen the cracks begin to show, hence why he was so worried now. Tracey wasn't cut out for their world. Yes, she had a temper on her, one that made even him and Jamie wary at times, but if the culprits responsible for the arson attack were as unhinged as Ricky believed them to be, then he didn't want his mother involved in any way, shape or form. The hard part however would be convincing Tracey to keep out of harm's reach. If he knew his mum as well as he thought he did then he knew that she would have something to say on the matter. Her and Max were close, a little too close for his liking. She'd had enough heartache over the past few years to last her a lifetime and the last thing she needed was to jump head first into bed with a new man.

Steepling his fingers, Ricky brought his hands up to his face as he pondered the events that had taken place just a few days earlier. Other than when his father had been brutally gunned down, he and his family had never been involved in any active feuds. Oh, there had been falling outs over the years, plenty of them, but nothing so bad that Ricky's life or the lives of his family were in any actual danger. Terry would have never stood for it. He and his business partner Kenny Kempton had ruled Dagenham with an iron fist and would have considered allowing someone to get the better of them as a sign of being weak and in their world, showing weakness was as good as signing your own death warrant. Terry would have laid down the law and used brute force if need be to show people exactly who was the boss. Ricky had seen his dad in action enough times to know that his reputation had been warranted, and that those around him had every right to be cautious.

'Daddy.'

Pulled out of his reverie, Ricky gave his five-year-old son, Mason, a warm smile as the little boy scrambled up onto his lap.

'Are you ready for school, champ?' Ricky asked as he hugged his son's small frame into his chest.

Nodding, Mason took a bite of an apple. 'Can you pick me up from school Daddy? Please?' Chewing on the fruit, Mason looked up at his father, his eyes wide and pleading.

'Maybe.' Seeing the longing in his son's face, Ricky gave a gentle sigh. As a child he could remember asking his own father the exact same question. Not that Terry had ever picked him up from school, other than the one time after Ricky had been hauled into the headmaster's office for fighting. Terry had been furious, and after arriving home, he'd given his eldest son a good hiding that he wouldn't forget in a hurry. Ironically, Terry hadn't been angry because his son had lashed out at another child. No, the only reason Terry had been so livid was because Ricky had actually allowed the other child the opportunity to go running to the headmaster to tell tales. It was a lesson well learned, one that Ricky had held in good stead ever since. 'I'll see what I can do, okay, but I can't promise anything; you know that Daddy has to go to work.'

Placated, Mason jumped off Ricky's lap, dropping the apple onto the sofa as he did so. As the little boy raced back out of the lounge, he almost collided with his mother.

'Hey, be careful,' Kayla gently warned. Shaking her head, she stepped inside the lounge. 'He's got too much energy that boy,' she laughed. 'And I wonder who he gets that from, eh?'

Ricky couldn't help but grin. By all accounts, he'd been just as energetic as a child. Mason clearly took after his father rather than his mother, and not just when it came to the looks department either. 'Maybe he needs a playmate?' Ricky said, reaching out to retrieve the discarded fruit.

'No.' Holding up her hand, Kayla vehemently shook her head. 'We have already discussed this, and we both agreed that one child is more than enough for us, and let's face it,' she laughed, jerking her head towards the hallway, 'the thought of having two kids with Mason's energy is exhausting, let alone us having to actually deal with it on a daily basis. We'd never get a wink of sleep for a start, and I don't know about you, but for me that is one thing that is definitely not up for negotiation.'

Ricky gave a small smile, one that didn't quite reach his eyes. In all honesty, he wouldn't have minded a second child, and maybe even a third. It was Kayla who was adamant that she didn't want any more children, not that he entirely blamed her. Mason's birth had been horrific in every possible aspect that you could think of.

As for Kayla's well thought out birth plan, well that went out of the window within five minutes of the contractions starting. All in all it would be fair to say that it was an experience neither of them wanted to repeat any time soon. 'I was talking about getting a dog; I dunno, a puppy or something.'

'Maybe,' Kayla conceded. 'But something small.'

'It would be small; it's a puppy.'

Kayla rolled her eyes. 'They don't stay puppies for long sweetheart and we've hardly got the room for a dog that when fully grown would be the size of a small horse. Maybe a Chihuahua or something like that.'

Ricky screwed up his face. 'Leave it out?'

'What?' Kayla protested as she made to walk into the hallway to answer the knock at the front door. 'A little Chihuahua would be perfect for us,' she said, gesturing around her.

Ricky's scowl deepened. 'Well don't expect me to walk it,' he shouted after her. 'If we get a dog then it's got to be a man's dog, not some scrawny little rat. If anyone saw me I'd never live it down.'

'What wouldn't you live down?'

Taking note of his brother standing at the lounge door, Ricky sighed. 'We were talking about getting a dog to keep Mason company, and Kayla,' he said, screwing up his face again, 'suggested a Chihuahua.'

'I don't know bruv,' Jamie said, pretending to think the situation over. 'Personally, I think one would suit you. You could even get one of those bags that you tie around your waist to put the dog treats in,' he added, throwing Kayla a wink. 'And if you're really, really lucky they might even sell a nice pink one.'

Groaning out loud, Ricky rolled his eyes. It was so typical of Jamie to take the piss; he never took anything serious, and in fact seemed to think that life was one long joke, until you pissed him off of course and then an entirely different person emerged.

Grasping the apple in his fist, Ricky launched it in the direction of his brother's head. To his annoyance, Jamie had already anticipated the action and ducked down out of harm's way. 'What are you doing here anyway?' Ricky asked. 'Why aren't you at the betting shop?'

Straightening up, Jamie tossed the apple into a waste basket then wiped the sticky residue away from his hand. 'You can talk,' he said, nodding to his brother's position on the sofa. 'I'm not the only one who should have been at work by now. Max called me; he wants us to meet him at The Ship and Anchor.'

Ricky's forehead furrowed. 'What for?'

'Why do you think?' Aware that Kayla and Mason were within earshot, Jamie lowered his voice a fraction. 'To talk about the arson attack. You know, the big, scary orange flames and the thick, black smoke that we saw the other night. It wasn't exactly hard to miss, was it.'

Ricky growled. 'The point I was trying to make is why does he want to meet here in Dagenham? Why not start asking around in Leigh-on-Sea where the arson attack actually took place? Or better still, why doesn't he give the Dixons what they want and arrange a meet with them? It doesn't make any sense.'

'Fuck if I know what's going on.' Jamie shrugged. 'All I know is that he wants us to meet him there in a couple of hours.'

Thoughtful, Ricky resumed chewing on his thumbnail. 'What about Mum?'

'What about her?' Jamie frowned.

Ricky took a deep breath. Jamie was even more protective of their mother than he was, if that was possible, and after witnessing Michael Murphy punch her to the floor two years prior, that protective streak had increased tenfold. 'I don't want her involved in any of this.'

Jamie snorted with derision. 'Yeah well that's a given.' He gave a shrug. 'She doesn't need to be involved. The car lot is Max's business, it's nothing to do with Dad, or even us come to think of it. We might work for Max, but we weren't the intended targets, were we?'

As Ricky nodded he couldn't help but ponder over his brother's words. As far as he could tell, Jamie was spot on; the car showroom didn't concern their mum, so why had Max called her first? And he must have done for her to have already been at the car lot before they arrived. Fair enough, they were friends, you could even say that they were close friends, but his mum hadn't needed to be there.

'Well come on,' Jamie said, oblivious to the dark thoughts running through his brother's head. 'Are we going to get a move on or what?'

Ricky heaved himself off the sofa. 'Before we head over to the boozer I just want to swing by Mum's place first, and make sure that she's okay.'

Jamie shrugged and as he playfully chased his nephew down the hallway, the sound of Mason's squeals and Jamie's laughter resonated throughout the house. In that instant, Ricky didn't know which one out of the two was the bigger kid, his five-year-old son or his brother.

* * *

As he and Tracey exited his apartment building in Leigh-on-Sea, Max couldn't help but glance around him. Were his movements being monitored? Were the bastards who'd burnt down his business watching him, perhaps even contemplating a second attack?

Satisfied that he could see no one loitering in the vicinity, Max walked Tracey to her car.

Once she was seated behind the wheel of the Audi, he bent down to speak to her through the open window. Ever hopeful that she had forgiven him for not telling her the truth about knocking the tax man, he offered a bright smile. 'I want to make it up to you. I mean, our date turned out to be a bit of a disaster didn't it? So how about tonight, let me take you out. I know this great little jazz club in Soho that belongs to a mate of mine; you'll love it there.'

Tracey paused, her lips set into a thin line. For the briefest of moments Max thought she was going to refuse him, that during the course of the two days she had spent with him after the arson attack she had decided their relationship was over before it had even begun.

'Sounds perfect,' she finally answered, offering him a dazzling smile.

'That's a date then.' Straightening up, Max tapped the car roof, and as Tracey pulled away from the kerb, he continued watching until the Audi had turned the corner of the street. Walking towards his own car, he pulled out his mobile phone. Despite telling Tracey that there was no way Kenny could have been involved in the arson attack, a niggling thought at the back of his mind told him that the answers he craved could be found in Dagenham, his and Kenny's old hunting ground, hence why he'd instructed Tracey's sons to meet him at the boozer.

Scrolling through his contact list, he located the telephone number for an old pal of his, Eddie Winters. Born and raised in Dagenham, Eddie had his finger on the pulse. Not only was he well respected and given his due by those who knew him, but he was also a hard bastard, one who didn't take fools gladly. Without giving the matter a second's thought, Max typed out a message, telling Eddie that he wanted a meet. As far as he was concerned, the quicker he was given answers, the better it would be for all of them.

* * *

Pulling up outside his mother's house, Ricky surveyed the drive. The Audi was missing, a clear indication that his mother wasn't home.

'Did Mum say she was going out?' Ricky asked as he unclipped his seat belt and threw open the car door.

'Not to me.' Jamie shrugged. Following suit and climbing out of the car, Jamie looked around him. 'What are we hanging around for?' he asked his brother, his eyebrows rising. 'Mum's not home.'

'I just want to check on something.' Letting himself into the house, Ricky walked through to the kitchen. As usual, it was spotlessly clean, not that he'd expected any different; the kitchen had always been his mother's domain, her pride and joy. He pressed the back of his hand against the kettle, and just as he'd suspected it would be, it was stone cold, something which was highly unusual seeing as his mother was unable to function without having her morning coffee first. 'She hasn't been here all night.'

'Eh?' Jamie whipped his head around to face his brother. 'What do you mean she hasn't been here all night? Where the fuck is she then?'

'That,' Ricky said with a raise of his eyebrows, 'is exactly what I'd like to know.' He glanced at his watch and, noting that they still had some time to kill before meeting Max at the pub, pulled out one of the dining chairs, took a seat, then, kicking out his long legs in front of him, made himself comfortable. 'And believe me bruv,' he said, his face twisting into a snarl. 'Mum had best start talking and fast before I end up blowing a gasket.'

6

The Ship and Anchor public house in Dagenham was typical of the boozers in the area. Situated on the corner of a busy junction, the pub could easily be accessed from all directions, hence why it was somewhat of a goldmine and had once been owned by a local face, Paul Mooney. Pulling into the pub car park, Max pressed his foot down on the brake then switched off the ignition. Purposely, he'd told Ricky and Jamie to meet him at least an hour after he'd arrived. He wanted to suss out the lay of the land for himself before Ricky and Jamie made an appearance and more importantly he wanted to speak in private with his old pal Eddie Winters without an audience listening in on their conversation.

If anyone would have heard something about the arson attack then it was bound to be Eddie; he had a lot of fingers in a lot of pies, and as a result made it his business to be in the know. The difficult part however would be convincing his friend to divulge the information he had, at least without there being a hefty price tag attached, or a favour to be owed, and a very large favour at that. And the last thing Max wanted was to be indebted to someone, friend or not.

As for the car showroom itself, or rather the plight of the showroom, Max knew for a fact that it was common knowledge that so-called gangsters were unable to keep their mouths firmly shut. No, they liked to brag about the crimes they'd participated in, believing that it made their reputations all the more warranted, and Max had a sinking feeling in the pit of his stomach that someone would be talking about the attack on both himself and his business. Max had a reputation of his own, especially in regards to the crime he'd committed as a teenager, a murder that his so-called pal Terry Tempest had helped him to execute. The very same Terry Tempest who had actually been the one to inform the old bill of Max's involvement in the death of his mother's partner.

Max had always believed that he and Terry were good friends, and that their friendship was rock solid. They had known one another since childhood, and Max had trusted Terry with his life, they had even made a pact that if one of them was ever questioned over the murder that they would keep the other's name out of the enquiry. And just as he'd promised he would, Max had stuck to the plan, he'd been loyal to Terry until the very end, it was just a pity the same couldn't be said about Terry.

Still to this day, Max was unable to get his head around the revelation that Terry was the reason he'd spent eighteen years of his life locked up. Fair enough, he'd committed the brutal murder, but there had been nothing to link him to the crime, at least nothing that would have made the filth suspicious of him. If it hadn't been for Terry grassing him up he would have literally got away with murder.

Entering the pub, Max took a look around him and, spotting Eddie's large, muscular frame standing at the bar, he made a beeline for his old friend.

'You all right Max?' Eddie smiled in a greeting. 'Long time no see, mate.' Pulling out a wad of notes from his trouser pocket, he turned his head to look at Max expectantly. 'What can I get you?'

Max cast his gaze across the optics and noting the brandy that had been placed in front of Eddie, he nodded down at the glass. 'I'll have what you're having.'

Eddie grinned and as the barmaid busied herself pouring the drink, he gestured around him. 'So what brings you back to Dagenham? It's not like you to be in the manor.'

Max allowed himself to smile. Eddie had a point; in recent years he'd frequented the area on a number of occasions all thanks to his friendship with Tracey and her sons. 'I may not live around here any more but I still like to keep a hand in; it is my old stomping ground after all, and you know how the old saying goes.' He grinned. 'Don't shit on your own doorstep.'

Eddie gave a thoughtful nod. 'And there was me thinking it could have something to do with that car showroom of yours?'

Max raised his eyebrows. Just as he'd suspected, news had obviously travelled fast. 'There are no flies on you are there, pal,' Max laughed.

Eddie puffed out his chest. 'You know me Max, I make it my business to know what's going down.' He spread open his arms, the gesture coming across as almost apologetic. 'What with Terry out of the equation and Kenny incarcerated at Her Majesty's pleasure for the considerable future, someone had to take over the reins of the manor, didn't they?'

Taking the glass of brandy, Max downed the drink in one large gulp, enjoying the burn as the alcohol slipped down his throat. 'And let me guess,' he said, his expression deadpan. 'That person would be you.'

'Let me put it this way.' Eddie shrugged. 'I was more than happy to step in, not that I was willing to give any other fucker the chance of taking over. For years I've bided my time and waited for my chance to prove myself worthy as the top dog, and' – he looked around him, the faint hint of a smile tweaking at the corners of his lips – 'now that I've got my hands on the prize I'm not about to give up the crown any time soon, at least not without a fight.'

Max laughed out loud at the veiled threat. Not that he could say he was entirely surprised. Eddie along with his two brothers were well known in the area, and it would be true to say that Eddie's reputation was on a par with Terry's, not that Max could ever envisage Eddie involving himself with prostitution mind; drugs, yes, even money laundering, or bank robberies if the Carter brothers ever decided to hang up their gloves and let someone else have a look in once in a while. But as for forcing a woman to sell her body for money, then no, Eddie Winters had too much respect for the opposite sex. He adored his four daughters and worshipped the ground that his wife Nancy walked on. 'I'm not interested in a turf war if that's what you were thinking, and the same goes for Terry's sons.'

Eddie visibly relaxed. 'I'm glad to hear it. So, what is it I can do for you then? Because I know you Max Hardcastle,' he said with a grin, 'and you wouldn't be here now unless you wanted something from me, and if it's not the manor you're after then it's bound to be something else.'

Max didn't need to be asked twice; he was more than keen to get back down to business, and the arson attack was his number one priority. 'You heard about the showroom being torched.'

'You'd have to be deaf and blind not to have heard, and trust me,' Eddie said in a gruff voice as he sipped at his drink, 'I'm neither.'

Gesturing to the barmaid for another round of drinks, Max leant casually against the bar. 'So, what have you heard?'

Setting his glass down, Eddie took a moment to study Max. 'Word on the street is that someone is out to destroy you.'

Max lifted his eyebrows, his steely grey eyes boring into Eddie's skull with an intensity that would make most men avert their gaze. 'And would that word be from the horse's mouth by any chance?'

'Don't be daft,' Eddie laughed. 'Do you really think I wouldn't have paid you a visit before now if I had concrete information? We go way back Max; we were pals long before Terry ever came on the scene, and your mum was good to me and my family. When you were banged up, she looked after my brothers after our mum died. Our dad had already fucked off by then and what did I know about bringing up kids? They were only nippers, barely out of nappies, and I was still a kid myself, only eighteen. I was more interested in earning a name for myself; the money to pay for the rent had to come from somewhere didn't it, and it wasn't like my old man was going to trouble himself and make sure that we had a roof over our heads. He didn't give two shits about us; all he cared about was propping up the bar, which he did on a nightly basis might I add, probably still does if the fucker is still alive.' He gave a slight shrug and turned up his nose. 'But as for your old mum, she stepped in when no one else wanted to; everyone else might have looked down on us and treated us like scum, but not her. Whenever she could, she made sure that my brothers' clothes were clean, that they went to school, and that they had food in their bellies, that's not something I'm likely to forget. She was a good woman, an absolute diamond, and I had a lot of respect for her.'

The familiar sense of guilt he felt surrounding his mother once again engulfed Max. His mum had been devastated when he'd been handed down a life sentence and all these years later Max couldn't help but wonder if he'd somehow contributed to her death. He'd broken her heart, he knew that much, smashed it to smithereens in fact; he'd denied her a future, denied her not only having her son in her life but also the joy of grandchildren. Perhaps her grief had been so all-consuming that she had never fully recovered. She'd certainly never lived long enough to see her only son released from prison. Instead, she'd died alone, a fate he would never in a million years have wanted or chosen for her.

'And another thing,' Eddie continued with a wicked gleam in his eyes. 'I choose my enemies wisely, and the last thing I want or need is for you and me to be at loggerheads. Besides, I like my kneecaps where they are, thank you very much.' He paused for a moment to study Max. 'But that wasn't really your style, was it? Too quick, and too impersonal.' Leaning back slightly, Eddie shook his head. 'Nah, it was Terry who had a penchant for kneecapping people, but you' – he stabbed his finger forward, amusement dancing in his eyes – 'if I remember rightly, liked to take your time when it came to dishing out your own form of retribution, and when I say take your time, I'm talking about ripping out fingernails one by bloody one, driving nails through body parts, slicing off noses, or' – he cocked his head to one side, his forehead furrowing – 'was it ears?

'Both,' Max sighed. It had been a long time since he'd felt the need to torture anyone and he certainly hoped he would never have that need again. The acts he'd once committed had been truly barbaric, not that the men in question hadn't deserved their violent fates, because they had. Still, this fact did nothing to help ease Max's conscience. He couldn't help but feel a great sense of shame. Bottom line was that he wasn't proud of what he'd done in the past, but at the time the brutal acts he'd once carried out had been a necessity. More often than not it was a case of kill or be killed, and Max had chosen the former.

Eddie shrugged and screwed up his face. 'Either way, the end result would have still been the same I suppose.' He made a slicing motion across his neck and shook his head. 'So all in all I hope that answers your question,' Eddie continued. 'If I knew something I would have been upfront and told you from the off.'

Max nodded again. He should have guessed this would be the case. Eddie may have been a lot of things, but he wasn't stupid. If he'd had any information surrounding the arson attack he would have been one of the first to pay Max a visit. As for the culprit, all along Max had been right; someone was talking, the question was, who?

'Oi, over here.' Turning to look in the direction of the entrance, Eddie beckoned his two younger brothers, Charlie and Alfie, over as they entered the pub. 'You remember my old pal Max Hardcastle?' he said, gesturing towards Max. 'His mum helped us out after Mum died.'

'Yeah of course,' Charlie answered as he shook Max's hand. 'I heard you've had some trouble down your way.'

Max couldn't help but laugh; news certainly did travel fast. He went on to shake Alfie's hand. 'I was just asking Eddie here if he had any names for me?'

Charlie shook his head. 'Whoever it is, the dirty bastards are remaining tight lipped.'

'And it's not like we actually associate with arsonists,' Alfie added with a nonchalant shrug. 'And there must been more than one person involved considering there was nothing salvageable, the entire car lot was burnt to a crisp.'

Turning his gaze on the youngest of the Winters brothers, Max frowned. Not once had he mentioned the extent of the damage let alone the fact that he suspected there to be more than one culprit.

As the conversation turned to other interests, unease settled in the pit of Max's stomach, his mind working overtime. As hard as he tried not to, he couldn't help but steal furtive glances in the direction of Alfie Winters. Significantly younger than him, Alfie was a carbon copy of Eddie and Charlie: same stocky build, same mousey brown, cropped hair, and the same rounded nose that appeared to have been broken more than once, if the prominent bent bridge was anything to go by. Only unlike his brothers, Alfie came across as quieter, more reserved, and other than when he'd first mentioned the arson attack, he barely uttered more than two words to contribute to the conversation.

If Max hadn't known any better, he would have sworn that he could sense a hint of hostility coming off the younger man, perhaps even disdain. It was so subtle that he doubted any other man would have picked up on it, but Max being the kind of person he was had; not that he had any inkling as to why his presence could have caused such a reaction. He hardly knew the man and other than the odd few times he'd bumped into Eddie over the years, he and Alfie Winters had certainly never interacted with one another, at least not enough for either of them to have formed an opinion or cast a judgement against the other.

With a glance down at his watch, Max noted the time. Seeing as Alfie was nearer to Ricky and Jamie's age and that they were from the same area, they were bound to have crossed paths at some point. There and then he made a mental note to ask Tracey's sons just how well they knew the youngest Winters' brother. And like Eddie had already stated, the last thing either of them needed was a reason to be at loggerheads; as it was, Max apparently had enough enemies to contend with without adding another one to the mix, especially when that enemy went by the surname Winters.

Tracey Tempest tilted her head to one side, her eyes narrowed into mere slits. To say that she was seething would be the understatement of the century. In fact, she was so furious that she didn't know whether to laugh out loud at the sheer audacity of her sons or whether to slap them across their handsome faces.

'Well, come on,' Ricky demanded. 'Answer me. Where the fuck have you been?' He crossed his arms over his chest, his eyes hard. 'Or is that a stupid question?' he added, looking his mother up and down with a measure of disgust.

Remaining silent, Tracey placed her handbag on the kitchen table and slipped off her jacket with slow deliberate movements. As angry as she was, she couldn't help but feel her cheeks redden. It wasn't as though her sons didn't know where she'd been. They had last seen her with Max and the fact she had only just returned home two days later was a dead giveaway to the fact that she had spent the nights with Max, not that she and Max had actually done much bar argue.

'Well come on,' Ricky shouted. 'Say something. Admit it; you've been with Max all this time.' He screwed up his face, repulsion written across his features. 'How could you Mum?' he spat. 'What about Dad?'

A snort of laughter escaped from Tracey's lips. Terry had done more than his fair share of screwing around throughout their marriage, whilst she hadn't so much as looked at another man. 'Don't,' she warned, her eyes flashing dangerously. 'Just don't, okay.'

For a few moments they remained silent, the atmosphere crackling with tension. Wearily closing her eyes, Tracey bowed her head. She deserved some happiness, didn't she? And despite his shady past, Max was a good man. Her sons liked him and more importantly, she liked him too, so where was the harm in them becoming more than just friends? They weren't doing anything wrong; they weren't hurting anyone. They were adults for Christ's sake and it wasn't as though they were creeping around and seeing one another behind their spouses' backs. She was a widow and Max was single through choice.

'You just don't get it, do you Mum?' Jamie butted in. 'What

about us, eh?' He poked himself in the chest with a stiff finger. 'We work for Max, so what happens when this...' He looked around, trying to find the right word. 'When this sordid affair of yours,' he spat, 'comes to an end? Are we supposed to become collateral damage? We'll be out on our ears, and you know it. What are we supposed to do without an income eh, live on fresh air? We can't even work from Dad's scrap yard since you sold his business, so where exactly is the money going to come from? And what about your grandson? You go on and on about how Mason is the apple of your eye; are you really willing to see him go without a roof over his head all because you couldn't keep your knickers on?'

Tracey's hand flew out and as her palm connected with Jamie's cheek, the harsh slap was loud in the small confines of the kitchen. Almost immediately she took a large, shuddering intake of breath, her eyes wide and filled with horror. She hadn't meant to lash out, at least not as hard as she had, and as she tentatively reached out her arm for her youngest son, her palm burned, bringing with it further testament to just how hard she'd slapped him.

Shrugging himself away from her grasp, Jamie held a hand to his smarting cheek, not that it did much to conceal the stark red handprint that stained his skin.

Tracey's heart sank. She could think of only one other time when she had physically lashed out at her boys, and that had been when she had discovered what an evil, wicked man her husband had been, and even then she had only taken her fists to them because she had been terrified that they too could have followed on in their father's footsteps and been involved in the prostitution racket. 'I'm so sorry my darling,' she croaked out, her tone pleading. 'I didn't mean to do that, truly I didn't.' She looked down at her hand as though the limb were alien to her, wishing more than anything else that she could turn back time. 'I would never willingly harm you; you know I wouldn't. You may be grown men but you're still my babies.'

'What the fuck is wrong with you Mum?' Ricky barked out as his hard stare went from Tracey to his brother. 'You're swinging for us now; you're actually lamping us.'

There and then, shame washed over Tracey. As difficult as it was to admit it, the truth hurt, and the only reason she had lashed out in the first place was because everything Jamie had said was true. What would become of her boys if she and Max fell out? Would he no longer have a need for them? Not that this gave Jamie the right to speak to her the way he had. She had raised her boys to respect women, not treat them with disregard, and above all else, she was their mother.

'Is that what you really think of me?' she asked, her voice barely louder than a whisper. 'All because I want someone in my life, it's sordid, something dirty. After everything I've been through with your father, I deserve to be happy.'

'What else do you expect us to call it?' Ricky said, screwing up his face. 'It's wrong, it's... it's sick. Dad would turn in his grave.'

Jamie waved his brother's words away. 'I didn't mean it like that,' he mumbled. 'I was out of order and I'm sorry, but you have to see where we're coming from. You're not thinking straight Mum, and Ricky's right. Dad wouldn't have wanted this for you, especially not with Max; he was Dad's mate for fuck's sake.'

'No.' Tracey took a step forward, her body becoming rigid. The shame she'd felt was quickly replaced once again with anger. 'You, either of you,' she said, wagging her finger between her two sons, 'will not dictate to me. Don't you think I've suffered enough without the two of you interfering with my life? And as for your dad,' she said, her face contorting with anger. 'That man all but broke me. He flipped my world upside down without a second's thought. I loved him, I gave him everything there was to give of myself and it wasn't enough, nothing would have been enough, he would have still wanted more, would still have shagged anything with a pulse. So don't you dare stand there telling me that your father would have disapproved. He gave up the right to have any kind of say over my life the very moment he betrayed my trust and made a mockery of our wedding vows.'

'But that's just it, Mum,' Ricky cried. 'Do you really believe that Max is going to stick around for the long haul? Yeah, he might be a good bloke for the majority, but he spent half his life locked up. If he wanted to settle down, don't you think he would have done it long before now?'

Tracey snapped her lips closed. Just as Jamie had before him, her eldest son had hit the proverbial nail on the head. Max had never given her the impression that he wanted to settle down; in fact, he seemed content living alone in his bachelor pad. Perhaps their relationship was destined to never progress further than a few dates; maybe she would never be anything more to him other than a quick fling, a quick shag, another notch on his bedpost. Her shoulders sagged. Was she being selfish and putting her own happiness above that of her boys? Was she really prepared to go against them, perhaps even fall out with them, and all for a quick fumble between the sheets that at the end of the day might turn out to be meaningless? And what were they going to do if Max decided that he no longer had a need for them? Not that she thought he would actually do something as callous as that. Max not only had morals, but he was also loyal to those he cared about, and he did care, she knew he did, why else would he have stuck around and offered Ricky and Jamie employment after discovering just how depraved their father had been? 'I appreciate your concern,' she said, her tone clipped. 'But I am a grown woman and I certainly do not want or need your advice.'

His face a mask of anger, Ricky nodded. 'Fair enough,' he said, getting to his feet and turning to look at his brother. 'We'll see what Max has to say about this instead then, because I can tell you now Mum, this ain't happening.'

Tracey's blood ran cold. 'Just who the fuck do you think you are talking to?' she demanded. 'You say one word about any of this to Max,' she said, slamming her hands down onto the table and glaring at her eldest son, 'and there will be hell to pay, do you hear me?'

As the nerve in Ricky's jaw pulsated, he gave a soft laugh and shook his head. 'Did you really think that we were going to give you our blessing, that we would tell Max to crack on. You're our mum for fuck's sake; which part of that don't you understand?'

'That's right,' Tracey answered, straightening up. 'I'm your mum, that doesn't give you the right to speak to me like this. And let me tell you something else for nothing, sweetheart, I will see who I want, when I want, with or without your blessing, is that understood?'

When her sons didn't answer, Tracey's nostrils flared. 'I said, is that understood?' she shouted. All along, she should have known that this would be their reaction; it wasn't even about Max, not really, it was all to do with the fact that she was their mother and they didn't like the idea of her being with any man other than their father. Well if they thought that by throwing their dummies out of the pram she would give in to their demands, then they had another think coming. She wouldn't be bullied, especially not by her own flesh and blood.

With one last searing glance in his mother's direction, Ricky jerked his head towards the door, indicating for his brother to follow him.

'I meant what I said,' Tracey yelled after them as they walked from the kitchen. 'Just one word Ricky and I will come down on you so bloody hard that your feet won't even touch the floor. You might think that you're some kind of tough man out there,' she said, pointing in the direction of the front door, 'but in here you're my son, not my bloody keeper, and believe me I am not scared of you and never will be.'

She didn't receive a reply, not that she had really expected one. Her sons could be pig headed and stubborn when the mood took them; they took after her in that respect. As the front door slammed closed, Tracey gripped on to the edge of the kitchen table so tightly that her knuckles turned white. Anger surged through her veins and as the sound of tyres screeching away from the kerb filtered through to the kitchen, she resisted the urge to swipe her arm across the table and knock everything before her to the floor. Should she warn Max that her boys were on the warpath? If they were anything like their father then she knew instinctively that they wouldn't hold back when it came to giving Max a piece of their minds; maybe they would even come to blows. A new sense of fear ravaged through her body and, rummaging through her handbag, she located her mobile phone and tapped out a series of digits. As she pressed dial and brought the device up to her ear, her hands ever so slightly trembled. 'Come on,' she urged Max. 'Answer your bloody phone.'

To Tracey's dismay, the call went to voicemail and without leaving a message, she slumped heavily on to a chair. As childishly as they were behaving, in the two years since Terry's death, Ricky and Jamie had been her rocks. They had been there for her without question and had stood by her side as she had mourned the loss of their father and then subsequently come to terms with the allegations that had been made against him. They had even stood by her when Bianca Murphy had announced that she was pregnant with Terry's child, and to Tracey's knowledge, neither Ricky nor Jamie had enquired after their half sibling, even though she suspected the child to be residing in the local area, more than likely with Bianca's parents. If they wanted to, they could easily track the baby down. They could even forge a relationship with their sibling, only deep down in her heart Tracey knew that they wouldn't; they would class any kind of interaction with Terry and Bianca's child as being disrespectful to her.

As she placed her head in her hands, a lone tear rolled down Tracey's cheek and she angrily wiped it away, annoyed at herself for not being stronger. She should have stopped them from leaving the house; better still, she should have sat them down and told them that she would live her life as she saw fit, not how they wanted her to live it. She was still a relatively young woman; after all, fifty was the new forty or so they said, so why should she be expected to live out the remainder of her life as though she were a nun? Not only that, but she didn't intrude or interfere in her sons' lives; was it too much for her to expect the same curtesy back from them?

She picked up her phone again and pressed redial, biting down on her lip as the call went to voicemail a second time. The boys would come around, she told herself as she placed the device back on the dining table. They had to. They had no other choice than to respect her wishes, and although it might take some time, eventually they would see that Max was a good man, that he could be trusted, and that he was nothing like their father. For a start, Max didn't use people to his own advantage, nor would he ever contemplate pimping out a woman. Max had even given evidence in court against Kenny and the Murphy family, something that she knew went against the grain and was bound to cause mistrust amongst his associates. He came from a world where it was frowned upon to become an informer, a grass, and yet he'd done so willingly in order to save the women who had been trafficked into the country. Those weren't the actions of a man who only wanted to look out for himself. No, Max's one and only thought had been to gain justice for those who had had crimes committed against them. As a direct result of Max's testimony, Kenny and the Murphys had been handed down lengthy prison sentences and the women had been returned to their home countries. If nothing else, Max had done society a favour, and Ricky and Jamie should take that into account instead of throwing their weight around and acting like spoilt children throwing a tantrum.

Determined not to allow her sons to treat her as though she were nothing other than their property, Tracey straightened up and dragged her fingertips underneath her eyes, wiping away any stray smears of mascara. She was Tracey Tempest, not someone who was spineless or weak minded. If nothing else, Terry's murder had forced her to learn how to stand on her own two feet. She wasn't clueless to the world around her any more, she'd seen evil with her own two eyes, and had even shared a bed with a man who as far as she was concerned could only be described as the devil incarnate. Whether her sons liked it or not, she'd had to toughen up, and the quicker Ricky and Jamie understood that, the better it would be for everyone concerned.

* * *

After saying his goodbyes to the Winters brothers, Max walked from the pub, the muscles across his shoulder blades rigid. Clutching his car keys tightly in his fist he made his way across the car park. Where the fuck were Ricky and Jamie? He'd specifically instructed Jamie to meet him at the boozer, and the fact that they hadn't bothered to turn up grated heavily on his nerves. They weren't in the habit of letting him down, and unlike their father they were loyal; they had proven as much when they had taken over the reins of his businesses when he'd served a short stint inside Pentonville prison for his role in battering Kenny Kempton half to death. His thoughts wandered to the showroom, and unease edged its way down his spine. Was it possible that the bastard responsible for burning down the car dealership had upped his game and targeted the betting shops? What other possible reason could there be for the brothers to have not met with him?

As he unlocked his car, he took out his mobile phone, his brow furrowing. Three missed calls from Tracey. He was about to return the calls when the squeal of tyres across the gravelled ground, followed by the unmistakable scent of burning rubber as the car skidded to a halt, caused Max to turn his head. 'Where the fuck have you been?' he shouted, his shoulders slightly relaxing as he recognised Ricky's car. He tapped at his watch and shook his head. 'I told you to meet me here at eleven, not midday.'

'You bastard.' As he jumped out of the car, Ricky's expression was murderous. His anger was so palpable that even the knowledge of what Max was capable of was wiped from his mind. 'My mum,' he roared. 'My fucking mum.'

Momentarily taken aback, Max narrowed his eyes. The fist that shot out, taking him unawares, connected with his jaw and as he staggered backwards, he automatically brought his hand up to his face. The punch had been hard, not that he would have expected any different from Ricky.

'Leave it,' Jamie shouted, yanking on his brother's arm. 'Just leave it, okay, Mum wouldn't want this.'

'Nah,' Ricky snarled, shaking his head. 'I'm warning you now.' He screwed up his face and bounded forward a second time. 'This ends now do you hear me? You go near my mum again and I'll kill you.'

For the briefest of moments, a shiver of fear ran down Max's spine and screwing up his face, he glanced back down at the phone. Had something happened to Tracey? She'd been fine when they'd said goodbye that morning; maybe not entirely happy considering he'd lied to her about the cars, but she had agreed to another date, so she couldn't have been that upset with him, could she?

'Do you hear me?' Ricky hissed as Jamie hauled him several feet away. 'Go near her again and I'll fucking have you.'

Max hastily composed himself and, slipping the phone back into his pocket, he took a step forward. 'I'll let you have that first shot for free,' he said, working his jaw open and closed, to check that no lasting damage had been caused. 'But swing for me a second time,' he added, his grey eyes hard, 'and I won't hold back; it'll be game on and believe me, you don't want that because I'll put you on your arse and not even break out in a sweat.'

Ricky's lips twisted into a snarl and as he made to break free from his brother's grasp, Jamie tightened his grip.

'Leave it,' Jamie repeated, throwing a wary glance in Max's direction. 'Just calm down bruv; this isn't going to get us anywhere, is it.'

Still rubbing at his jaw, Max lifted his head slightly. Out of the two brothers, he would have put money on Jamie being the one to steam in with his fists, not the other way around. Jamie was hot headed and had a quick temper on him, whereas Ricky on the other hand was what Max would call a thinker and it was common knowledge that the thinkers of the world were the more dangerous. 'Is your mum okay?'

Ricky's expression hardened and as he blew out his cheeks, he shrugged his younger brother away from him with so much force that Jamie almost toppled to the ground. 'Stay away from her,' he warned, his chest heaving with every word he spat out. 'She's off limits, have you got that? If you're after a quick shag then go and find some other slapper to get your kicks with but keep my mum out of it.'

Lifting his eyebrows, Max gave a slight shake of his head. That wasn't going to happen, no matter how much Tracey's sons might threaten him, and he had a sneaky suspicion they already knew that. And as for a quick shag, Tracey was anything but that. He had feelings for her that over time had grown stronger and stronger. He wouldn't be able to walk away from her even if he wanted to, not that he did want to, of course. He was more than content to see where his and Tracey's relationship took them, a first for him considering that in the past he would have been one of the first to hold his hands up and admit that he didn't want to settle down any time soon. He glanced across to the pub, his hard gaze scanning the grainy windows.

'Is your mum okay?' he repeated as he gestured towards his phone. 'I had some missed calls from her.

'Yeah,' Jamie answered as he automatically brought his hand up to the side of his face. 'Believe me, she's fine.'

Taking note of the red mark across Jamie's cheek, Max nodded. It didn't take a genius to work out where the injury had come from, and if he knew Tracey as well as he thought he did, then he wouldn't be surprised if she'd been the one to have marked him. 'Right then,' Max said with an air of caution. 'Can we all calm the fuck down?' He jerked his thumb behind him to the pub. 'You're late, and regardless of how angry you might be with me at this precise moment in time, if I tell you to meet me here at eleven then I expect you to be here, have you got that?'

Ricky gave an agitated sigh, and as he opened his mouth to answer, the muscles across his shoulders and forearms tightened.

'We were caught up with something,' Jamie quickly interrupted, jerking his head towards his brother.

'I can see that,' Max answered, pointing towards the red mark on Jamie's cheek, 'and from the look of it, I'd say that you came off worse.'

'Yeah you could say that,' Jamie groaned. 'A word of warning for you: don't ever get on my mum's bad side, because I can promise you now, it doesn't end well.'

Despite the dire situation, Max couldn't help but chuckle. From their very first meeting, when she'd stormed inside his office wanting answers about her husband's business interests and murder, Max had gathered that despite her petiteness, Tracey was a feisty woman and nothing he'd learnt about her since then had altered his mind on that front. She was fearless, and the fact that she had been prepared to take on Kenny and the Murphy family single-handedly was more than enough to prove that point. 'Noted. So what the fuck is all of this about eh?'

'As if you didn't know,' Ricky spat. 'You and my mum.'

It was exactly as Max had guessed, not that he wasn't glad that everything was out in the open; he'd told Tracey numerous times that they should tell Ricky and Jamie that their feelings had shifted. 'Your mum means a lot to me,' Max said, giving a small smile, 'and don't worry,' he added, holding up his hands. 'I don't need the third degree; it goes without saying that I'll treat her right.'

'Too fucking right you will,' Jamie piped up.

'And don't think that we're happy about this either,' Ricky added as he shook out the tension in his fist. 'One wrong move on your part and it'll be game over for you.'

'I'll bear that in mind,' Max answered. Keen to get back down to business, he nodded towards the pub. 'What do you know about Alfie Winters?'

Jamie shrugged. 'Not a lot, other than that he's a lairy bastard. It goes with the surname I suppose; they've all got a lot to say for themselves if you know what I mean.'

Instinctively, Max knew exactly what Jamie meant and as much as he liked Eddie, it would be fair to say that his mouth had always been one of his biggest downfalls.

Ricky leant against his car, his earlier anger slowly ebbing away. 'Alfie Winters hangs about with that nutcase doesn't he, what's his name?' he asked, tilting his head towards Jamie.

'Raymond Cole,' Jamie volunteered.

'Yeah that's it, Raymond Cole, he's a proper nutter.'

'I've never heard of him.' Max frowned as he tried to rack his brain and put a face to the name. Coming up empty handed, he rubbed his hand across his jaw, the dark stubble rough to his touch. 'He's not a mate of yours then I take it.'

'Are you having a bubble?' Jamie answered, screwing up his face. 'As if we'd hang around with the likes of him. Even as a kid he wasn't all the ticket; he's got a screw loose. He set fire to his old girl's gaff; she was in bed at the time, and if it hadn't have been for the neighbours raising the alarm, he would have ended up killing her.'

Ricky opened his mouth to agree before snapping it closed again and shifting his gaze back to Max. 'Why the sudden interest in Alfie Winters?'

'I don't know.' Max shook his head. 'I just get the impression he doesn't like me very much.'

Ricky snorted. 'Yeah well that makes two of us.'

Max rolled his eyes; the fact Ricky was no longer trying to swing for him told him otherwise. Twirling his car key around his index finger, he chewed on the inside of his cheek, deep in thought. 'I've just got this feeling in my gut.' He paused for a moment and looked back to the pub. 'What are the chances that Alfie Winters could have had something to do with the arson attack?'

'Leave it out,' Jamie laughed. 'Him and Raymond Cole might be a pair of nutters, but they're not suicidal and, let's face it, they'd have to be to think they could pull off something as big as this without bringing repercussions down on themselves. They're bound to know that you would go ape shit, and as nutty as they are, I just can't see them being that stupid.'

'Yeah, well.' Max sighed. In any normal circumstance, the Winters surname would be more than enough to guarantee that Alfie would be given a swerve, and it went without saying that his elder brothers would protect him from the repercussions of any wrong doings that he participated in; they were family after all, and from what Max knew of them, a close-knit family at that. Only, these weren't normal circumstances; the attack on himself warranted revenge and he'd never shied away from dishing out retribution in the past. It was this fact alone that made people wary of him.

He began to make his way back to his car. 'Keep your ears and eyes peeled,' he called over his shoulder, 'and if you hear anything, you know the drill.'

'We've got it.' Jamie made a mock salute. 'If we hear anything, you'll be the first to know.'

Climbing into his car, Max waited for Ricky to reverse out of the car park, then pushing the key into the ignition, he started the car. As much as he didn't want there to be, a seed of suspicion had been firmly planted in his mind, and he began mentally ticking off his concerns. Not only had Alfie known the extent of the damage and the fact there had been more than one culprit, but he'd also been hostile. Fair enough, it hadn't come across as glaringly obvious but it had still been there and Max had picked up on it. The problem he had was: *why* would Alfie want to destroy him? It made no sense; they barely knew one another. The muscles in Max's stomach tightened as he tried to think back. Could it be possible that he'd read the situation wrong? And what about Eddie? Could he have been involved? Could the attack have been about the manor all along, or to be more precise, who was going to run it?

As he flicked the indicator to turn out onto the road, Max gave the pub one final glance. As hard as it was for him to even try and comprehend, just maybe the answers he so desperately craved weren't as far out of reach as he'd first believed them to be. It was both a sobering and depressing thought, and above all else it really went to show that you couldn't trust anyone, even those who in any normal circumstances you would trust with your life. Max knew better than anyone about being stabbed in the back, and if Terry could betray him, anyone and everyone could be capable of treachery.

* * *

Eddie Winters narrowed his eyes as he studied his youngest brother. 'What the fuck is up with you?' he asked. 'You've barely said more than two words since you got here.'

Downing the remainder of his lager, Alfie slammed the empty pint glass down on the bar and screwed up his face. 'Him,' he said, jerking his head towards the door that Max had exited just moments earlier. 'Amongst other things, Hardcastle is a grass, a rat. Why the fuck you would stand here having a friendly conversation with the cunt is beyond me.' He glanced around him and lowered his voice. 'If we're not careful we'll be labelled the same as him; is that what you want?' he asked, his eyes flashing dangerously. 'For all and sundry to think that we are Judases, that we are just like that ponce and that we can't be trusted?'

Taken aback by his brother's outburst, Eddie ever so slightly rocked back on his heels. It was true, Max had given evidence in court against Kenny Kempton and the Murphy clan, but as far as Eddie could tell it had been warranted; at least, this was the common consensus amongst their associates. No matter which way you looked at the situation, Kenny had been bang out of order and had deserved everything he'd had coming to him. Max had only done what any other man would have done in the same situation and at least he'd had the bollocks to stand up for the women involved, especially since it would have been far easier and a lot less troublesome on his part to turn a blind eye.

As he continued to study his brother, Eddie jabbed a finger forward. 'This had better not have had anything to do with you and that nutcase pal of yours, because the attack on Hardcastle's car dealership has got his name written all over it. Raymond's not right in the head and you know it.'

Alfie raised his eyebrows at the slur. 'He's all right,' he answered, forever on the defensive when it came to his best mate. 'Besides, he's had a hard life, you know he has. His mum didn't want him and he was still only a kid when she kicked him out on the streets and as for his old man...' He paused for a moment, just catching himself in time before he let slip that Ray's father had been Terry Tempest. 'Well, he hardly ever saw his dad, did he?'

'Hard life?' Eddie exclaimed, his voice incredulous. 'He almost burnt his mother's house down to the ground, with her still in it might I add. Is it any wonder that she threw him out on his ear? And like I said, the attack on Hardcastle's showroom has got his name written all over it. He's got a nasty little habit of burning things down.'

Charlie shook his head. 'Eddie's right,' he said. 'Cole has got a screw loose, and you mark my words bruv, sooner or later he's going to drag you down with him.'

His back up, Alfie glared at his brothers. 'Well just maybe that's where you're wrong,' he said with a smug smirk. 'Ray is well connected and he has a lot of muscle on his side, not that he needs it in all fairness, he knows how to take care of himself.' He shoved his hands into his pockets and puffed out his chest. 'Besides, Ray is going places, and any day now he'll be coming into some money, and a lot of it.' He glanced back towards the exit, his expression one of pure hatred. 'And when he does, grasses like Hardcastle had better watch their backs.'

As he digested his brother's words, concern was at the forefront of Eddie's mind. It didn't escape his notice that Alfie hadn't denied his involvement concerning the arson attack, and if he knew Max Hardcastle as well as he thought he did then he knew without a doubt that the man would leave no stone unturned in his hunt for the culprits responsible. Eddie could only hope and pray that Max wouldn't point fingers in their direction. Unlike his brothers, Eddie knew the Max from old, and he knew for a fact that Max wouldn't allow something as simple as friendship to get in the way of dishing out his own form of retribution. And considering he also had Terry's two sons on board, the end result was bound to end up messy, or to be more precise, if they weren't careful, the situation could end up resembling what could only be described as a blood bath.

'Well just rein it in a bit, yeah.' Eddie gestured around him. 'Max Hardcastle is added aggro we don't need; he can be a sly fucker when he needs to be, plays his cards close to his chest, and before you know it, he's got you on his radar, and then believe me, all hell will break loose.'

Alfie laughed out loud. 'And?' he sneered. 'Is that supposed to scare me into toeing the line, or would you rather I bow down to him? I'll tell you what,' he said, laughing even harder, 'maybe you'd prefer it if I quaked in my boots whenever he's in the near vicinity; would that be more to your liking?' To prove his point he held out his hand and purposely made it waver.

Eddie sighed; it hadn't been what he'd meant at all and as he threw his arm around Alfie's shoulders, he pulled him in close.

'Just don't go making an enemy of him,' he chastised. 'Like I've already said, he's aggravation that we can do without.'

Rolling his eyes, Alfie allowed himself to be pulled into his brother's embrace. 'Yeah, well, I still think that he's a no-good dirty cunt,' he mumbled under his breath. 'And sooner rather than later he's going to get what's coming to him.'

7

Tracey eyed Max suspiciously, her eager gaze on the lookout for any tell-tale signs that he and her sons had come to blows, even though her boys had reassured her over and over again that their meeting with Max hadn't turned ugly.

'What the bloody hell is that?' she asked, standing on tiptoes and leaning in closer to scrutinise the faint bruise that was still visible across Max's jaw.

'It's nothing,' Max said, waving his hand dismissively.

'What do you mean it's nothing?' Tracey cried. 'Did one of my boys do this?' she asked, reaching out to tentatively touch the bruised skin. 'Because it sure as hell wasn't there this morning. Was it Ricky?' she spat as she unclasped her handbag and pulled out her mobile phone, more than ready to give her eldest son an ear bashing that he wouldn't forget in a hurry. 'I should have known that he would try and pull a stunt like this. I'm going to bloody kill him when I get my hands on him; they swore to me that nothing untoward took place, that it didn't come to blows between you.'

'Stop.' Gently catching hold of her wrist, Max shook his head.

'Just leave it, darling,' he said. 'Everything has been sorted out; that's all you need to know.'

Tracey was about to open her mouth and protest when Max shook his head a second time. 'They're looking out for you sweetheart, and I wouldn't expect anything less from them. They're good lads and they think the world of you; you should be proud of them. They had every right to have a pop at me, you're their mum at the end of the day and all they want is for you is to be treated right, and I wholeheartedly agree with them; you deserve the best.'

Still unsure, Tracey tore her gaze away from the bruise. She hadn't brought her sons up to be thugs and the mere thought that they had followed through with their threat and lashed out at Max was almost enough to make her feel ashamed of them, even if, as Max had just stated, they were only looking out for her best interests. 'Yeah... but...'

'No but's.' Max smiled. 'Take it from me, no real harm was done, at least nothing that I can't handle anyway.' He passed across her fitted black jacket and, taking out his car keys, he signalled that it was the end of their conversation.

Tracey sighed in defeat. She knew Max well enough to know that he wouldn't elaborate any further on what had taken place between him and her sons. Shrugging on the jacket, she smoothed down the leopard print silk shirt that she wore underneath. 'Where are we going again?' she asked as she rummaged through her handbag to check that she had her front door keys.

'A little club that I know in Soho.' Max grinned. 'It's owned by a mate of mine and you're going to love it there.'

Tracey looked up, her eyebrows ever so slightly rising, and as she followed Max out of the house it briefly crossed her mind as to why she'd never heard him mention the club before, especially seeing as it was owned by one of his friends. Pushing the thought away, she allowed herself to relax. It wasn't a big deal, she supposed, and it wasn't as if she'd known all of her husband's friends. She hadn't even known of Max's existence until after Terry's death and yet by all accounts they had been good mates.

* * *

Thirty minutes later, Max brought the car to a halt and switched off the ignition. Unclipping his seatbelt, he motioned towards a premises across the street.

'The Soho Club.' Tracey frowned, and as she turned in her seat to look at Max, alarm filtered across her face. Surely he hadn't brought her to a strip club? 'This is owned by Tommy Carter, isn't it?' she asked, scandalised. 'Or rather, it belongs to the Carter family.'

'It did,' Max answered with a sigh as he looked through the window and studied the club. 'My mate bought it from them a year or so ago and turned it into a jazz club. Come on.' Sensing Tracey's trepidation, he gave her hand a gentle squeeze before throwing open the car door and climbing out.

Clutching her handbag tightly, Tracey followed suit and, as she waited for Max to join her on the pavement, she peered up at the club with suspicion. 'Are you sure that this isn't a strip club?'

Max shook his head, and grasping her hand in his, they made their way across the busy street. 'You'll see.' He grinned.

As they bypassed the queue that snaked the length of the club and stepped inside the foyer, Tracey's eyes ever so slightly widened. Decked out with a rich burgundy and bronze swirling patterned carpet that was so thick her heels sank into the luxurious fibres, and pale bronze coloured walls, with deeper bronze sconces strategically placed behind an art deco style reception desk, the entrance hall itself was what she could only describe as impressive. The large, dazzling crystal chandelier complete with matching bronze fittings hanging above their heads screamed opulence and from her first impressions of the club she could tell that money hadn't been an issue when it came to the décor.

'This way.' After shaking the burly doorman's hands, Max gave her a wink, and gently pressing his hand to the small of her back, he led the way through a set of double doors.

Immediately the scent of expensive perfume assaulted Tracey's nostrils. Astounded, she looked around her. Set off to one side was a long bar area, the crystal glasses so pristine that they actually sparkled beneath the dim lighting, and taking pride of place in the middle of the vast room was a stage that housed an assortment of instruments. Surrounding the stage were at least thirty round tables that could comfortably seat six people, each table adorned with small crystal lanterns that gave the club a soft hue.

'It's beautiful,' Tracey gasped. 'Why have you never brought me here before?' she asked as they weaved their way through the tables.

Max grinned and, giving a slight shrug, he gestured to one of the VIP tables directly in front of the stage. 'I don't come here often,' he admitted, his gaze surveying the club as though he was on the lookout for something or someone.

Once seated, and a bottle of champagne had been placed in front of them, Tracey turned her attention back to the stage. The atmosphere crackled with anticipation and as she took a sip of her drink she almost jumped out of her skin when a deep, booming male voice that spoke with an East London accent came from directly behind them.

'Fuck me, Max Hardcastle, it's about time that you showed your face in here you fucker. It's good to see you mate.'

Max laughed out loud and shook the outstretched hand. 'This is my old friend, Vince... Vincent Daly,' he said to Tracey with a grin. 'This is his club.'

Placing her glass on the table, Tracey looked up. Standing well over six feet tall, the man before her offered a bright smile, his dark brown skin almost glistening underneath the dim lighting. 'Nice to meet you,' she said, thrusting out her hand. 'I'm Tracey... Tracey Tempest.'

For the briefest of moments Vincent faltered, before he hastily took her tiny hand in his. 'Tracey Tempest, eh?' He shot Max a surreptitious glance, the smile filtering back across his face. 'I knew your husband; not as well as Max here,' he said, flashing a row of even white teeth. 'But our paths had crossed over the years.'

Tracey smiled, although it would be fair to say that it was a smile that didn't quite reach her eyes. The mere mention of her late husband often had that effect on her. It was the pity and mistrust written across other people's faces that she disliked the most, however much they tried to hide it from her. Not that she blamed them; how could she when if the roles were reversed, she too would find it all too easy to judge. It was almost as though she could see the cogs turning in their heads, as if they were weighing her up or trying to somehow decipher whether or not she could have had any prior knowledge about what her husband had been getting up, or more to the point, whether or not she too could have been involved in the prostitution racket. Of course the answer was no, she'd had no idea; how could she have when Terry had deceived her just as much as he had deceived everyone else around him?

'Have you got everything you need?' Always the impeccable host, Vincent motioned towards the champagne bottle. 'Can I get you anything else to drink?'

'We're fine,' Max reassured him. 'But I do need to have a word before the night is over.'

Vincent nodded, his smile not faltering. If he was surprised by

Max's request then he hid it well, Tracey noted. Perhaps a little too well.

'I thought as much,' Vincent answered, confirming Tracey's suspicions. 'Whenever you're ready, come into the office,' he added, pointing towards the rear of the club, 'and I'll be waiting for you.'

As they said their goodbyes, Tracey picked up her glass and took a long sip of the champagne. 'He seems nice.'

'He is,' Max was quick to answer, his expression becoming closed off. 'He's a good bloke.'

'And how do you know him?' she probed.

Max waved his hand dismissively. 'I've known him for years, both him and his brother.'

It was a vague answer to her question and as she studied Vincent's retreating back, Tracey bit down on her bottom lip. Why all the secrecy? she wondered. It also didn't escape her notice how Max could barely look her in the eyes, a sure sign if ever there was one that he was keeping something from her, what that was though, for the life of her she had no idea.

Before Tracey could ask any further questions, the stage lights sprang on, and as the musicians walked out on to the stage, a raucous applause went up around them. Well aware that the moment was lost, Tracey made herself more comfortable, all the while mentally reminding herself to dig a little deeper into Vincent Daly.

An hour later, after promising Tracey that he wouldn't be too long, Max made his way through the club. Outside Vincent's office, he lightly tapped his knuckles on the door then without waiting for permission to enter, he pulled down on the handle.

Looking up from a stack of paperwork on his desk, Vincent grinned and, getting up out of his chair, walked around the desk and perched his backside on the edge of the table. 'Have a seat,' he told Max as he gestured to a wine-coloured chesterfield sofa. 'I've been expecting a visit from you.'

Sitting down, Max leant his forearms on his knees. 'I take it you heard about the car showroom then?'

With a deep sigh, Vincent nodded. 'Put it this way, news of your impending downfall is certainly doing the rounds and if it's reached my ears then you can guarantee that every other fucker out there has also heard a whisper or two.' He paused for a moment and, tilting his head to one side, he studied Max. 'Is Kenny's name in the frame? Because from what I know of the bastard, he went down a little too quietly for my liking, and I told you as much right from the get-go,' he added, pointing a finger forward. 'He's bound to want revenge and let's face it, he's got plenty of time on his hands to scheme and plot out his retaliation.'

'You tell me.' Max nodded towards the telephone on the desk, then sinking further onto the sofa, he blew out his cheeks. 'I don't know... maybe,' he finally admitted as his thoughts turned to the possibility of either Kenny or Eddie Winters and his brothers being behind the attack. 'We both know that Kenny wouldn't be able to pull off a stunt like this though, at least not without help anyway, and it's not like he's in a position to waltz out of nick whenever he feels like it, is it. So the question is, who the fuck would he have on his side? It's no one from the Murphy family, I know that much, and from my understanding, Kenny is more or less considered a social pariah, so who would even want to back him and more to the point why? What would they be getting out of this? Because no one would involve themselves in something as colossal as this unless they are going to benefit from it somehow.'

As he thought the question over, Vincent shrugged. 'You've got a point,' he conceded. 'But if it's not Kenny, then who else would have the audacity to try and take you on? I mean, they're bound to know that you're not going to sit back and allow someone to take the piss out of you. And let's be honest here, torching the car show-room is the biggest piss take of them all; it's your livelihood, your main source of income, and by torching the gaff it's pretty obvious that they went straight for the jugular, that they mean business and that they're not going to stop until you either suss out who was behind the attack and deal with it, or' – he looked Max in the eyes and shook his head – 'they take you out first, however small the likelihood of that happening might be.'

For a few moments, Max remained silent. Vincent hadn't told him anything that he didn't already know. He'd been hit where it hurt the most and considering the car dealership was where the majority of his money came from, then whoever had set out to destroy it knew him well, or at least well enough to know that he spent the majority of his time at the car lot rather than the bookies. He jerked his head back towards the telephone on the desk. 'Have you heard from your brother?'

'Not for a few days.' Reaching into his back pocket, Vincent pulled out a burner phone. 'Do you want me to give him a bell? Just say the word and Kenny will be taken care of. Think of it this way,' he said, grinning, 'at least it will be one suspect crossed off the list. It'll be a win-win situation for all concerned. And you know as well as I do what Cain is like,' he said, referring to his younger brother. 'He's bound to be bouncing off the walls; he wants to see Kenny taken out as much as anyone else. As it is, the slimy fucker is beginning to throw his weight around a bit too much for Cain's liking; the way he's carrying on, anyone would think he's the top dog. In fact, just a few days ago he almost topped a bloke, beat him to a bloody pulp then threw him over the railing, all because he hasn't repaid a debt. I wouldn't mind but the poor bastard only owes a couple of measly quid, the same price as a can of tuna. It's hardly a small fortune is it, or something worth having your life extinguished over.'

After glancing down at his grazed knuckles, Max lifted his eyebrows. He'd witnessed men being shanked for a lot less when he'd been inside, and when it came to debts, it was the number one rule that you pay back what you owe no matter how big or small the debt might be. As for Kenny, he couldn't say that he was entirely surprised to hear that he'd been throwing his weight around. Kenny had always been a bully, and even when they had been kids Kenny had got off on intimidating those he considered to be weaker than himself.

'Have you forgotten what it's like inside already?' Max asked. 'When we were in Belmarsh, how many times did we witness someone being sliced open all thanks to a debt that hadn't been repaid.'

'True,' Vincent sighed as he thought back to his younger years. 'Look, just give me the nod and by this time tomorrow I can guarantee you that Kenny will be brown bread.' Dangling the mobile phone in front of Max's face, Vincent grinned. 'Come on,' he coaxed, his eyes flashing mischievously. 'You know you want to; just say the word and it's as good as done.'

Max couldn't help but laugh. As tempting as the offer was to seal Kenny's fate, he couldn't, at least not yet anyway, not until he'd found out who was behind the arson attack.

'No.' Max held up his hands as though to ward off Vincent's protests. 'Kenny isn't likely to go anywhere anytime soon, not unless he does something to put himself on to the segregation wing and knowing that sly fucker he'd do anything and everything in his power if it meant saving his own arse. No, we're better off keeping him sweet, and more importantly keeping him where Cain can keep an eye on the cunt. The last thing I want is for him to slip through our fingers and end up being shipped off to another wing or a different nick.'

'And that,' Vincent said, pointing a finger in Max's direction, 'is where our friendly screw will come in handy. All we have to do is put the hard word on the bastard and tell him to make sure that Kenny stays put.'

'Maybe,' Max answered, getting to his feet. Having spent eighteen years of his life banged up, he'd come to learn that there was no such thing as a friendly screw, at least none that were so corrupt that they would actually commit a crime on a prisoner's or ex-prisoner's behalf as the case happened to be. 'We'll see.'

As they walked to the door, Vincent slung his arm around Max's shoulder. 'You know what your trouble is, don't you?' he said, his voice jovial. 'You need to learn how to trust more, and yeah, fair enough, I'd be the first to hold my hands up and agree that a screw may not be the first person you would automatically trust with a problem like Kenny, but you have to remember this bloke is in your pocket. We've got so much shit on this geezer that he'd be stupid not to do your bidding; as it is, the prick shits himself whenever Cain so much as looks at him the wrong way, and—'

Max shook his head, cutting Vincent off. 'You're forgetting something,' he said bitterly. 'It was trusting someone that got me into this situation in the first place. So, you've got that much right; other than a select few, I don't trust any fucker. I've been stabbed in the back one too many times and like fuck am I ever going to willingly put myself in that position again.'

Vincent's smile fell and as he released his arm from around Max's shoulders, he sighed. 'Look, I'll give Cain a bell anyway and tell him to have a word in the screw's ear. At least that way he'll know the score, and more importantly, he'll know when to turn a blind eye. It's not like it would be the first time, is it?' He shrugged.

'Half the screws are as bent as the cons themselves, and you know that as well as I do. When we were banged up we witnessed the bastards in action on a daily basis. As for trust, you know that me and my brother have got your back. Cain has put his neck on the line for you, he's the one holed up with Kenny, and the last thing any of us want is for the low life fucker to suss out where Cain's loyalties really lie before he's had the chance to iron him out.'

Thinking it over, Max nodded. 'Fair enough,' he answered. 'Tell Cain to be on standby. And as for the screw,' he said with a raise of his eyebrows. 'Make sure that he knows what's expected of him. I don't care how much you have to threaten the bastard, just make sure he understands that it's in his best interests to do exactly what I tell him to do.'

Vincent grinned and, cracking his knuckles, he gave a nod of his head. 'I had a feeling you would say that.' He winked.

* * *

In Belmarsh Prison, Cain Daly leaned casually against the door frame to his cell and began the process of rolling himself a cigarette. After having been in and out of the prison system for most of his adult life, he was no stranger to being locked up. Despite his predicament, it was the noise of the prison that he detested the most and other than his freedom of course, one of the few things that he longed for was a reprieve from the constant chatter, laughter, angry shouts, and whenever a new bloke was brought onto the wing, the pitiful sound of his sobs that were sure to come once reality had finally set in and he'd come to realise that this was to be his life for the considerable future. As much as Cain joined in with every other prisoner and shouted at the bloke to shut the fuck up, the truth was, he couldn't help but feel depressed. It was the sense of being helpless he supposed, that and the knowledge that whether they liked it or not, there was no escape, that the prison and the four walls they had been assigned to would become the be-all and end-all of their existence for however many years they had been sentenced to. As if that wasn't bad enough, the endless stream of monotony was enough to break even the toughest of men, especially those handed out life sentences.

Out of the corner of Cain's eye he caught sight of a man slowly hobbling along the landing, his swollen face a mass of purple and black bruises. A sense of irritation swept through Cain's body, and placing the matchstick thin cigarette between his full lips, he glanced towards Kenny's cell just a few doors along. To the outside world, Cain appeared calm and as he lit up and lazily drew the smoke deep into his lungs, he contemplated what the evening ahead had in store for him; instinctively, he knew that whatever was about to go down wouldn't be pretty and, turning back to look at the man still painstakingly making his way to his cell, he felt a moment of pity for him.

Why the fuck he had even been given the go ahead to return to the wing so soon after the injuries he'd sustained, Cain couldn't fathom out. As it was, the bloke was a sitting duck and that was without the added fact he could barely walk further than two paces without needing to hold on to the iron railing for support, the very same iron railing that just days earlier Kenny Kempton had thrown him over.

As the man neared Cain, he bowed his balding head, avoiding eye contact with those around him, his wiry body physically trembling so much so that in Cain's opinion he looked in grave danger of collapsing to the floor. Whether the tremors were through fear or pain, Cain had no idea; perhaps it was a combination of the two, seeing as his return to the wing was the equivalent of walking into a lion's den.

Catching a prison officer's eye, Cain gave a look of sheer

contempt. The screw, a non-descript man in his early forties, with a bulbous nose that he was constantly wiping, rheumy blue eyes and short mousey brown hair, named Simon Peters, or Mr Peters as they were forced to call him, had the grace to look away, not that Cain hadn't got his number first. He was on Max Hardcastle's payroll, or rather he was in Max's pocket all thanks to a very large gambling debt he'd rather his employer and family knew nothing about.

'Well, well, well, look who it is.'

Cain turned to look over his shoulder, his heartbeat picking up pace. Unlike Kenny, he was no bully, and despite his sheer size and menacing presence, he wasn't in the habit of intimidating others, especially men like the poor fucker who was still heavily limping towards his cell and who was in no position to fight back.

A wicked grin spread across Kenny's face and as he sauntered along the landing, there was a cockiness about him that made Cain want to pull back his fist and fell him to the floor, just for the sheer fun of it.

'You owe me,' Kenny snarled, the smile quickly slipping from his face. 'And no one,' he continued, his voice rising, 'treats me like a mug and gets away with it.'

The atmosphere around them became suddenly tense and as conversations fizzled out, all eyes turned towards the injured man, awaiting his response, or to be more precise, awaiting Kenny's next move, keen to know how he was going to handle the situation. After all, it was a break from the routine and the majority of prisoners would even consider the fallout to be a light form of entertainment, a welcome relief to ease the boredom of their day.

Cain steeled himself, not that he was in a position to help the man out however much he might want to, and as every instinct inside of him screamed out for him to come to the man's defence, he knew instinctively that he wouldn't, *couldn't,* without blowing his cover. Kenny believed that they were allies, and that if any trouble should arise, then Cain would be one of the first to fight in his corner. Instead, Cain flashed a glance towards the prison officer, silently willing him to move the injured man along and out of Kenny's reach. To his dismay, the officer hesitated. Cain narrowed his eyes, his expression hardening. What the fuck was going on? Why wasn't the screw ordering Kenny back to his cell? Why was he allowing the fiasco to continue?

'I said that you owe me.' Kenny stepped forward, his fists clenching then unclenching in rapid succession. 'Unless of course' – he flicked his gaze towards the railing, his eyes flashing dangerously – 'you want to take another unfortunate tumble. You never know, this time you might not be quite so lucky; you could actually break your neck or at the very least suffer some lasting damage up here.' He tapped the side of his head and flashed a sly grin, thoroughly believing that he was the star of his own show and those around him were his captive audience, hanging off his every word. 'Or you could pay back what you owe, with some added interest on top for my inconvenience of course. I mean,' he said, taking a step even closer, the smug grin intensifying. 'I don't do charity and I sure as hell don't help out snivelling little pricks like you.'

Amid laughter, the man looked down at the floor, his slim frame shaking so violently that Cain could actually hear his teeth chattering. 'I have no money,' he answered in broken English, his voice surprisingly strong considering how much his body shook.

'Then it looks like you and me have got a problem, doesn't it.' The glee in Kenny's voice became more apparent and as the atmosphere around them became even more charged, Kenny gave a sadistic grin. 'Because from the look of things you obviously didn't learn the first time around.'

Kenny made to charge forward, and in a last-minute decision,

Cain swore under his breath and brought out his meaty forearm, bringing Kenny to a grinding halt.

'Leave it out,' he hissed in Kenny's ear, his eyes darting towards the screw. 'Not here man, not like this; you'll be carted off to the block.'

It was enough to make Kenny pause, and shrugging Cain away from him, he smoothed down his T-shirt. 'Another time,' he said with a snarl, his wary gaze following Cain's to the prison guard. 'But sooner or later I will have you, let's make no mistake about that.'

With the situation temporarily under control, Cain ignored the disappointed groans that came from the other prisoners and gave the screw one final look of disdain as he finally got his act together and ushered Kenny back to his cell. Cain strolled nonchalantly towards his own cell, his fingers itching to grab the burner phone from its hiding place so he could get in contact with his brother and tell him that enough was enough, that Kenny's days on earth were numbered, even if that meant bringing Max Hardcastle's wrath down on top of him in the process.

8

Standing in front of his grandmother's fireplace, Raymond Cole stared at the framed photographs of his late father Terry Tempest, which took up every available inch of spare space on top of the mantlepiece. He had no real interest in looking at them; he'd seen the photos a hundred times before and if he was being honest with himself, he was sick to the back teeth of looking at his father's grinning face staring back at him. It was only the fact Patricia expected it from him that as soon as Raymond entered her home he made a bee line for them. No matter what, he had to keep up the act of the doting grandson, and even more than that it was crucial to his plan that Patricia not only trusted him but that she also believed his intentions were pure.

'Here you go sweetheart, a cup of tea, just how you like it, nice and strong with two sugars.'

'Cheers Nan.' Carefully taking the cup and saucer from her, Raymond smiled. 'I can't stay for too long today though,' he warned. 'I'm off out tonight.'

Patricia's eyes lit up. 'Are you going out on a date?' she asked.

'That's exactly what you need darling, a nice girlfriend, and you make sure that she's a nice girl too, not some cheap trollop.'

Raymond laughed. 'You know me, Nan.' He winked. 'I haven't got time for a bird; I'd rather be out earning some dough.' Although that wasn't strictly true; he'd actually been seeing a woman on and off for a couple of months. He'd met her on one of his visits to see Kenny and the fact her old man was inside was a large part of the attraction. He actually got a kick out of knowing he had one over the geezer and that while he was sweating his bollocks off in a concrete cell with nothing else to do but think about his girl and life on the outside, Raymond was the one in their bed giving her one. 'Nah I'm seeing my mates tonight; we'll probably end up going to a club or something.'

'Well you enjoy yourself sweetheart.' Nodding thoughtfully, Patricia gestured towards the mantelpiece. 'Were you looking at your dad's photos again?' She cast her gaze over the framed images that showcased her only child's life from infancy right up to just a few months before his death. 'Like two peas in a bleeding pod the pair of you,' she sighed. 'He was a good man your dad and he would have been proud of you; I know that much.' Taking a used tissue out from her sleeve, she dabbed at her watery eyes. 'I still can't get over it; I don't suppose I ever will. When you lose a child it hits you in here.' She thumped her fist against her breast bone to drive her point home. 'It's like a knife twisting in your heart. I mean, it's just not right, is it? My Terry was in the prime of his life and still had so much to live for and on his birthday an' all of all days.'

Irritation swept through Raymond and, stifling the urge to roll his eyes, he placed the cup and saucer on a side table and then took a seat beside Patricia on the sofa. Every single time he visited her, Patricia would spout the same old crap, so much so that he could recite her words off by heart. She missed Terry, she loved Terry, she wished that she had died in Terry's place, blah, blah, fucking blah.

'Come on now,' he said gently. 'Don't go upsetting yourself Nan.' He passed across a fresh tissue. 'My dad wouldn't want to see you like this, would he? He'd want you to get on with your life, to be happy.'

Patricia continued to dab at her tears. 'You are a good boy,' she said, clasping Raymond's hand in hers and giving it a squeeze, her bony fingers holding on for dear life. 'You're the only one who comes to visit me now. The other two, Ricky and Jamie, they couldn't give two monkeys about me. My own grandsons, my own flesh and blood and they couldn't care less if I lived or died. Maybe that's what they're waiting for, they're counting down the days until I'm six feet under.' She looked around the lounge, her eyes wandering over her possessions. Not that she had a great deal to show for her seventy years on earth, just a flat screen television and a stereo, both of which had once belonged to Terry, and a few knick-knacks, or toot, as her son had liked to call the china ornaments that she had collected over the years. 'I bet they would soon come running then, more than likely hoping that I'd left them a few quid in my will, not that I've even got much to leave; I've barely got enough money to feed myself, let alone leave anything for those two ungrateful buggers.'

'If you're strapped for cash Nan you only have to ask.' Making a show of pushing his hand into his pocket, Raymond pulled out a handful of notes. 'You know that I'll look after you.'

'No.' Patricia waved her hand in the air, her eyes remaining firmly riveted on the cash in her grandson's hand. 'I wouldn't dream of asking you for money my darling,' she lied. 'I've still got some pride left inside of me. But if your dad were still here,' she said, craftily eyeing up the money, 'he would have made sure that I'm okay, that I've at least got enough money to look after myself and pay the bills. I can't even afford to go to bingo any more, my only pleasure in life. It used to do me good getting out of the house once in a while to see my mates, it gave me something to live for.' Lighting a cigarette, she inhaled the smoke deep into her lungs before loudly exhaling. 'Even the price of a loaf of bread and a pint of milk has gone through the roof. How they expect us pensioners to get by I'll never know; it's pure greed,' she said, pointing the cigarette in Raymond's direction, 'that's what it is.'

Hiding his annoyance, Raymond rolled off two fifty-pound notes and placed the money on the side table, if for no other reason than to shut her up. It also didn't escape his notice how considering she was so hard up, she always found the money to buy a never ending supply of Benson and Hedges. 'There you go Nan, and there's plenty more where that came from,' he said, lightly tapping his finger on the cash. 'So in future just ask, you're my nan and it's my job to make sure that you're all right. I wouldn't want to see you go without.'

Patricia didn't need to be told twice, and greedily snatching up the money, she tucked the notes into her bra strap then patted Raymond's hand before nodding towards her son's wedding photograph that took centre stage on the mantlepiece.

'I blame her, that Tracey,' she spat, screwing up her face. 'She's never liked me. From day one that bitch did everything in her power to sink her claws into my Terry and take him away from me, and she wasn't content in that either; oh no, she also had to poison my own grandsons against me too; she must have done, otherwise they would come and see me every now and then.' She stubbed out the cigarette in an overflowing glass ashtray then proceeded to noisily blow her nose. 'At least I've got you with me my darling,' she said, tucking the dirty tissue back up her sleeve. 'That's something to be thankful for I suppose.'

Raymond cleared his throat and, seeing this as his chance to bring up the subject of meeting his half-brothers, he pulled his lips down at the corners into what he hoped resembled a sad smile. 'When are you going to introduce me to my brothers Nan?' he asked. 'I mean, if I met them then I could have a word in their ears, I could make sure that they come and see you a bit more often; you'd like that wouldn't you?'

About to flap her hand dismissively, Patricia paused. The longing in Raymond's voice was her undoing and as selfish as it was to want to keep him all to herself, it was only right that he met his half siblings; not only that, but in the long run it would be another yard stick to beat her daughter-in-law with.

'I'll tell you what,' she said, her eyes flashing with malice. 'I'll introduce you to them tomorrow; it's about time the three of you were acquainted and it's only what your dad would have wanted, to have his three boys all together under the one roof.' She glanced up at the ceiling, tears welling in her eyes again. 'I just wish that he could have been here to introduce you to your brothers himself.'

Nodding his head, it took every ounce of Raymond's willpower not to smirk. By the time he'd finished with them, Ricky and Jamie weren't going to know what had hit them. As far as Raymond was concerned, they had taken his dad away from him. Even now, all these years later, he could still recall how Terry had always been in a hurry to get back home to his boys, his *real* sons, the ones who bore the Tempest surname. No matter how many times as a child he had begged Terry to let him come and stay with them or at the very least visit on the weekends, the answer had always been the same, a very firm no. Was it any wonder that he felt nothing but bitterness and hatred towards the sons Terry had wanted, welcomed even, whilst he had been kicked to the kerb with so little thought, as though he were nothing but an inconvenience to his father, a burden? Fair enough, Terry may have put his hand in his pocket every now and then and provided for his son. There were times when he'd even taken Raymond out shopping and bought him new outfits and the latest designer trainers, but only because his previous shoes had holes in the soles and his clothes had become too small for him. When it came down to it, Terry had never had his son's best interests at heart, he'd only ever thought of himself and he'd proved that point time after time. No, Terry had never been what Raymond would call a stable presence in his life, and yet despite all of this, Raymond had loved his dad, he'd wanted to grow up to be just like him, and more than anything else he'd wanted to make him proud.

'That's a date then.' Patricia broke Raymond's reverie, and rummaging through her handbag, she pulled out her mobile phone and began typing out a message. 'We'll see what lady muck thinks about her so-called perfect marriage now shall we,' she said, giving a wide grin. 'Once she finds out all about you and how your dad kept you hidden away for all these years.'

The smile Raymond gave in return was tinged with sadness. Unbeknownst to her, Patricia had just hit the nail on the head. When it came down to it, he was nothing but Terry's dirty little secret and the knowledge that his very existence had been a mistake, and that he hadn't been wanted by either of his parents, hung over Raymond like a thick, dark cloud.

A familiar sense of anger began to build within him, a rage that was so tangible he could practically feel it oozing out of his pores. Fuck Ricky and Jamie, and fuck Max Hardcastle. He was going to make them pay, every last one of them, if it was the last thing he ever did; even the tiny woman sitting beside him wouldn't be able to escape his wrath.

* * *

Tracey glanced down at her mobile phone and groaned out loud. What with everything else going on, Patricia was the last person she was in the mood to deal with. As it was, she and her mother-in-law had never been what she would particularly call close; to put a finer point on things, they positively loathed one another and had done so from their very first meeting.

'Who's that?' Jamie asked, flicking his head towards the phone.

'Who do you bloody think?' Tracey replied, groaning a second time. 'Your nan. She wants to pop over tomorrow morning.' Switching the phone off without replying to the message, she slipped the device back into her pocket. 'She wants to see you and Ricky, reckons that she has something important to tell you both.'

Jamie raised his eyebrows; in his mind he could think of nothing worse. 'Fuck that,' he said, screwing up his face. 'You can count me out for a start. She'll only cause hag; it's all she ever does. Anyway, I've got things to do tomorrow.' He took his own phone out of his pocket and tapped the screen. 'I'm meeting someone.'

'What and leaving me all on my own to deal with her? Cheers for that Jamie.'

'Meeting who?' Ricky butted in, his eyes narrowed into slits.

'Just someone,' Jamie answered, giving a nonchalant shrug.

'Why are you being so cagey?'

'I'm not.'

'Yeah you are.' Ricky's hard gaze snapped back to the phone in his brother's hand. 'You're hiding something. I know you better than you know yourself and you've been acting weird for weeks. Every time I look at you you've got your head in your phone. Who are you messaging?'

'Fuck me, what is this, a Spanish inquisition?' Jamie's cheeks flushed pink and turning his face away from their inquisitive stares, he shoved the phone back into his pocket and out of sight. 'I don't have to tell you everything you know; I am allowed to have a life of my own, one that doesn't include any of you lot.'

As the old saying, the pot calling the kettle black, sprang to Tracey's mind, she lifted her eyebrows and gave her youngest son a knowing look. So, it was all right for her sons to have a private life but what about her? Wasn't she entitled to the same privilege?

'We'll be here Mum,' Ricky said, silently daring his brother to argue the case. 'Both of us, even if I have to drag him here myself.'

Tracey nodded, feeling somewhat relieved, and turning to look at Max she raised her eyebrows. 'What do you think?' she asked. 'The cat is already out of the bag with these two,' she said, motioning towards Ricky and Jamie. 'We might as well go the whole hog and get it over and done with and tell Pat our news. She's bound to find out sooner rather than later and you know what they're like around here,' she said, gesturing to the houses on either side of her home. 'The neighbours live for a bit of gossip, and I'd rather tell her myself than give any of this lot the satisfaction of telling her first. I'm actually surprised that no one has let slip before now. Every time I step outside the front door I can see their curtains twitching, watching my every move, the nosy bastards.'

Max hesitated and, rubbing his hand over his jaw, he shrugged. 'It's your call darling but I can tell you now, it's not going to go down well. Pat is hardly my biggest fan, is she. She's still convinced that I had a hand in Terry's murder and nothing you or I say is ever going to change her mindset.'

Thinking it over, Tracey pulled her phone back out and began typing out a reply. 'Fuck her,' she said, looking up and locking eyes with Max. 'I don't owe her anything. She's been nothing but the bane of my life since the day I met her. Right from the start she had it in for me; no one would have been good enough for her precious son and she actually told me that to my face.'

'Right then,' Max said with a raise of his eyebrows. 'Now that that's sorted out, back to business.' He took a seat on the sofa and rested his forearms on his knees. 'If... and it's still a big if in my book, because I'm not 100 per cent convinced that Dixon is as innocent as he tried to make out, but if,' he sighed, 'it wasn't him, then who else could have been behind the arson attack?'

Tracey shook her head and as she joined Max on the sofa, she gently rubbed the palm of her hand over his tense shoulder. 'I can't get my head around it. None of this makes any sense to me.'

'Yeah and that's the problem Mum,' Jamie agreed. 'It doesn't make sense, no matter which way you look at the situation.' He paused for a moment and shoved his hands into his pockets. 'And what about the Dixons?' he asked, lifting his chin slightly. 'They're gunning for you; they want revenge and they're not going to stop until they've dished out their own form of retribution.'

The muscles in Max's forearms tightened, and running his tongue over his teeth, he sank back onto the sofa. 'Fuck the Dixons,' he retorted. 'I'm this close to losing my rag and believe me, those pricks are the least of my worries. This no-good cunt has got me running around like a blue-arsed fly. Someone out there knows something.' He stabbed his finger towards the lounge window, his grey eyes hardening. 'And if I have to start kicking the shit out of people to get answers, then so fucking be it, because I've had it up to here,' he said, pointing to his head.

Tracey gave an involuntary shiver. As much as she tried to convince herself that she had become stronger since her husband's murder, she had never and would never condone violence. It was meaningless in her opinion and did nothing, other than cause further animosity. Not that she could say she entirely blamed Max for wanting revenge, he had come under attack after all, and if it hadn't been for the fact he had planned to take her out for the evening, the final outcome could have been so very different. A workaholic, Max often stayed at the car lot late into the night. Perhaps the culprits had even been banking on the fact that he would still be there. Maybe if the circumstances had been different, she would have been mourning his death. The mere thought was enough to turn her insides to ice and, grasping his hand in hers, she gave it a gentle squeeze; whether it was more for his benefit or hers she didn't know, the only thing she knew for certain was that she was thankful he was still beside her and in one piece.

As he continued to study Jamie, Ricky chewed on his thumbnail. 'So who is this person you're supposedly meeting tomorrow?'

Jamie sighed with agitation. 'Are you still banging on about that? We had this conversation over ten minutes ago.'

'It's a fair question,' Ricky retorted. 'And I can't work out why you're keeping schtum, unless,' he said, giving his brother a hard stare. 'You've got something to hide.'

'Enough,' Tracey barked out in a bid to quieten them down. 'Can we just concentrate on the car lot for a few minutes without the two of you bickering like a pair of bloody kids? You're meant to be grown men for fuck's sake, not children.' A moment of silence followed and as she made a point of looking at her eldest son, Tracey raised her voice slightly. 'What are you thinking?' she asked.

'About what?' Tearing his gaze away from Jamie, Ricky turned his attention back to his mother.

'The car lot,' she said, throwing up her arms. 'What else do you think we've been bloody talking about all this time? Who do you think could have been behind the attack?'

'I don't know,' Ricky answered, glancing back towards his brother again, his forehead furrowing as he tried to work out what it was his brother was hiding. 'But whoever it is, they must have a death wish; either that or they are fucking stupid.'

Thirty minutes later, once they had left their mother's house, Ricky sucked in his bottom lip. The fact Jamie was acting so out of character didn't sit right with him. Under normal circumstances, Jamie was like an open book, he always had been; even as kids Ricky had been able to see right through him.

'Nan's going to go ballistic,' Jamie said, pulling out his car keys.

'Yeah probably,' Ricky answered, still deep in thought.

'I can tell you now that she's going to go off her trolley.' Jamie let out a light laugh. 'I'll bet you a score,' he said, holding out his hand, 'that she'll try to swing for Max. As it is, she can't stand him and that's without her finding out about him and Mum.'

Ricky ignored his brother's outstretched hand, his eyes flashing dangerously. 'And what about you?' he asked casually.

Jamie frowned. 'What about me?'

'Max.' Ricky jerked his head towards the house. 'Do you like him?'

Jamie's frown deepened. 'What kind of question is that? You know I like him; he's a good bloke. Fair enough, I can't say that I was thrilled about him and Mum at first but if he makes her happy and he treats her right then I'm okay with it. We don't really have much of a choice, do we, other than to accept it. You know what Mum's like, she's not going to listen to a word we say.'

With a quick glance back at the house, Ricky chewed on the inside of his cheek then, grasping his brother's shirt in his fist, he hauled him roughly around to face him before proceeding to slam him up against the car. 'Was it you?' he hissed through gritted teeth.

Shock resonated across Jamie's face and, yanking his shirt out of Ricky's fist, he shook his head. 'What the fuck are you talking about?'

'You,' Ricky continued in a low growl. 'Was it you who burned down the car lot? And don't even bother trying to lie to me Jay,' he said, reinforcing his grip. 'I know you better than you think I do, just remember that; you've been acting weird for weeks.'

'Of course it wasn't me.' Shoving Ricky away from him, Jamie straightened up. 'Are you all right in the head?' he asked pointing to his temple. 'Have you gone doo-fucking-lally? I was with you remember. You were the one who drove us to Leigh-on-Sea. How the fuck am I supposed to have been in two places at the same time, and why would I even want to destroy Max's business? He's my boss; without him I wouldn't have a job, would I?'

Ricky dragged a hand over his face. He'd totally forgotten that he'd been the one to drive them to Leigh-on-Sea, but that didn't mean Jamie couldn't have been involved somehow. Perhaps he could have even been the brains behind the outfit; after all, he had first-hand knowledge of Max's businesses, of all the businesses in fact, and it was more than a little bit suspicious how only the car lot had come under attack, especially seeing as he and his brother worked at the bookies. 'So what's with all the secrecy then? I know you're hiding something.'

'Yeah and like I said,' Jamie answered, shouldering Ricky out of his path. 'It's none of your business.'

'Hey.' Tugging on his brother's arm, Ricky shook his head. 'Come on bruv,' he implored. 'I'm not stupid and if I've noticed it then you can guarantee that Max has as well and it's only a matter of time until he starts asking questions. Something's going on, I know it is.'

'What, other than the fact that you don't trust me?' Jamie stabbed his finger in the direction of the house. 'That you think I'd purposely burn down the car lot. Despite what you might think of me, I'm not sick in the fucking head.'

Briefly closing his eyes, Ricky wanted to kick himself. It was so unlike him not to get his facts straight first before going in all guns blazing. He liked to think through his actions, and even more than that he liked to be level headed when he went in for the kill. It was just one of the many reasons he and Jamie worked so well together; he was the calm to Jamie's storm. 'What do you expect me to think? You've been acting weird, really fucking weird and every time I look at you you've got your nose in your phone.'

'And since when did that become a crime, eh?'

At a loss for something to say, Ricky glanced away. 'I dunno,' he sighed. 'I just thought... I don't know... that if you'd been involved then I could have at least tried to cover it up, maybe have a word with Max and...'

'Cheers for that bruv,' Jamie snarled. 'Thanks for trusting me. You're meant to be my brother, and that means we're supposed to look out for one another, not accuse each other of shit that we haven't even done.'

'Jay.' Pulling on Jamie's arm again and forcing him to a halt, Ricky blew out his cheeks. 'Don't be like this,' he implored. 'I was only trying to look out for you and even you've got to admit that you've been secretive lately. You don't tell anyone where you're going or who you're meeting, then you disappear off the face of the earth for hours on end and no one can get hold of you. What did you expect me to think?'

'That I'm not a little kid any more; I don't have to explain my actions.' Giving a bitter laugh, Jamie kissed his teeth. 'I'm not listening to this bullshit,' he said, shrugging Ricky away from him. 'So do yourself a favour and fuck off before I end up lamping you one.'

'Jamie,' Ricky called after his brother. When he didn't get a response he slumped heavily against his car and rubbed at his temples. Moments later, the screech of tyres pulling away from the kerb rang loudly in his ears, and slipping his hand into his pocket, he pulled out his cigarettes. To say that he had the feeling he'd just made one of the biggest fuck ups of his life was the understatement of the century.

9

As he and his elder brother exited the lift and stepped out into the foyer of The Room at the Top nightclub in Ilford, Essex, Marc Dixon thoroughly believed that he was the dog's gonads. He and Barry were onto a nice little earner, one that they hadn't even told their dad about, not so much because Dickie would be averse to the crime they had participated in, but more so because he had big mouth and couldn't be trusted to keep schtum. Not only were they about to be paid out the equivalent of a small fortune but they were also on the brink of mapping out a grisly end for their dad's arch rival Max Hardcastle and his two sidekicks Ricky and Jamie Tempest, hence why they hadn't let Dickie in on their plans; no doubt their old man would want to broadcast it from the rooftops. He would get a kick out of all and sundry knowing that his sons were the ones to have brought Hardcastle down.

'Over there,' Barry shouted in an attempt to be heard above the music as he indicated to two men standing at the bar.

Strolling across the dance floor with a confident swagger, the brothers bounded up a short flight of steps and after shaking hands with the men, Marc leant casually against the bar. To begin with he'd wanted nothing to do with them; he didn't trust them as far as he could throw them, still didn't to a certain degree, and as far as he was concerned that was half the problem. Until recently they had been strangers, and there was still a large part of Marc that was suspicious of their motives. It was Barry who'd been the one to convince him that they were on to a winner, and in the end it hadn't even been about the money, although he had to admit it was a strong factor considering the men had offered up a great deal of cash in return for him and his brother to obliterate Hardcastle's showroom. Eventually, the only thing to have swayed his mind was the fact that the men took after his own heart and detested Hardcastle and the Tempests almost as much as he and his family did, if not even more so if that was even possible.

Barry's lips curled into a snarl, and as he slipped his hand into his trouser pocket, he pulled out his wallet. 'That bastard Hardcastle,' he growled. 'He's a dead man. He did my old man over in front of the entire fucking boozer, made him look like a right mug.' He took out a twenty-pound note and waved it in the air in an attempt to gain the bar staff's attention. 'I want the cunt destroyed. Him and the Tempests. By all accounts, the no-good, sly bastards got a couple of digs in an' all.'

Raymond Cole raised his eyebrows towards Alfie Winters and, hiding the smirk that threatened to etch across his face, he shook his head. 'The no-good fuckers,' he sympathised. 'And your old man must be what...' He leaned back slightly, a mock pained expression replacing the smirk. 'In his sixties if he's a day.'

'That's right,' Marc stated. 'He turns sixty next year and those bastards beat the living daylights out of him. Three against one,' he hissed. 'He didn't stand a chance; it's only by some miracle that they didn't kill him. As it is, his rep is in tatters all thanks to those cunts.'

Raymond tutted. 'What's the world coming to, eh?' he asked,

throwing Alfie a surreptitious wink. 'They need stringing up by their fucking bollocks.'

'Yeah you can say that again,' Barry agreed. 'Oi, over here,' he called out to the barman. 'What's everyone having?'

Once they had their drinks in front of them, Marc eyed Raymond over the rim of his glass. 'Where's our dough?' he asked. 'We did our bit; when do we get paid?'

Raymond waved his hand dismissively. 'Don't you worry.' He grinned. 'You'll get your money; in fact, I left it back at my place for safe keeping. Once we leave here we can go back to mine and I'll settle you in. And from what I've heard, you did well. Hardcastle hasn't got a clue who targeted him; I've even heard one or two whispers that he's been asking around in Dagenham. Like I said' – he shrugged – 'the prick doesn't know what's hit him.' He placed his arms around Marc and Barry's shoulders and grinned even wider. 'And to think all along the culprits were on his own doorstep,' he laughed.

'Well, sort of,' Marc answered, squirming underneath Raymond's strong grip. 'You're from Dagenham, aren't you? Sounds like he's on the right track to me?'

Ignoring the comment, Raymond released his grasp on their shoulders and rubbed his hands together. 'Who's for another drink?' he asked, nodding towards Marc. 'It's your round, ain't it?'

Marc reluctantly pushed his hand into his pocket, all the while giving his brother a sidelong glance. There was something about Cole that he didn't trust and it was more than just the sense of feeling uncomfortable whenever they were in his presence. Cole had an unhealthy hint of menace about him, and no matter how much he might try to hide it from them, he reminded Marc of a predator who was merely toying with them and waiting for just the right moment to unleash the madness and destroy them. Marc was amazed Barry hadn't also picked up on the negative vibes

Raymond Cole gave off. But that was Barry all over; he'd never been able to look at the bigger picture, especially when money was brought into the equation. Still, Marc reasoned, as soon as they were given their cash, they wouldn't have to have any more dealings with the nutter, and as far as Marc was concerned, the quicker they collected their dough and returned to their own manor, the better it would be for everyone.

By the end of the night, Marc and Barry had sunk enough booze to sink a ship, and laden down with a carrier bag containing even more beer and takeaway kebabs, all sense of unease had well and truly gone out of the window. Not only had they let their guards down but they were so drunk they had eagerly followed Raymond and Alfie into a block of run-down flats. They hadn't any idea where they actually were; it could have been the ends of the earth for all they knew or even cared for that matter.

Sinking onto a worn sofa, Barry was oblivious to the cigarette burns that peppered the threadbare arms, and as he opened the carrier bag and took out a can of lager, he snapped open the ring pull and took a deep drink. 'You know what Hardcastle's trouble is, don't you?' he said, bringing his fist up to his lips as he belched. 'He thinks that he's untouchable.'

Marc nodded. 'Both him and the Tempests,' he said, tucking into his kebab. 'All because their old man was some kind of gangster.' He chewed on the doner meat, oblivious to how deathly silent both Raymond and Alfie had become. 'I mean,' he continued, 'who the fuck was their old man anyway?' He looked up, his lips covered in grease. 'He was nothing but a plastic gangster, a wannabe. Now our old man on the other hand,' he said, pointing a greasy finger forward, 'is the real deal; he could have wiped out Terry Tempest in the blink of an eye.'

'He could have an' all,' Barry agreed as he took another long slurp of the beer. 'In fact, he would have done it with one hand tied behind his back. The Tempests are fuck all, they're has beens, everyone knows that.'

Raymond stiffened, and as he sat forward in the chair, the pulse in his jaw began to pulsate. 'Is that so,' he said, giving the brothers a hard stare. 'Because from what I've heard, Terry Tempest was a handful; he had a rep that would make most men piss themselves through fear as soon as he so much as looked at them the wrong way.'

The anger in Raymond's voice was enough to make Marc look up and, for the first time since his arrival, he looked around him and took in his surroundings. Other than a mismatched sofa and two armchairs, the lounge was completely bare, no television, no curtains or carpet, there weren't even any personal possessions, at least nothing to prove that anyone actually lived in the flat. Taking note of the squalor, he momentarily frowned. Considering Raymond Cole was paying out the equivalent of a small fortune, his home left a lot to be desired and if he hadn't known any better, Marc would have sworn that he and his brother had been brought to some kind of doss house. Desperately, he tried to think back. Had Cole even used a key to let them in or had the front door already been jammed open?

'Where's our dough?' he asked, his voice holding a note of suspicion.

'It's here.' As he gestured vaguely around him, Raymond gave a menacing smile. 'That's the second time that you've asked me where the money is.' He glanced across to Alfie and lifted his shoulders in a shrug, his lips pulled down at the corners, disguising the wicked gleam in his eyes. 'Anyone would think that you don't trust me or something the way you're carrying on.'

Marc narrowed his eyes, his gaze once again darting around the room and settling on a can of petrol that had been placed beside the lounge door. The battered, rusting can looked so out of place that he was barely able to drag his eyes away from it. Who in their right mind would keep petrol in their home and for what purpose? He glanced back to Raymond, and taking note of the knowing look in his eyes, he swallowed deeply. Unease snaked its way down the length of Marc's spine, his body becoming suddenly tense. From somewhere at the back of his drink-addled mind, his brain screamed at him to be cautious, that incoming danger in the form of the two men sitting across from him could very well be imminent.

'Of course we trust you,' Barry slurred, nudging his brother in the ribs. Oblivious to the concern at the forefront of Marc's mind, he opened a second can of lager and guzzled down half the contents. 'What's not to trust? You're men after our own hearts,' he said, wiping the back of his hand across his lips. 'Your enemy is our enemy, and the quicker those bastards are wiped off the face of the earth, the better.' Draining his drink, he placed the empty can on the floor then unsteadily got to his feet. 'I need a piss.'

'Toilet's that way.' Pointing towards the lounge door, Raymond watched as Barry left the room then turned his steely gaze back to Marc. 'I've got a feeling that you don't like me.'

Marc attempted to smile. 'Nah, don't be daft,' he said, giving a nervous laugh, his voice a lot higher than usual. 'Of course I do.'

In return, Raymond gave a chilling grin. 'I'll let you into a little secret,' he said, standing up, his large physique filling the small room. 'You were right not to trust me.'

As he processed the words, Marc blinked in rapid succession. The greasy kebab he had been happily munching on just moments earlier lay heavy on his chest, and as acrid bile forced its way up his throat he hastily swallowed it back down, grimacing as he did so. 'What do you mean?' he asked, his eyes darting nervously back towards the can of petrol then to the lounge door in the hope that his brother would hurry back.

'The Tempests,' Raymond answered. He slipped his hand inside his jacket and pulled out a six-inch carving knife. 'They're mine,' he hissed, turning the knife over in his hand and inspecting the metal. 'No one gets to fuck with them apart from me. Let's just say that I've got a personal beef with the Tempest brothers and as for Hardcastle...' He pointed the knife forward, the steely tip glistening under the naked lightbulb. 'Once I've finished with the bastard, he's going to wish that he'd never been born.'

Marc's terrified gaze snapped towards the blade. Where the hell had the knife come from? Surely to God the nutter hadn't had it with him the whole time he and Barry had been in his presence? 'You can have them, the Tempest brothers I mean.' Beads of cold sweat broke out across Marc's forehead and holding up his hands, he gave an involuntary shiver. 'Just hand over our money and me and Barry will walk out of here and pretend that none of this ever happened. I swear to you, we won't breathe a word of this to anyone. As for Hardcastle he's clueless,' he continued, his breath catching in his throat, 'he hasn't got the first idea of who could have targeted him.'

Alfie chuckled and, raising his eyebrows, he looked across to Raymond. 'What money?' He made a point of patting down his pockets before shrugging. 'I haven't got any money, have you Ray?'

Raymond shook his head, the menace in his eyes intensifying. 'There is no money you stupid prick. Did you really believe that I was going to hand over twenty grand for something that I could have easily done myself? In the end,' he said, 'it made more sense to get someone else to do my dirty work, and that's where you greedy pair of fuckers came in. You fell for it hook, line and sinker. You see, it was always going to end like this, but no hard feelings though.' He grinned. 'It's nothing personal. You and soppy bollocks through there,' he said, pointing the knife in the direction of the hallway, 'were always going to end up becoming collateral damage; you were nothing more than a means to an end, only you were too stupid to see what was going on right underneath your nose. A little tip for you for future reference, not that you'll actually need it where you're going,' he laughed, 'if something appears too good to be true then it usually is.'

There and then, Marc's blood ran cold. Admittedly, he and Barry may not have been the sharpest tools in the box, but not for one single moment had it crossed their minds that they were being set up. 'Nah, leave it out,' he cried, throwing the half-eaten kebab into the air and jumping up from the sofa. Despite every instinct screaming at him to get out of the flat and away from danger, the principle of the matter gnawed away at Marc. He and Barry were owed money, they'd done their bit, they'd burnt down the car lot and now they wanted their cash, they'd earned it. 'You can't do that,' he yelled. 'You owe us.'

'I think you'll find that I can do whatever the fuck I like.' Lunging forward, Raymond slammed the knife heavily into Marc's gut and as his lips opened into a silent scream, Ray viciously twisted the blade upwards. 'This is the end of the line for you and that dense prick you call a brother,' he hissed in Marc's ear. Pulling out the blade, he pushed Marc roughly away from him, and as the injured man fell to the sofa in a crumpled heap, frothy blood-stained bubbles billowed out of his slack mouth, and the death rattle wheezing out of his throat as he took his final breaths was so loud that it echoed around the small room.

'I'd say that's one down and one to go, wouldn't you?' Raymond grinned maniacally, the knife at his side dripping claret onto the bare concrete floor.

From behind them the sound of the chain flushing followed by heavy footsteps made both Raymond and Alfie turn their heads expectantly towards the lounge door.

'That's better.' At the doorway to the lounge, Barry wiped his hands down his jeans. As he took in the scene before him, he rocked back on his heels, his eyes almost bulging out of his head. 'What the fuck…?' he screamed, backing away, a mixture of both panic and fear clearly evident in his voice.

A sickening grin spread across Raymond's face, and opening out his arms, he jerked his head in the direction of Marc's body. 'Welcome to the party.' He winked. Taking a menacing step forward, he grasped the blood-stained knife tightly in his fist. 'And guess what, it's your turn next.'

* * *

Lucie Burke yawned loudly and, dragging herself out of bed, she padded down the hallway towards the front door. Dressed in nothing but a short, pale pink satin dressing gown that barely covered her backside, she was a beautiful young woman with straight, shiny dark hair that hung just above her collarbone.

'Who is it?' she called out, her voice still thick from sleep.

'It's me, Raymond.'

'For fuck's sake,' she groaned, yanking open the front door. 'Do you know what bleeding time it is?' On seeing the blood splattered over Raymond's shirt and jeans, the words died in her throat. 'Oh my God,' she gasped, bringing her hands up to her lips. 'What the hell has happened to you?'

Barging his way inside the flat, Raymond gave a nonchalant shrug. 'We just ran into a bit of trouble that's all,' he answered, nodding towards Alfie. 'You don't mind if we sort ourselves out do you, get cleaned up a bit, maybe even have a bath.' He gestured down at his soiled clothes. 'These could do with a wash as well.'

Her eyes wide, Lucie ran a hand through her hair. As much as she liked Raymond, a shiver of fear ran down the length of her spine. Her partner of ten years would go absolutely ballistic if he was to find out that she'd cheated on him and he would find out, there was no doubt in her mind about that. Cain was like a dog with a bone once he'd set his mind to something and seeing as their six-year-old daughter was fast asleep in the bedroom next door, she had a nasty feeling that he wouldn't take too kindly to another man coming into his home and making himself comfortable, let alone getting cosy with his missus.

'I don't know Ray...' she began, her eyes darting towards the bedroom where her and Cain's daughter was sleeping. 'You know that I don't like you coming here when I've got Alisha with me; she's a light sleeper and...'

Flashing a wide grin, Raymond pulled Lucie roughly into his arms. 'Come on darling,' he said, copping a feel of her pert backside. 'You know it makes sense babe.'

'You stink of petrol.' Wrinkling her nose, Lucie pushed Raymond away from her.

'Do I?' Raymond sniffed his shirt. 'Did I forget to mention that there was a fire? Some doss house on the other side of the estate; it went up like a bonfire.' Spreading open his arms, his face lit up. 'Petrol would be my guess, I mean,' he said, laughing. 'As if you'd be so careless as to leave petrol lying around; it's an accident waiting to happen, everyone knows that.'

Lucie's eyes widened and, glancing out of the lounge window, she wrapped her arms around herself and inwardly shuddered. 'I hope that no one was hurt?'

'Who gives a fuck if they were.' Raymond shrugged. 'They're

only dossers, either that or junkies; it's not like anyone would actually miss them, is it.' He pulled Lucie back into his arms and nuzzled his face in her hair, ignoring her protests to get away from him. 'And how about something to eat as well? I could murder a bacon sarnie, how about you Alf?'

'I wouldn't say no,' Alfie agreed. 'With a nice dollop of tomato ketchup.'

Reluctantly, Lucie sighed in defeat. As wrong as it was of her to even entertain another man there was something about Raymond that she couldn't help but feel drawn to. Not only was he handsome but he also had a hint of danger about him, and she had always been attracted to the bad boys, hence why she and Cain had got together, not that he had been around much throughout their relationship. Perhaps that was the problem, she was lonely, and when Raymond had chatted her up whilst they had queued to go into Belmarsh Prison, she'd found herself flirting back with him. Only the flirting had progressed to her sleeping with him and on more than one occasion too. As much as she still loved Cain, she thoroughly believed herself to be in love with Raymond too. Was it even possible to love two men at the same time? She was sure it was; she'd read about it once in one of her magazines.

Her gaze darted towards her daughter's bedroom and she pressed her finger to her lips. 'Just be quiet,' she warned. 'I don't want Alisha to wake up. The last thing either of us need is for her to blurt out in front of Cain that Mummy's friends woke her up in the middle of the night.'

Raymond chuckled. 'Do I look like I give a flying fuck what your old man thinks?' Kicking off his shoes, he stripped down to his boxer shorts and made himself comfortable on the sofa. 'Have you got any green?' he asked, flicking on the stereo.

Lucie sighed, then crossing the lounge, she opened the window slightly to let in some fresh air before reaching up on top of a cabinet. Taking down a small metal tin, she prised open the lid and passed across a small, sealed bag of cannabis. With her backside perched on the arm of the sofa, she tugged her dressing gown down her thighs and pursed her lips together. 'I mean it Ray,' she said, leaning over him to turn down the volume on the stereo. 'You can't just turn up whenever you feel like it. What if Cain's brother had been here? He drops by every now and then to see Alisha and give me a bit of money. How the hell am I supposed to explain who you are? He's not daft; he's bound to think that it's a bit suspect.'

Raymond's expression hardened. 'Then you'd best make sure that he doesn't. Next time he turns up tell him to fuck off or better still send him my way and I'll deal with him.' Breaking out into a smile, he pulled Lucie on to his lap. 'You've got me now, aintcha darling? You don't need that cunt any more; it's not like he's going to get out of nick anytime soon anyway is it.' Tipping Lucie back off his lap he began the process of building a joint. 'What's happening with that bacon sandwich?' he asked, lifting an eyebrow. 'Me and my pal are starving; we've grafted our arses off tonight.'

'Yeah, you could say that we've worked up an appetite,' Alfie sniggered.

Raymond chuckled at the hidden meaning behind Alfie's words and, sparking up, he inhaled the smoke deep into his lungs. 'And that's another thing,' he said, screwing up his face. 'Where the fuck did you get this crap from?' He lazily exhaled two thick tendrils of smoke through his nostrils and gestured towards the smouldering joint held between his fingers. 'It's shit.'

'Well it's not like you had to pay for it, did you.' Placing her hands on her hips, Lucie rolled her eyes in annoyance. As for the cannabis, she would be having words with Austin Fletcher the next time she saw him. He must have known the weed he'd sold her was no good, and to make matters even worse, he'd charged her over the odds for it too.

'Too fucking right I didn't. Next time you want to score, come and see me or Alfie and we'll sort you out, and if you play your cards right,' he said, looking her up and down and licking his lips, 'I might even give you a discount, if I'm feeling generous.' Passing the joint across to Alfie, Raymond nodded towards the kitchen. 'Come on babe,' he said, giving her a wink. 'Sort us out. I'm so hungry I could eat a scabby horse.'

Bending down to pick up the soiled clothes, Lucie made her way into the kitchen. Once there she bit down on her bottom lip and stared at the blood that covered their shirts and jeans. There was so much of it; far too much for it to have come from a busted lip or a bloody nose. The iron scent turned her stomach and giving a shiver she hastily threw the clothes into the washing machine, then switching on the hot water tap, she meticulously scrubbed her hands clean. Had she inadvertently become an accessory to whatever crime Ray and Alfie had committed? The mere thought was enough to make her want to throw up.

Opening the fridge, she took out a pack of bacon and a tub of margarine, all the while averting her gaze away from the photograph of her and Cain pinned to the fridge door. As exciting as Ray was, she couldn't help but think that he sailed a bit too close to the wind for her liking and considering Cain had a ferocious temper on him, one that even she was loath to get on the wrong side of, she had a nasty feeling that if she wasn't careful, Ray could very well end up becoming her downfall.

10

The next morning in Belmarsh Prison, Cain Daly rinsed the soap from his hair then, switching off the water, he grabbed a towel and rubbed the thin material over his head.

'Yeah but you're not the one holed up with him though are you?'

Stepping out of the shower cubicle, Cain groaned. 'Are you still whining?' he complained.

Warren Harris rolled his eyes in agitation. 'It's all right for you,' he hissed. 'But if Kenny decides to go for him, then it's me who's going to end up copping it. I share a cell with the nutter and I can tell you now that I don't fancy having a kettle of boiling water flung over my boat race all because of that bastard and that's if the nutcase doesn't try to do me in first. He's not right in the head,' he continued. 'He walks around muttering to himself.' He gave an inward shudder and tapped his temple. 'I'm telling you mate, there's something not quite right up here. I've started sleeping with one eye open just in case he goes for me in the middle of the night. The last thing I want to see when I wake up is his face bearing down on me with a blade held up to my throat; it'd be enough to give me a heart attack.'

'Would defeat the object a bit that, wouldn't it,' Cain answered, suppressing a grin.

'I'm being serious man,' Warren continued, his voice becoming more desperate. 'I even caught him talking to the wall, like actually having a full blown conversation with it.'

'Listen.' Checking that no one else was within earshot of their conversation, Cain lowered his voice. 'You're getting worked up over nothing.' He dried himself off then slipped on a fresh pair of boxer shorts and jeans. 'If Kenny was going to seriously maim the bloke,' he said, pulling a T-shirt over his head, 'he would have done it long before now.' It was a lie, but Warren didn't need to know that. Kenny was the type of man who got a kick out of intimidating others, and unless Warren's cellmate fought back, the bullying and violence would only escalate.

'Getting worked up over nothing,' Warren exclaimed. Quickening his pace to keep up with Cain's long strides, he tugged on his arm. 'Trust me, when it comes down to it, Kenny is the least of my worries. Do you even know what the nutter I'm holed up with is in here for?' he asked.

Cain shrugged. He'd heard one or two whispers about Warren's cellmate that ranged from petty theft, to fraud, to embezzlement, not that the man in question had actually confirmed or denied whether or not the rumours were true. All in all he'd remained tight lipped when it came to the reason he'd been imprisoned, not that Cain had actually seen him speak to anyone come to think of it. Other than Kenny of course, when he'd asked him to acquire a can of tuna for him on tic and when you look at the amount of aggravation that had caused, was it any wonder that he kept himself to himself?

'Look, he can't be that bad.' He motioned around him. 'They'd hardly house him in here if he's a bonafide nutcase would they? Besides, there's nothing of him. I could snap him in half with one hand and you saw yourself the way Kenny beat him to a pulp; the bloke didn't even attempt to protect himself, he just stood there, taking the blows.'

'What and you think that's normal behaviour, do you?' Warren tapped the side of his head again. 'Any other man would have fought back or at least tried to defend themselves. I'm telling you, he ain't right, and they reckon he killed someone,' he added, his eyes widening.

Cain laughed out loud and, nodding towards the cells, he raised his eyebrows. 'Take your pick,' he said, spreading his arms out. 'The entire wing is crawling with murderers, what makes this bloke any different from everyone else in here?'

'Yeah,' Warren answered, his voice becoming a lot higher than usual, 'but the majority of this lot didn't go on a killing spree, did they? I even heard that when the old bill finally caught up with him, he was in the process of tucking into one of the corpses.'

Cain laughed again. 'I think someone is having you on mate; it's a wind up.'

'Nah, it's the truth, straight up.' As they stopped outside Warren's cell, he nudged Cain in the side. 'Have a look at him yourself,' he said, jerking his head towards his cellmate. 'And then tell me whether or not you think he's still all the ticket.'

Lying flat on his back, Albert Nowak, a middle-aged Polish migrant, stared up at the ceiling with a blank expression, his wiry body so still that in Cain's opinion, he looked more like a corpse than a living, breathing human being.

'You all right mate?' Cain called out to him.

Slowly turning his head, Albert gripped on to the bedding so hard that his knuckles turned white. Next to his pillow was an open can of tuna and as the remnants of the rotting fish assaulted Cain's nostrils, he wrinkled his nose.

'Do you see what I mean now?' Warren hissed, giving Cain a knowing look. 'That sodding can is stinking the place out but he won't get rid of it no matter how many times I've told him to bin it.'

Cain nodded, his eyes going from Albert to the can. It was no secret that the metal tin could be used as a weapon, the sharp edges of the lid turning it into the perfect blade. They were allowed to order it in their canteen, but Cain had no idea why, considering how strict the rules were about prisoners having weapons in their possession. 'Better you than me then mate.' Cain shook his head, and stepping back outside the cell, he made his way along the landing.

'Hey,' Warren called after him. 'What am I supposed to do about the nut...' he began before quickly snapping his lips closed and nodding towards his cellmate.

Cain shrugged, the hint of a grin tugging at the corners of his lips. 'I dunno mate,' he answered, 'but I'm sure you'll think of something. And I don't know about you,' he called over his shoulder, 'but I've got a visit to go and get ready for.'

Throwing his arms up into the air, Warren gingerly stepped back into his cell. 'That's it mate,' he said, careful not to make any sudden movements. 'Nice and easy pal, nice and fucking easy.' Ever so slowly he lowered himself on to his bunk and, laying down, he placed one hand behind his head, his free hand retrieving a matchstick thin cigarette and placing it between his lips. 'My mate's got a visit,' he said for something to say as he lit up. 'Lucky bastard; I'd give anything to see my kids.' He offered out the cigarette and as Albert took it from him, he exhaled a shaky breath. 'You got any kids mate?' As soon as the words left his mouth, Warren wanted to kick himself; of course the nutter wouldn't have kids.

'A daughter,' Albert answered, his voice barely louder than a whisper.

Surprised, Warren nodded. 'Don't suppose you get to see her much, bit like me really. My missus won't bring the kids here, reckons it's not a good environment for them, not that I blame her. Who in their right mind would want to bring their kids to a place like this?' He took the cigarette back and puffed on it. 'Nah, if I want to point fingers then I'd best start pointing them at myself I suppose; it was me who did the crime. I tried to do over a post office van, "tried" being the operative word. Why should my kids have to suffer for my mistakes? The missus has told them that I'm working away on an oil rig; in the long run, it's got to be a lot better than them ever finding out the truth, hasn't it? That their old man is a blagger,' he sighed, 'and not a very good one at that considering where I've ended up.'

'My daughter is dead.'

A cold chill ran down the length of Warren's spine. He knew it, the rumours were true after all. The nutter had killed and devoured his own daughter, the sick bastard. 'What... what happened to her?' he stuttered, curiosity getting the better of him.

A long silence followed and, bracing himself to get ready to run from the cell as if his life depended on it, Warren clenched his fist into a tight ball. He may not have been considered a tough man like Cain but that didn't mean he was willing to go down without a fight.

'She took her own life.' Albert's voice wavered. 'My baby was just nineteen. They ruined her, made her feel worthless, made her believe that life wasn't worth living.'

At a loss for words, Warren swallowed deeply and, uncurling his fist, he ground the cigarette out on a foil ashtray then rolled over on to his side. Studying the photographs of his children taped to the wall, he let out a long sigh. The mere thought of losing one of his own didn't even bare thinking about. 'I'm sorry for your loss mate,' he said sincerely. He didn't receive a reply; in all honesty, he hadn't expected one.

* * *

Standing beside the open kitchen window that overlooked the entrance to her block of flats, Lucie Burke exhaled a cloud of smoke. With the cigarette still dangling from the corner of her lips, she screwed up her eyes, walked across the kitchen, took a bowl out of the cupboard then filled it with Coco Pops.

'Alisha,' she called out to her daughter. Placing the bowl on the table, she opened a milk bottle and gave the contents a quick sniff. Deeming it fit for purpose, she poured the milk over the cereal. 'Come and get your breakfast, babe.'

Still dressed in her pyjamas, six-year-old Alisha padded bare-foot into the kitchen, her light brown hair a mass of tight curls framing her face. Tucked underneath her arm was a fluffy pink toy rabbit, although fluffy was a bit of an exaggeration considering the state of the toy. Having been washed so many times that the pink fur had become tatty and bald in places, Lucie was in half a mind to throw it out. It was only the fact that Alisha was bound to throw a tantrum of epic proportions that stopped her from chucking it in the bin. She could do without the hassle if truth be told and was a great advocate of doing anything and everything in her power for a quiet life, or at least, she had been until Raymond had entered her life.

'Come on, Leesh,' Lucie coaxed, glancing up at the clock on the wall. 'Get a move on sweetheart; it's nearly time to go and get ready for school.'

Once her daughter was seated at the table, Lucie resumed her position by the window, and sipping at a cup of lukewarm black coffee, she idly flicked cigarette ash down on to the pavement below.

'Mummy, who's that man?'

Lucie turned her head and, seeing Raymond standing in the doorway to the kitchen, she almost choked on her coffee. 'He's no one sweetheart,' she said hastily, composing herself and giving her daughter a bright smile. 'Just one of Mummy's friends.'

As Lucie turned her attention back to Raymond, she gave him a glare and jerked her head towards the bedroom, her eyes silently beseeching him to leave and more importantly get away from her daughter. As far as Lucie was concerned, the less Alisha knew about Raymond the less likely she was to repeat anything back to Cain. Alisha had always been a daddy's girl; she and Cain adored one another and as a result she had him wrapped around her tiny little finger.

'Is he my daddy's friend too?'

The innocence in her daughter's voice was almost enough to make Lucie want to cry. Once more, guilt ate away at her and, glancing at the photograph of her and Cain pinned to the fridge, she gave a tight smile. 'Of course he is sweetheart.' Moving back to her position at the window, she rested her forearms on the window frame, hoping that Alisha would soon forget all about the strange man she'd seen in the kitchen.

The sight of a familiar car pulling into the car park below was enough to send Lucie into a wild panic and in her haste to get to the bedroom, she knocked her coffee mug to the floor, soaking the front of her dressing gown and smashing the cup to smithereens in the process.

'You need to leave,' she shouted at Raymond, her eyes wild with fear and her chest heaving. 'Cain's brother's just turned up.' She breathed heavily. 'He can't see you here; it'd be more than my life is worth, and yours too come to think of it.'

A slow smile crept across Raymond's face and, lounging back on the bed, he gave a nonchalant shrug. 'And?' He smirked, pulling the duvet up to his neck and closing his eyes as though he were contemplating going back to sleep. 'I thought we'd already had this conversation last night and I told you that if he turns up, to tell him to fuck off.'

'I mean it Ray. Cain and his brothers are not men that you want to get on the wrong side of.' Tears glistened in Lucie's eyes, and tugging on his arm, she attempted to pull him off the bed. 'Please,' she begged of him. 'You need to get out of here.' Rushing into the lounge, she shoved Alfie awake. Throwing his clothes at him, she looked around her. Ever since Raymond had entered her life, she'd neglected her housework, preferring to spend her free time at Raymond's beck and call and smoking as much green as she could possibly lay her hands on. Now, not only was her home beginning to resemble a pigsty, but the stale, pungent scent of the cannabis they had smoked the night before still lingered heavily in the air. 'Get dressed,' she all but screamed at him as she darted back into the kitchen to retrieve a can of air freshener from under the kitchen sink, 'and get out, both of you.'

* * *

Bounding up a flight of steps, Vincent Daly wrinkled his nose. No matter how many times the council disinfected the communal area, the underlying scent of decay was ever present and served as a constant reminder to the residents that they were living in what most people would consider to be squalor. Not that Vincent believed he was above council housing because he didn't. Despite his recent wealth, all thanks to owning the jazz club and his other business interests, he and his younger brothers had grown up on a similar council estate in North East London, and he had fond memories of his childhood. The Daly surname had been notorious on their estate and growing up in the area had also given them an education of sorts, albeit the wrong kind of education. From an early age, both he and his brothers had been street wise and despite their mother's best efforts to teach her sons right from wrong, as a single mother she'd been left with no choice but to leave them to their own devices whilst she went out to work. As a result, they'd had to learn how to stand on their own two feet and take care of themselves, and thankfully they could. They would never have been able to survive the tough London estate if they couldn't.

The sound of footsteps descending the stairs made Vincent look up, and flattening his back against the wall, he watched as two men with muscular builds passed him by. Frowning, he took a moment to study them before continuing up the stairs to what had been his brother's home before his imprisonment. With just two flats on the upper floor, Vincent looked between the two properties, his frown deepening. The men had come from somewhere, he knew that much, and considering his brother's neighbour was an elderly woman who lived alone, he had a sneaky suspicion that they hadn't come from her flat.

Lightly rapping his knuckles on the front door, Vincent chewed on the inside of his cheek. Within a matter of moments, the door was flung open and flashing a wide grin, he stepped across the threshold. 'You all right Luce?'

Lucie nodded, her skin flushed and as his niece Alisha screamed out his name, he gave his sister-in-law a chaste kiss on the cheek before making his way into the kitchen.

Picking the little girl up and hugging her to him, Vincent affectionately kissed the top of Alisha's head. 'Hello princess.' He turned then to look at Lucie. 'It's just a flying visit. I'm going in to see Cain this morning, so thought that I'd pop by to see if you had any messages you want passed on.'

'Are you going to see my daddy?' Alisha asked, her face lighting up with excitement.

'That's right, I am.' Vincent smiled.

'Can I come too? Please?' she asked, giving a heart-stopping, gappy grin. 'I want to see my daddy... please Uncle Vincent.'

'No, not today sweetheart, you have to go to school.' On seeing her face fall, Vincent dug his hand into his pocket and pulled out a small bar of chocolate. 'You can come next time,' he said, plonking her on the floor and handing over the chocolate. 'I promise.'

Placated with her uncle's answer, Alisha skipped happily from the kitchen, ripping open the chocolate bar packaging as she did so.

'You spoil her,' Lucie scolded, barely able to look her brother-in-law in the eyes. 'She'll be on a sugar high now and right before she goes to school too. I already get it in the neck from her teacher because she reckons that she's too hyper and disrupts the class. I swear she's becoming more and more like her father by the day.'

'She's worth spoiling.' Vincent grinned. 'Besides, I'm only doing what Cain would do if he was around. You know how much he idolises her.'

At the mention of her partner and daughter's closeness, Lucie's cheeks turned a deeper shade of red and grabbing a roll of kitchen paper off the worktop, she bent down and began mopping up the spilt coffee and retrieving the broken pieces of the mug.

'Who were the two geezers who passed me by on the stairs?' Vincent asked, watching her reaction closely.

Lucie momentarily froze, the colour draining from her face. 'I don't know.' She shrugged, biting down on her bottom lip. 'I didn't see anyone.' She straightened up, crossed the kitchen and threw the soiled paper towel and mug into the pedal bin. 'Maybe they were visiting Mabel next door,' she added, plucking out a cigarette, her fingers ever so slightly shaking as she placed it between her lips before offering the box across. 'They could have been from the council; she did mention to me that she had a leaking tap.'

As he took the cigarette packet, Vincent inwardly groaned; he'd known her long enough to know that she was lying to him and it wasn't a particularly good lie at that, and as for claiming that the men had been from the council, Vincent knew for a fact they hadn't been plumbers.

Lighting the cigarette, Vincent narrowed his eyes as he continued to study his sister-in-law. It was no secret that in the past Lucie had run up a number of debts, and no matter how many times his brother had bailed her out she still wasn't able to curb her spending habits. Catalogues and store cards in particular were her weakness. At the click of a button it was all too easy to rack up a mountain of debt and no matter how good her initial intentions were to repay the money owed, she never did, hence why bailiffs had often turned up, demanding payment or threatening court action. And now that he came to think of it, the men he had passed on the stairs had looked like typical heavies, the type of men who wouldn't think twice about barging inside a premises and taking everything that could be sold on regardless of whether or not a defenceless woman or young child were in the property. 'At least give me some credit.' He tapped the side of his nose. 'I'm not a complete idiot, I know exactly what's been going on around here.'

Terror filled Lucie's eyes and as her heart began to hammer inside her chest, her mouth hung slightly open as she grappled for an answer.

'For fuck's sake Lucie,' he growled. 'Didn't you learn your lesson the last time you had bailiffs on the doorstep? How much do you owe this time?' he asked, pulling out his wallet.

Eyeing the money in her brother-in-law's hand, Lucie swallowed deeply. Despite the shame that engulfed her, the relief she felt was very much evident as she allowed her shoulders to slightly relax. 'I don't need any money,' she protested.

'How much?' Vincent barked out, not in the mood to argue with her.

'Fifty,' Lucie answered, spitting out the first figure that sprang to her mind.

'Fifty?' Vincent repeated back with a raise of his eyebrows. 'Is that all, fifty quid?'

Lucie nodded.

He passed across the money, not taking his eyes away from her face. 'Sort yourself out,' he chastised, 'if not for your sake then for Alisha's. What kind of an example are you setting her, eh?'

Without answering, Lucie took the money, the expression written across her face said it all.

'Yeah fair point,' Vincent answered as an image of his brother incarcerated for armed robbery sprang to his mind. With Cain and Lucie for parents then what hope did little Alisha have? Not that either one of them were what he would consider to be bad people, they, himself included, had just made the wrong choices, repeatedly; it was nothing more than a coping mechanism, a way to survive the hard life they had been dealt.

He glanced around the kitchen; it also hadn't escaped his notice that the flat reeked of cannabis, although he had to admit she'd done a pretty good job of trying to disguise it if the overpowering stench of lavender air freshener was anything to go by. 'Can I ask you something?' he said, slipping the wallet back into his pocket. 'And be honest with me. Is there something else going on here?' He motioned around the kitchen then held up his hands. 'I'm not averse to a smoke myself and you know what me and Cain were like back in the day, but have you got a problem Luce? Because this,' he said, sniffing the air, 'is excessive, even for me. I could smell it before you'd even opened the front door and coming from someone who's been there, done it, and got the bloody T-shirt, this is more than just one blunt. Have you been on a bender?'

'No, of course I haven't,' Lucie was quick to answer, her cheeks flushing even redder. 'What do you take me for?' She pointed down at her soaked dressing gown. 'It's just been one of those mornings that's all,' she lied. 'I don't know if I'm coming or going and I needed something to take the edge off, you know, what with Alisha and everything. It's hard work being a single parent and then there's Cain.' She glanced away and rubbed her hand over her face. 'Well you know full well how the situation is; Cain isn't around to help out is he, and it all gets a bit too much sometimes. I need a release, something to take my mind off how shit my life has turned out.' Turning on the waterworks, she allowed hot salty tears to slip freely down her cheeks. 'I didn't ask for this,' she cried. 'Why couldn't Cain have got himself a nine-to-five job, something legal? Why did he have to be so bloody greedy? And he promised me after Alisha was born that he was going to go straight, that he would put a life of crime behind him.'

Vincent sighed, not knowing how best to respond. All he and Cain had ever known was the life they had led and between them they had been in and out of youth detention centres and prison more times than they'd had hot dinners and that was saying something. 'Come on now,' he said, pulling her into his arms and stroking her hair, his voice becoming gentle. 'He'll be out soon enough and then you can get on with your lives, be a proper family; it won't always be like this.'

Lucie scoffed between sobs. 'He's still got at least another five years to serve, and what about me and Alisha, eh? We're the ones stuck on the outside waiting for him,' she spat, angrily wiping the tears away. 'It's like living in bloody limbo.'

As much as Vincent sympathised, and he really did considering he had watched his own mother struggle to bring up four sons single-handedly, all of who had dabbled on the wrong side of the law and had in one way or another brought her more heartache than any mother deserved, it was on the tip of his tongue to tell her that she might want to lay off the green if it was making her this emotional, especially since she was taking care of his niece on a daily basis. 'It'll be all right,' he soothed. Glancing towards the front door, he paused for a moment, his forehead furrowing. 'Those blokes,' he asked, jabbing his finger forward, his expression hardening. 'They weren't here because of drug debts were they? Because if they were then just let me know, and me and the boys,' he said, referring to his and Cain's younger brothers, 'will have a word with them and tell them to back off.'

Alarm filtered back across Lucie's face and vehemently shaking her head, she stepped out of Vincent's embrace and wrapped her arms around her slim frame. 'You know what I'm like,' she said, the words coming out in a rush. 'I just wanted to buy a few bits for Alisha, that's all; she's growing up so fast that nothing fits her any more.'

Satisfied with her answer, Vincent took note of the half-eaten bowl of cereal on the kitchen table and nodded. 'I'll let you get on then and get the little one off to school. I'll tell Cain that you said hello, shall I?'

Lucie gave a small smile. 'Tell him...' She looked down at the money grasped in her fist, her eyes welling up with fresh tears. 'Tell him that I'll be in to see him as soon as I can.'

'Will do.' Stepping out into the hallway, Vincent called out to his niece, 'See you later alligator.'

'Not if I see you first crocodile,' Alisha playfully called back, her mouth still full of chocolate.

Once outside his brother's flat, Vincent quietly closed the front door behind him then stood for a few moments just thinking.

Concern was at the forefront of his mind. In recent months, Lucie had become more and more distant; she'd even stopped visiting his mother, and in the past the two women had always been close, more like mother and daughter than mother and daughter-in-law, and when it came to Cain, Lucie would usually have a couple of messages that she would want passed on to his brother. More often than not, updates on how Alisha was doing at school or at the very least she would want him to tell Cain that both she and Alisha loved and missed him.

Making his way back down the stairs, Vincent sighed, then glancing at his watch and noting the time, he cursed under his breath before charging down the remainder of the steps. By the time he'd climbed behind the wheel of his car and sped out of the car park, the fact his sister-in-law had been acting so out of character was completely wiped from his mind, as were the two men who had passed him on the stairs.

11

The best way to deal with her mother-in-law, Tracey decided, was to go all-out mob-handed. Not only did she have Max and her two sons with her, but Ricky's wife Kayla had also popped over to offer some much needed moral support and, when it came to Patricia, Tracey had a nasty feeling she was going to need all the support that she could get.

Sitting at the kitchen table, she and Kayla were sipping on a cup of coffee awaiting Patricia's arrival with bated breath.

'Any news on the car showroom?' Kayla asked as she blew on her drink in an attempt to cool the hot liquid down.

Tracey shook her head, and giving the kitchen door a quick glance, she lowered her voice. 'I don't know what to make of it all,' she mused. 'I heard the recorded message myself and the bastard definitely hinted at destroying all of the businesses, so why haven't they done that? It just makes no sense. It's like they're toying with Max, like they're getting a kick out of riling him up.' She rested her elbows on the table and, wrapping her fingers around the mug, she took a long sip, contemplating the situation. 'They wanted a reaction out of him and now that they've got one they've completely dropped off the radar. They've got to be sick in the head, haven't they?'

For a few moments, Kayla watched her mother-in-law over the rim of the mug. 'You don't think...' She gave a little shrug, almost as though she were afraid to say the words out loud. 'That Kenny could be involved?' she whispered.

'I don't know darling,' Tracey sighed, although it would certainly explain why there had been no further onslaughts. Despite Max's insistence that Kenny wouldn't have the means to have had a hand in the arson attack, Tracey knew for a fact that there was enough bad blood between the two men to make Kenny a strong contender. Even now, two years on, it still seemed inconceivable to her that Kenny could have been responsible for Terry's murder; the two men hadn't just been business partners, but they had also been good friends. Not only had Terry trusted him, but she had too, so much so that she would never in a million years have suspected Kenny or his son Shaun of being behind the execution and that was exactly what it had been, an execution. Shot in the back, Terry hadn't stood a chance, let alone been in the position to fight back or try to defend himself.

Still, the burning question remained: what possible reason could there have been for Kenny to not only want to kill his best friend but to also see it through and have him murdered in cold blood? All through the trial Kenny had remained tight lipped and given no explanation for his actions. In fact, he'd denied his part in the killing until he was blue in the face. He'd been so convincing that at one point even Tracey herself had had doubts about his guilt. Nor had Kenny given any reason as to why he and Terry had felt the need to prostitute out women, let alone work in partnership with the Murphy family who were considered to be nothing less than scum by everyone who had the misfortune to come across them. It hadn't solely been about money, she knew that much; Terry had always been flush and business had been doing well, even Ricky and Jamie had been able to confirm that their father's business had been booming. The only thing that Tracey knew for sure was that Kenny had managed to tear her family apart single-handedly, leaving both her and her sons devastated, and her grandson Mason so traumatised that in the months following his grandfather's slaying he hadn't been able to sleep alone at night. Still to this day he suffered from the occasional nightmare and would wake up in a cold sweat, screaming that the bad man had killed his granddad.

With so many questions remaining unanswered, Tracey felt as though she had the weight of the world on her shoulders. It ate away at her day and night, even though by rights she knew that she should be able to leave the past behind her and concentrate on her future with Max. The problem she had was that she couldn't rest and didn't think she ever would; at least, not until she'd been given the answers she so desperately craved; she at least owed that to her family, or more to the point, Kenny did.

'What happened last night?' Kayla asked, breaking her thoughts.

Tracey glanced up and frowned. 'What do you mean?'

Draining her drink, Kayla stood up and walked over to the sink. 'Ricky,' she said, jerking her head towards the lounge as she rinsed her mug underneath the tap. 'He came home in a foul mood. Did something happen between him and Jamie?'

'No, not that I'm aware of.' About to question her daughter-in-law further, a knocking at the front door stopped Tracey dead in her tracks. Giving a little moan, she raised her eyes to the ceiling. 'I can do without this,' she complained. 'Haven't we got enough on our plates without Pat sticking her oar in and causing uproar?' A huge part of her had hoped that her mother-in-law wouldn't turn up; it would have certainly made her and her family's life a lot easier if that had been the case.

'I'll get it,' she shouted out, then rolling her eyes in annoyance, she grasped hold of Kayla's hand and gave it a gentle squeeze before making her way down the hallway.

Opening the front door, Tracey looked from her mother-in-law to the man standing beside her, and doing a double take, her breath caught in the back of her throat. It was almost like looking at Terry himself, or at least a younger, watered down version of Terry. 'What's going on?' she asked, trepidation clearly notable in her voice as she tilted her head to the side, her hard gaze snapping back to Pat.

'What does it look like?' Patricia retorted. In a cloud of overpowering cheap perfume, she breezed across the threshold. The smug grin plastered across her heavily made up face was almost enough to make Tracey want to throw her back out on her ear again. It's not as if it would be the first time that she'd had the satisfaction of throwing her mother-in-law out. In fact, one of her biggest regrets in life was that she hadn't done it sooner whilst her husband had still been alive, not that she hadn't been tempted on occasion, because she had. Every single time Patricia had visited, Tracey had practically had to bite her tongue to stop herself from berating her husband's mother. She was only thankful that Terry had been of the same opinion and had dreaded Pat's visits, too. It had even become a long-standing joke between them.

'Pat,' she hissed, glancing over her shoulder towards the lounge. 'What the bloody hell is going on? Who is this?' she asked, nodding towards the man standing beside her mother-in-law.

Patricia's smug grin intensified and patting her peroxide blonde beehive into place, she puffed out her chest. 'This,' she said, gesturing to Raymond, 'is what I wanted to talk to you and the boys about.' She slipped her arm through his and made to move forward.

'Oh no you don't,' Tracey hissed, her eyes flashing dangerously. 'Pat,' she warned. 'This is the last time that I'm going to ask you this. What the fuck is going on?'

'This is my Terry's son, Raymond.' Patricia grinned spitefully. 'His real son.'

Tracey placed her hand upon her chest, the tiny hairs on the back of her neck standing upright. 'What are you talking about?' she all but screamed. 'What bloody son?'

'Terry's son,' Pat reiterated, the smug grin once again filtering back into place. 'And like I already said, his real boy, unlike the cuckoo in the nest that you tried to palm off as my Terry's offspring.'

Tracey's blood ran cold. Not long after Terry's death, Patricia had accused her of having an affair, claiming that Jamie hadn't been Terry's biological son. She'd even gone as far as to say that Terry had had doubts about Jamie's parentage, too. How or why, Tracey had no idea, considering she had only ever been faithful to her husband and that both Jamie and Ricky had been Terry's double and not just when it came to looks either; they even shared the same mannerisms, so much so that at times it took her breath away.

'And it's only right that he,' Patricia said, motioning towards Raymond, 'becomes acquainted with his brothers, or should that be brother?' she asked, tilting her head to one side as though thinking the question over. 'After all, it's only what my Terry would have wanted. To have his real sons, his flesh and blood, together under the one roof.'

Looking Raymond up and down, Tracey shook her head, her mind desperately trying to take in what she was being told. A small part of her had always known that this day would come, that her and her mother-in-law's dislike of one another would one day come to a head. Patricia was so vindictive that she would do and say anything to score a point, even if that meant blowing her own grandsons' world apart in the process.

'Is he here?' Patricia asked innocently. 'The cuckoo I mean, just in case you didn't know who I'm referring to. It's about time you told him all about his parentage, isn't it? After all, it's only right that Jamie should know where he comes from. That's if' – she smirked – 'you even know yourself who his real father is and let's face it, given your track record, I highly doubt that's the case.'

'Mum?'

Goose flesh covered Tracey's skin and as she turned to look over her shoulder, the colour drained from her face. How long had Jamie been standing there, and how much exactly had he heard? 'Go inside,' she urged him, her voice a lot higher than usual. 'I'll be in soon.'

Jamie narrowed his eyes. 'What's going on Mum?' There was an edge to his voice and turning back to look at her mother-in-law and in particular the man beside her, Tracey resisted the urge to push them back outside the house and slam the front door in their faces. 'Don't you dare,' she hissed, her eyes not wavering from Pat's smug face. 'I'm warning you, utter one word, just one,' she spat, 'or do anything that so much as threatens to break my baby's heart and I will personally hammer the life out of you, is that understood?'

Patricia returned the hard stare and turning to give her youngest grandson a sickening grin, she nodded towards Raymond. 'I've got something to tell you and your brother sweetheart,' she said as she flounced past Tracey and made her way into the lounge. 'Something very important.'

* * *

As she entered her son's lounge, and it always would be Terry's lounge in Patricia's eyes, considering it had been his hard-earned money that had paid for it, and that included the state-of-the-art kitchen that Tracey was so proud of, the sight of Max Hardcastle as large as life sitting on her Terry's sofa was enough to wipe the smug smirk from Patricia's face.

'What are you doing here?' she demanded. 'You're not family.' She looked around, her jaw dropping open. 'He ain't family,' she screeched at the top of her lungs. 'Get him out of here.'

Walking into the room, Tracey grasped hold of Max's hand. 'He's got as much right to be here as anyone else Pat,' she said, pulling herself up to her full height and giving her mother-in-law a hard stare. 'He's my partner, we're together, we have been for a while.' It was a slight exaggeration, not that Patricia needed to know the ins and outs of her and Max's relationship.

'Do what?' Patricia snarled. 'Oh I see.' She gave a sarcastic laugh and shook her head. 'I should have seen this coming. All along I knew there was something going on between you and him, that he was your fancy man,' she spat, glaring at Max, the contempt she felt for him written across her face, clear for them all to see. 'My Terry was barely cold in the ground and you and him were at it like rabbits. And I'll tell you something else for nothing lady,' she added, focusing her attention back on Tracey. 'You've got no shame; you'd drop your knickers for anyone. And you condone this, do you?' She turned to look at her eldest grandson. 'You're all right about this? This bastard murdered my son, your father, and you're allowing him to waltz in here and make himself comfortable in your dad's home, in his bed,' she shouted.

'Come on now Pat,' Max said, holding up his hands. 'Deep down you know that's not true; it wasn't me who killed Terry.'

'Oh, he finally speaks does he.' Every inch of Patricia's body bristled, the anger that ran through her veins so tangible that it took everything inside of her not to pummel her fists into the murdering bastard's face. 'I wondered how long it would take for you to open that trap of yours, and let's face it, you had plenty to say in court didn't you? Right from day one I knew that you were a wrong'un, but a snake in the grass,' she said, giving an overly exaggerated high pitched cackle, 'that's low even by your standards; that's if you even have any standards. I know you; just you remember that Maxwell Hardcastle, and I rue the day my son ever met you. You're a wrong'un, always have been, not that I can say I'm entirely surprised considering that mother of yours was nothing but a dirty slut.' She screwed up her face, disgust etched across her features. 'Night after night she sold her body down at the docks and allowed men to paw at her with their filthy hands. She didn't have an ounce of decency inside of her, and certainly had no self-respect. Is it any wonder that she raised you to be nothing more than an animal? Not that I can say she brought you up; more like she dragged you up. If I didn't despise you so much I'd pity you.'

'Pat,' Tracey roared. 'Enough.'

Max held up his hand, and giving a slight shake of his head, he sighed. 'Let her get it out of her system; the quicker we get this over and done with, the better it will be for everyone concerned.' He turned to look at Patricia and spreading open his arms, he gave a nod, his voice calm despite the steely look in his grey eyes. 'If you want to take a pop at me then go ahead,' he said, pointing at his jaw. 'We've already established the fact that you don't like me, that you think I somehow led Terry astray, that my mum was a prostitute, oh and let's not forget the fact I was dragged up rather than brought up. Any other words of wisdom that you might want to add to that Pat? Why don't you go the whole hog and accuse me of being the devil incarnate? Or how about we get down to the crux of the matter and you stand there blaming me for the fact your son was one of the biggest villains this side of the water? I mean' – he shrugged – 'I was in nick for eighteen years of my life, so I can't really see how I could have had that much of an influence over Terry if I was banged up, keeping my head down and minding my own business might I add. I didn't hear from Terry for years, seventeen years to be precise. So, if you want to point fingers then why don't you start with yourself? You were his mother; where were you when he was establishing a name for himself, selling knocked off gear, dealing drugs, pimping out women. Or how about when he and Kenny were threatening all and sundry that they would kill them if they came within a two-mile radius of their territory? From my understanding, one or two of the bodies were buried in the foundations of the flyover on the A13 and that's without the ones who were fed to the pigs or thrown overboard into the sea with weights tied around their ankles. So come on Pat,' he said, sitting forward in the chair, the nerve in his strong jaw pulsating. 'Answer the fucking question: where were you?'

Two pink spots appeared on Patricia's cheeks and turning her face away, she placed her hands on her hips. 'Well,' she demanded of Ricky in an attempt to avoid the question. 'Are you going to just sit there and allow this murdering bastard to talk to me like this? I'm your grandmother, not some stranger you've just met. Where's your loyalty, eh? We're family. That has to count for something, doesn't it?'

Ricky sighed and staring at Raymond, his forehead furrowed. 'Talking of strangers,' he barked out. 'What's he doing here?'

Patricia ran her tongue over her teeth, the wicked gleam in her eyes intensifying as she turned her attention back to her daughter-in-law. 'This is your brother.' She smirked. 'Raymond. Not that he actually needs an introduction. I would have thought it was obvious; he's like the spit out of your dad's mouth.' She gave Raymond a warm smile and reached out to clutch his hand.

A deathly silence fell over the room as they tried to digest what they had just been told.

'Is this a joke?' Jamie piped up, looking around him.

'It's no Joke,' Raymond said, giving them his best smile. 'Terry was my dad.'

'Like fuck he was,' Jamie retorted. 'Mum,' he said, his voice wavering, 'tell me this isn't true?'

Still staring at her mother-in-law, Tracey gave a slight shrug. 'I don't know darling,' she sighed, casting a glance towards Raymond, her mind still reeling with the news that amongst other things, Terry had also been a murderer. 'This is the first I've heard anything about it, as is the fact that not only did my husband run a brothel but that he also killed people,' she added, giving Max a glare.

'But how?' Jamie cried. 'I mean,' he said as he began to mentally calculate their ages. 'You and dad would have been married, wouldn't you?'

Ricky raised his eyebrows and as he waited for his brother to get a handle on the situation, he took a moment to study Raymond. As much as he didn't want to admit it, even he could see the similarities between them. Raymond was a walking clone of their father: same height, same build, same blue eyes, even the same shade of dark hair. More than anything, he was amazed that he had never made the connection before now, that he hadn't seen the likeness for himself. It wasn't as though he hadn't seen Raymond around because he had, perhaps he'd never looked at him long or hard enough, or maybe he just hadn't wanted to see the resemblance between himself and the local nutter. He glanced across to his mother, gauging her reaction to the news that Terry's infidelity went back even further than any of them could have imagined, and as Kayla perched on the arm of the chair, he instinctively grabbed hold of her hand, using the contact with his wife as a crutch of sorts.

'I didn't get to see him often, our dad I mean,' Raymond said, breaking the silence. 'But he tried to keep in touch whenever he could. He would often take me over to West Ham to watch a game or take me to Wimpy for something to eat. One year him and Kenny took me to watch the boxing; I can't even remember who was fighting now,' he said, giving a slight shrug. 'The only thing that mattered to me was that I was with my dad. I've got nothing but good memories of him, he was a good man.'

Giving Jamie a surreptitious glance, Ricky shook his head, their falling out momentarily forgotten about. 'You weren't at the funeral,' he said, narrowing his eyes.

'No.' Giving them a pained expression, Raymond shifted his weight from one foot to the other. 'Uncle Kenny asked me not to come; he didn't want to upset you,' he said, turning to Tracey and giving her a sad smile. 'He thought it would be best if I stay away, and' – he placed his hand upon his chest – 'the last thing I would ever want to do is to cause any upset, especially at a time like that. It must have been difficult enough without me turning up and making matters even worse. I did go to the grave afterwards though to pay my respects and lay some flowers.'

'Uncle Kenny?' Jamie scoffed. 'You do know that that bastard murdered my dad, our dad,' he corrected, making a point of excluding Raymond as he wagged his finger between himself and Ricky.

Raymond nodded, his startling blue eyes drifting towards Max. 'I know that he's in prison for murder if that's what you mean.'

'And we all know who should be there in his place,' Patricia butted in, her lips pressed into a thin line. 'You've got a bloody nerve,' she spat, her hard stare directed towards Max. 'My Kenny is as innocent as they come and you,' she said, her eyes flashing dangerously, 'not only did you get away with murder but you've also got the audacity to be living it up as though butter wouldn't melt in your mouth. And you've well and truly got your feet under the table here, haven't you? Even these two,' she said, indicating towards her grandsons, 'have fallen for your lies.'

'Oh give it a rest Pat,' Tracey barked out. 'Max had nothing to do with Terry's death and you know it.'

For the second time in as many minutes, Patricia's jaw dropped. 'You can bloody talk an' all.' Craftiness settled across her face. 'Just maybe,' she said, crossing her arms over her chest, 'I need to have a long overdue chat with the cuckoo, tell him some home truths; let's see how you'd bloody well like that.'

'Right that's it, out!' Tracey shouted, shoving her mother-in-law and Raymond out of the lounge and into the hallway.

'You can't throw me out; this is my Terry's house.' Patricia gasped.

'News flash Pat,' Tracey yelled, flinging open the front door. 'This is my house.' She held up her left hand, the gold wedding band that she still wore clearly visible for her mother-in-law to see. 'And I want you and that wicked, bastard tongue of yours to get out.'

Slamming the front door firmly closed behind them, Tracey leaned wearily against the wooden frame, and placing both of her hands upon her chest, she screwed her eyes shut tight and twirled her wedding ring around her finger. She would rather kill Patricia stone dead than ever allow her to spew her evil, spiteful lies into her sons' ears. Even if that meant living out the remainder of her life behind bars, it had to be better than the alternative, she decided. It would break Jamie's heart if he was to learn that Terry had had doubts that he was his father. Perhaps she and Max weren't so different after all, considering the only reason he'd murdered was to protect his mother, and she knew for a fact that despite what he'd told the parole board he felt no remorse for his actions, and why should he when he'd been merely looking out for his mother's best interests?

For a few moments she stood absent-mindedly chewing on the inside of her cheek, hoping that the thumping in her chest would soon return to its normal rhythm and even more than that, that her sons wouldn't notice just how rattled Patricia's visit had left her.

'What's she going on about?' Jamie asked when she finally returned to the lounge. 'What cuckoo?'

'Gawd knows.' Tracey flapped her hand dismissively, her cheeks reddening. 'You know what she's bloody like.'

'She's off her nut, I know that much,' Jamie said, screwing up his face. 'She thinks she can talk to birds now.'

Despite the situation, Tracey couldn't help but laugh. She was only thankful that her sons knew their grandmother well enough not to pay any attention to her ramblings; even Terry had taken everything Patricia had said with a pinch of salt.

'And as for Raymond Cole,' Jamie spat, 'what's he after eh, a kidney or something?'

'Jamie,' Tracey warned.

'What?' Jamie retorted. 'Who the fuck does he think he is? "Oh, Dad took me to watch West Ham play",' he said in a sing song tone. '"Dad took me to watch the boxing, Dad took me to Wimpy." Well bully for fucking you mate because you got a lot more out of him than we ever did.' His face a mask of anger, Jamie jerked his head towards his brother. 'How many times did we beg the old man to take us to a match? And what about my twelfth birthday?' he said, stabbing a finger towards Tracey. 'Dad promised that he would take me over Upton Park. All day I stood at that window,' he said, pointing across the room, 'waiting for him to get home from work early so that we could go and watch the match, and by the time he staggered through the front door he was so pissed he couldn't even walk in a straight line, or string a coherent sentence together, let alone take me anywhere, and all the while he was spending quality time with that nutter and taking him out. Well what about us, eh? Didn't we matter? We were his sons.'

Tracey sighed. Everything Jamie had said was true. As much as Terry had been a good father when it came to providing for his children, he hadn't been there for them emotionally. Time and time again he had let them down. As boys, they had been football mad; they'd lived and breathed the game, and all they had ever wanted was for Terry to take them to a match. In the end they'd given up asking, knowing full well that his promises were more often than not empty. Terry would have rather had the boys holed up at the scrap yard doing odd jobs for him than take them out and spend any actual quality time with them.

'Jamie's got a point,' Ricky said thoughtfully. 'Cole's after something, he has to be.'

Thinking the question over, Tracey shrugged. As much as it hurt her to know that Raymond had been conceived whilst she and Terry had been married, it wasn't Raymond's fault. He was as innocent as she and her sons were, and if she wanted to accuse anyone of treachery then Terry was the only one she could blame. He was the one who had been unfaithful, he was the one who had broken his wedding vows over and over again. And what about Raymond's mother? Had she been a victim of Terry's lies too? Had she been given no other choice but to raise her son single-handedly? In a roundabout way she felt sorry for Raymond; after all, he'd missed out on spending any length of time with his father, however selfish Terry may have been; he'd never had the chance to get to know his half-brothers, and he'd even grown up without knowing his paternal grandmother, not that he'd actually missed much on that front.

'Why don't you give him the benefit of the doubt?' she volunteered. 'He seems nice, and he must have something good going for him, or else Pat wouldn't be so taken with him, and you know what she's like; she would find fault with Jesus Christ himself.'

'Yeah too nice,' Jamie groaned. 'I don't trust him, and I'm telling you now,' he said, jerking his head towards Ricky, 'he's after something. That's not the Raymond Cole we know. The bloke is a nutcase and that's putting it mildly, and that's another thing,' he said, screwing up his face. 'There's no way that I'm admitting to anyone that I'm related to him. It's bad enough having Dad's reputation hanging over my head, let alone being associated to that nutter by blood.' His eyes became as hard as he gave his brother a glare, their argument from the previous evening once more at the forefront of his mind. 'There you go,' he said with a hint of sarcasm, 'another brother; maybe you'll trust this one a bit better.'

'Fuck off Jamie,' Ricky retorted.

'What?' Jamie answered, giving a nonchalant shrug. 'I'm only saying.'

'Yeah and like I said,' Ricky replied as he lounged back in the chair and ran his tongue over his teeth, the muscles in his forearms and shoulders tensing. 'Fuck off, because I'm seriously not in the mood for this.'

'Will you just pack it in?' Groaning in annoyance, Tracey glared at her sons. 'Haven't we got enough going on without the two of you being at each other's throats?' She took a seat beside Max on the sofa. 'Was any of that true?' she asked, her voice softening. 'What you said about Terry killing people?'

Max shrugged, then giving a sigh, he nodded. 'The part about bodies being buried under the flyover on the A13 is true; as for the others...' He gave another slight shrug. 'I have my suspicions but Terry neither confirmed or denied whether or not there were more bodies, although from my understanding there were; there had to be.'

'And did you know about this?' Tracey demanded of her sons, her eyes flashing dangerously.

'They would have been too young,' Max said, waving his hand dismissively. 'All of this happened while I was still banged up. The only reason I know anything about it is because Terry let slip one night when he was pissed.' Clearing his throat, Max leaned forward slightly. 'This Raymond,' he asked, changing the subject before Tracey could question him any further. 'Didn't you say that he's mates with Alfie Winters?'

'Yeah,' Ricky answered. 'They're joined at the bloody hip, both of them a pair of notrights. I know that Eddie Winters is your mate,' he said, holding up his hands as though to ward off Max's protests, 'and that the two of you go way back, but when it comes to Alfie, he's bad news. Always has been; even when we were kids there was something off about him. He's as unhinged as Cole is.'

Max nodded. He'd guessed as much and as the cogs began turning in his mind, he rested his forearms on his knees. 'So, presuming I'm right' – he paused for a moment and rubbed his thumb over his bottom lip – 'and that Alfie Winters has got some sort of an issue with me, then what's the betting that Raymond is of the same opinion?'

Jamie's eyes widened. 'I told you,' he said, jerking his thumb towards the front door. 'Something isn't right about any of this; he's definitely up to something.'

'Are you thinking that he could have been involved?' Ricky asked. 'That it was him and Winters who could have been behind the arson attack?'

'Could be.' Max shrugged. 'But if they are involved then my old pal Eddie is bound to know about it; he makes it his business to know what's going down. The burning question though is whether or not he could have been behind the attack. He would do anything to keep a tight rein on the manor and the first thing he would want to do is get rid of anyone who has the means to takeover, and not only does that include me but you two as well considering who your old man was.' Getting to his feet, he shrugged on his jacket. 'There's only one way to find out for sure though, isn't there?' he added with a raise of his eyebrows.

'Too fucking right there is,' Jamie chipped in, a hint of excitement audible in his voice. 'Any excuse to smash my fist into that mad fucker's face,' he said, referring to Raymond, 'and I'm in.'

'Hold up a minute,' Tracey protested. 'You can't go around just hitting people, and whether you like it or not, Raymond is your brother.'

'Half-brother,' Jamie corrected. 'Let's not get that twisted. Anyway, it was a joke Mum,' he lied. 'I wouldn't dream of smashing him in.' He gave her a wide smile that was so like his father's, then turning towards his brother, the smile slipped from his face and was quickly replaced with a snarl. 'Are you coming or not?'

'I thought you were supposed to be meeting someone?' Ricky lifted his eyebrows and glanced towards the outline of a phone in Jamie's pocket. 'You were making a big song and dance about it yesterday.'

A pink hue crept its way up Jamie's neck and as his fingers automatically reached inside his jeans pocket, he gave a carefree shrug. 'You just can't help sticking your nose into my business, can you?'

Before Ricky could answer, Kayla squeezed her husband's hand. 'Stop winding him up.'

'I am not,' Ricky protested. 'It was an observation that's all. I'm not the one who's being secretive.'

'It would take a lot more than him to wind me up,' Jamie

conceded as he pulled on his jacket, his expression hard. 'Are you coming or not?'

'Go on,' Kayla said gently. 'Go with them.'

'Do I actually have a choice?' Ricky groaned, as he reluctantly got to his feet.

'It's up to you.' Jamie shrugged. 'Do whatever you like; I'm not bothered either way.'

Shaking his head, Ricky let out a long sigh. 'Give it a rest bruv,' he groaned. 'Despite what you might think I'm not the enemy here.' Turning to Tracey he pulled her into a hug. 'See you later Mum.'

Tracey nodded. 'Keep an eye on him,' she mouthed, gesturing towards her youngest son. 'And make sure that he behaves himself.'

'I always do,' Ricky answered, looking over his shoulder in time to see his brother heading out the front door. 'Not that I ever get any thanks for it.'

Adrenaline coursed through Patricia's veins and as angry as she was with her daughter-in-law, Patricia could safely say that she felt as though she were on cloud nine. She would even go as far as to admit that she felt somewhat triumphant, as though she were the victor of a long drawn-out battle between the two women, a battle that had lasted decades and had been so bitter at times that it was only by some miracle they had never come to blows. Although, she had to admit that they had come close over the years and more than likely would have done if it wasn't for the fact that she hadn't wanted to fall out with Terry over it; after all, it stood to reason that her son would take his wife's side considering Tracey had been the mother of his children, or rather two of his children.

The only fly in the ointment as far as Patricia was concerned was Max Hardcastle. Oh, she had had her suspicions that something had been going on between him and Tracey, but to have actually come face to face with her son's murderer had unnerved Patricia a lot more than she was ever prepared to let on. Placing a cigarette between her lips, she lit up and inhaled the smoke deep into her lungs. 'The bitch,' she hissed as she noisily exhaled the smoke. 'I was right all along; I knew that there was something going on between her and that murdering fucker.'

Raymond gave an agitated sigh and, winding down the car window, he waved the smoke out of his face. 'Do you have to?' he complained, nodding towards the cigarette. 'It's barely been five minutes since you last sparked up.'

About to take another drag, Patricia stubbed the cigarette out and waved her hands in the air in an attempt to clear the fog. She actually felt like celebrating, not that she was much of a drinker, certainly not the hard stuff anyway; a couple of gins or a few glasses of white wine and soda was usually her limit.

'Why don't we go for a celebratory drink?' Patricia's asked, rubbing her hands together, her blue eyes twinkling. 'There's a nice little pub up the road. It used to be your dad's local. I could introduce you to his friends. It's about time I was able to show you off. You'd like that, wouldn't you darling?'

'I already know his friends,' Raymond barked back. 'And the majority of them are tossers, not that any of them know Terry was my old man. Let's not forget the fact that my dad did everything in his power to keep my existence a secret; he wouldn't have wanted to upset his perfect little family, would he?'

Patricia's face fell and giving her grandson a sidelong glance, she narrowed her eyes. He was his father's son all right and despite how much she had loved Terry, there were times when she'd had more than just an inkling that he had no time for her. He could go

weeks at a time without visiting or even getting in touch and when
he did eventually show his face it was usually because he wanted
something from her such as an alibi or somewhere to store the
knocked off gear he'd managed to get his hands on. 'Well how
about if we make a day of it? We could get a takeaway later and
have a night in front of the box instead then, just you and me; we
could watch a film, or I could even dig out your dad's wedding
video and point out who everyone is. How does that sound?'

'Sounds riveting,' Raymond answered through clenched teeth.

Oblivious to his sarcasm, Patricia smiled. 'So what do you fancy
then? Pizza, Chinese, or how about a curry?' she said, her eyes
lighting up. 'That was always your dad's favourite, but nothing too
spicy for me.' She rubbed her hand over her stomach. 'It goes
straight through me.'

Raymond's lips curled in disgust at the mental image. 'I can't,'
he said, glancing at his watch. 'I've got plans.'

Hiding her disappointment, Patricia nodded. 'Maybe another
time then.'

Flicking the indicator, he pulled the car into Patricia's road, and
slamming his foot on the brake, he turned in the seat to give his
grandmother a cold stare, his menacing gaze looking straight
through her. 'I'll pop over next week or something if I've got the
time.'

The change in Raymond was unnerving, and as much as
Patricia hated to admit it, there was something about him that
made her feel nervous, perhaps even a little afraid. Something she
had never noticed before and it was more than just the coldness in
his eyes. Racking her brain, she tried to think back. Had there
always been something off? Could it be that she had been so
thrilled to have another of Terry's sons in her life that she had
blindly overlooked his flaws? 'I know it must have been hard,' she
said, reaching out to lightly touch his arm. 'I mean, to come face to

face with your dad's murderer, but he will get his comeuppance, you mark my words darling, he will get what's coming to him.'

'I'm going to have the no-good cunt,' Raymond growled, shrugging Patricia's hand away from him. 'If it's the last thing I ever do and as for the other two,' he snarled, 'they'll pay for taking my dad away from me.'

'Who are you talking about?' As she shook her head, a cold chill ran down the length of Patricia's spine. 'What other two?'

'Ricky and that fucking cuckoo in the nest Jamie,' Raymond answered. 'Who else would I be talking about? If it wasn't for them my dad would have wanted me, he would have spent time with me and to think all along Jamie wasn't even his son.' He gave a malicious laugh. 'I can't wait to see the look on his face when he eventually finds out the truth, that he isn't even a Tempest, that he's nothing but the outcome of a dirty, sordid, illicit affair between his whore of a mother and some nobody.'

Fear clutched at Patricia's heart. She didn't doubt his threats when it came to Maxwell Hardcastle, not for one single second; after all, Hardcastle deserved everything he had coming to him and a lot more besides, but for Raymond to add his own brothers to the mix was enough to make Patricia feel nauseous. Ricky and Jamie had never done anything to harm Raymond; they hadn't even known that they had another brother, and if they had been told then they were bound to have welcomed Raymond into their lives with open arms. 'You don't mean that,' she cried. 'Ricky and Jamie are your brothers, they're your dad's sons. Terry would never have condoned you and the boys going against one another; you're family darling,' she pleaded with him. 'You're supposed to be one another's greatest allies, not enemies.'

Raymond gave a chilling grin, one that didn't reach his eyes. 'The boys,' he sniggered. 'All I ever heard growing up was, "my boys" this, "my boys" that. I'm sick to the back teeth of hearing about my dad's perfect boys.' He stabbed his thumb into his chest. 'What about me eh?' he snarled. 'Didn't I matter? I was his son too, but no,' he said, shaking his head. 'I obviously wasn't good enough for him, was I? So to answer your question, yeah I do mean it. Ricky and Jamie are going to pay for taking my dad away from me, they all are, and that includes that slapper Tracey, Hardcastle, Ricky's wife, even the kid Mason. What was it you called him? Oh yeah, that's right,' he sneered, 'the apple of my dad's eyes.'

Scrambling out of the car, Patricia stood on the pavement and grasped her handbag tightly to her chest, her mind reeling and her insides turning to ice. It wasn't until Raymond had screeched away from the kerb that she let out a terrified breath. Rushing towards her front door, she quickly let herself into the house before locking it behind her.

'You silly old fool,' she chastised herself. She must have misheard Raymond, or perhaps her mind was playing tricks on her and she'd merely imagined the coldness in her grandson's eyes and the hatred in his voice. After all, it had been an emotional day and surely to God he wouldn't have threatened to harm her great-grandson, an innocent child. Only deep down, she knew she wasn't being foolish; she had seen something in Raymond, something that she hadn't liked, something sinister that he'd obviously kept hidden away from her until now. She gave an inward shudder. Could it be that he'd been using her all along, that he'd only wanted to be near her so that he'd have an in with his brothers, perhaps even a means to punish them or even worse follow through with his threat and harm them?

Concern engulfed her and as she made her way through to the lounge, she made a beeline for the mantlepiece and stared at the photographs of her only son. As much as she hated to admit it, Terry and Raymond were cut from the same cloth. From an early age, Terry had had the same coldness about him, and no matter how many times she'd found excuses for his callous behaviour or tried to convince herself that she and Terry had had a close bond, there was no denying the fact that he had been a selfish bastard; his offhand treatment of her had been more than enough to drive that point home. And as easy as it had always been to blame her daughter-in-law, Tracey had never been the problem, not really. No, Terry had been the one who had kept her at a distance; even when it came to her grandsons Terry had never wanted her to be involved in their lives. He'd excluded her from the boys' birthday parties, and even at Christmas he'd been more than happy to leave her at home all alone rather than allow her to join in and celebrate the festivities with her family.

Her heart began to beat faster and slamming her hand over her mouth, she cast her gaze back over the photographs. Finally she found what she was looking for and as she reached out her hand, her fingers ever so slightly trembled. Clutching the image of her son and grandsons together, their arms wrapped around one another's shoulders, she studied their faces. All three men were so similar to one another that Terry wouldn't have been able to deny that he was Jamie's father even if he wanted to. Jamie's hair was a lighter shade of brown, but his face was all Terry's; the bone struc-ture and wide smile were identical, as was the colour of Jamie's and Terry's eyes, a brilliant, dazzling blue that they had inherited from her own father.

'Oh my God,' she cried, sinking heavily on to the sofa, her slim body shaking so much so that she had to physically restrain her legs to keep them from bouncing up and down. Raymond knew everything; she'd told him exactly what she had been told by Kenny, how Tracey had had an affair, and how Terry had highly doubted that Jamie was his son.

She'd only told Raymond about Tracey's supposed infidelity as a means for them to bond, a way for them to form a closeness.

She'd wanted Raymond to know everything there was to know about his family, the good and the bad, and the fact they both shared a mutual dislike of Tracey and a hatred for Maxwell Hardcastle had been enough to seal their relationship, or so she had thought. How could she have been so stupid, so blind as to not see for herself that Jamie was a Tempest through and through? And even more worrying, why would Terry have even claimed that Jamie hadn't been his son?

Hot tears slipped down Patricia's cheeks, the saltiness coating her dry lips. Could it be that Kenny had been lying to her all along? Perhaps Terry had never questioned Jamie's parentage, and if Kenny had lied about Jamie then what other lies could he have told?

The more Patricia thought the question over, the more uneasy she became. For what reason would Kenny have tried to deceive her and more to the point, what did Raymond plan to do with the information she had so willingly given him? Did he intend to inform Jamie that Terry wasn't his father? Did Raymond despise his brothers that much that he would purposely set out to break his younger brother's heart? As much as she had threatened to do the same, she would have never gone through with it; she loved her youngest grandson, always would, even if everything Kenny had said had turned out to be true and Terry hadn't been his father, she couldn't just switch off her feelings, she would have still classed Jamie as her grandson, as her family and even more than that she would have still wanted to be a part of his life. 'What have I done?' she sobbed, clutching the photograph to her chest, her tear-filled eyes staring up at the photographs lining the mantlepiece. 'Dear God, what have I done?'

12

After finally making his way through security, Vincent took a seat in the visiting room of Belmarsh Prison. On the small, low-rise table set in front of him, he placed a twenty-pound note and while awaiting his brother's arrival, he glanced towards the small canteen area. Already a queue was forming, and he groaned out loud. If he knew his brother as well as he thought he did then no doubt Vincent would spend a large chunk of the visit waiting in line to get served. As it was, Cain had a huge appetite and could eat like a horse, and he had a particular penchant for the chicken and mayonnaise wraps that the canteen sold. Not that Vincent blamed him considering he knew first-hand just how bad prison food could be.

'You all right bro?'

Vincent turned his head and as his brother approached, he got to his feet and pulled him into a bear hug. Similar in height and build, the brothers made an intimidating duo and had started out their life of crime as enforcers, until they had come to realise just how much money there was to be earned if they worked for themselves. They still would have been earning good money if Cain hadn't ended up caught bang to rights in the aftermath of the armed robbery that had finally seen him sentenced to ten years inside.

'How are you doing?' Vincent smiled.

Cain shrugged before returning the grin. 'I'm still alive,' he laughed, 'so I must be doing something right.' He released his brother and took a seat, his large frame appearing far too small for the chair. 'How are my girls doing?'

'They're good, better than good actually, they're both doing really well.' Vincent had been expecting the question and nodding enthusiastically, he forced a bright smile to crease his face. On the drive over to South London he'd decided not to mention to his brother that Lucie had become distant, nor was he inclined to tell Cain that his girlfriend of ten years had reverted back to her old habits and was running up debts like no one's business. As Cain had often pointed out in the past, Lucie splurging out on catalogues had to be a lot better than shoplifting which just so happened to be another of her favourite pastimes. Not that Vincent had ever been able to understand why she should feel the need to thieve from the high street when his brother had only ever been generous with his money. In their years together before Cain's imprisonment Lucie had wanted for nothing. She'd only had to bat her eyelashes at him or mention that she wanted to buy something and Cain would have thrust handfuls of money into her hands. 'Lucie said to tell you that she'll be in to see you soon, and that she and Alisha both love and miss you.' Of course, Lucie hadn't exactly said those words, especially the latter, but he wasn't about to tell his brother that. What was the point in causing any unnecessary worry or grief, when Cain wasn't in a position to do anything about the situation? How could he when he was confined to a prison cell for twenty-two hours of the day?

Satisfied with Vincent's answer, Cain lounged back on the chair. 'Any other news?' he asked with a raise of his eyebrows.

Taking a quick glance around him, Vincent waited for one of the prison officers to pass them by before answering. 'Max wants the hard word put on the screw,' he said, his eyes remaining firmly fixed on the officer's retreating back. 'He needs to know what's expected of him and when to turn a blind eye.'

'I thought as much,' Cain answered as his gaze drifted across the visiting room to where Kenny Kempton was sitting. 'The quicker this charade comes to an end the better.' His expression hardened and turning back to look at his brother, the anger that flashed in his dark eyes was more than enough to tell Vincent that Cain was nearing the end of his tether, and that his patience was beginning to wear thin. Not that Cain had ever had much patience to begin with in all fairness. No, it would be fair to say that Cain was the human equivalent of a Rottweiler; he could look friendly, but when pushed too far, his bite could be deadly.

Slightly angling himself better so that he could get a clear view of the room, Vincent lifted his eyebrows. 'Is he still throwing his weight around?' he asked, motioning towards Kenny.

Cain gave a hollow laugh. 'You could say that, or rather you could say that he's pushing his luck as far as I'm allowing him to.'

Vincent narrowed his eyes. The threat in Cain's words was more than evident. 'Just hang it out,' he implored. 'A few more weeks and then you'll have the go-ahead to end him.'

His gaze still focused on Kenny, Cain growled, 'I don't have weeks and seeing as I'm the one stuck in here with him, trust me when I say this, Kempton's demise can't come soon enough.' He curled his fist into a ball and ran his tongue across his teeth. 'I'm telling you bro, I'm this close,' he said, holding his thumb and fore-finger an inch apart to emphasise his point, 'to wiping him out.

Every time he opens that mouth of his all I want to do is smash my fist into his face and rip his head clean off his shoulders.'

Vincent sighed, and snatching up the twenty-pound note from the table, he got to his feet. 'I'll get you the usual, shall I?' he said casually gesturing to the canteen. 'Give you a few minutes to calm down.'

Cain nodded. 'And that's another thing,' he added, looking up at his brother. 'The screw isn't playing ball.'

'What do you mean he's not playing ball?' Vincent hissed.

Cain glanced across the room again. 'I don't know,' he answered, 'but I've got a feeling that his loyalties lie elsewhere.'

'Do fucking what?' Vincent snarled, his expression darkening as he sank heavily back onto the chair.

'Kenny.' Cain nodded across the room. 'I've just got this feeling in here' – he poked himself in the chest, his gaze remaining firmly riveted on Kenny's smug face – 'that he's somehow bought off the screw.'

Vincent reeled backwards. 'No, that's not possible.' He ran his hand over his head, the close cropped hair rough beneath his fingertips. He'd had a word in the screw's ear himself, he'd made the threat clear, so clear in fact that for a moment or two he'd actually believed that the prison guard was going to burst into tears, either that or shit himself, and he meant that literally. 'No,' he reiterated, his mind ticking over. 'No fucking way.'

'I'm telling you.' Cain leant forward slightly and lowered his voice. 'Something happened just a few days ago with Kenny and another con. And when it came to dealing with Kenny, the screw hesitated; I saw it with my own two eyes. He actually looked, I dunno...' Cain threw open his arms, leant back in the chair and shook his head as though he was trying to find the right word, 'like he was wary of him, maybe even afraid.'

Barely able to get his head around what he was being told,

Vincent turned in his seat to look at Kenny, not caring if the action came across as blatant or if any of the prison guards ordered him to turn back around. 'How the fuck did he manage to get to a screw?'

Cain shrugged. 'Your guess is as good as mine. But I can tell you one thing,' he added, sitting forward again. 'Do you see the geezer sitting with Kenny?'

Vincent nodded.

'I don't know who he is but what I do know is that he's becoming a regular visitor. That's the third time I've seen him here this month.'

As he continued to stare across the visiting room, Vincent narrowed his eyes. The man sitting with Kenny looked familiar and he was sure that he'd seen him somewhere before but where that was, for the life of him, he couldn't recall. He bit down on his bottom lip as though the action would somehow help to jog his memory. 'Find out who he is,' he said, turning back in his seat. 'I need a name and fast.'

Rubbing his hand over his stomach, Cain nodded, then jerking his head behind him towards the canteen, he lifted his eyebrows. 'I could murder a chicken and mayo wrap.'

Vincent rolled his eyes. After today's visit he had a feeling it wouldn't be the only murder his brother would be committing.

* * *

Arriving at Belmarsh Prison just in the nick of time, Raymond was still breathing heavily as he dropped onto the chair in front of Kenny.

'Where the fuck have you been?' Kenny snarled. 'Ten minutes I've been sitting here waiting for you to put in an appearance. You've made me look like a right prat.' As he shot a glance around the visiting room, Kenny's cheeks were flushed pink. He'd been waiting for so long he'd actually begun to think that Raymond had stood him up, and that as a result he would have to take the walk of shame back to his cell knowing that every prisoner in the room would have seen his humiliation. He would become a laughing stock, and even more worrying, the reputation he'd worked so hard to maintain would end up in tatters and all thanks to the arrogant little tosser sitting in front of him.

'I'm here, aren't I?' Raymond spat back. 'What are you getting your knickers in a twist for?'

Kenny narrowed his eyes; it was on the tip of his tongue to tell Raymond to fuck off, to put him in his place once and for all, and to remind him of who exactly was in charge. And he would have done too if it wasn't for the fact that he needed him so much and didn't want to risk Raymond turning on him, or even worse, for Raymond to take matters into his own hands and ultimately fuck up the plans that he had so carefully mapped out to end Hardcastle's miserable life. As much as it pained Kenny to admit it, other than Terry's illegitimate son and Patricia, he had no one on the outside, well other than his wife of course and she was about as much use to him as a chocolate teapot. When she did visit she alternated between being angry at him one moment and a snivelling wreck the next, so much so that her mood swings were almost enough to give him whiplash. And when she did actually make the effort to strike up a conversation, nine times out of ten all she wanted to talk about was their son Shaun and how well he was doing inside, how he'd made friends, and was by all accounts well-liked by both prisoners and officers. Kenny couldn't give a flying fuck about his son; Shaun had only ever been a disappointment to him. He was weak, a mummy's boy, and certainly not the son Kenny had wished for or deserved. As a result, more often than not by the time Kenny went back to his cell he felt even more depressed than he had before the start of the visit. 'Who's rattled your bleeding cage?'

'Who do think?'

Kenny's eyebrows rose a fraction. 'I'm seriously not in the mood to be playing guessing games. So stop acting like a first-class prick and start talking.'

Raymond sighed, and as he placed his arm across the back of the empty chair beside him, his face was a mask of anger. 'Hardcastle and the other two muppets, Ricky and Jamie.'

Kenny's eyes lit up. 'You've finally met them then?'

'Yeah for all of five minutes,' Raymond groaned. 'Before that stupid old bat Patricia fucked it all up. She started banging on about Jamie being a cuckoo in the nest and the next thing we knew Tracey was throwing us out of the house.'

Kenny chuckled out loud. So the ball had finally been put into motion, had it? 'And?' he asked, barely able to keep the excitement out of his voice.

'And what?' Raymond answered, confusion spreading across his features.

Fast on his way to losing his patience, Kenny's eyes widened. 'So what was the outcome?'

Raymond screwed up his face. 'I've just told you; Tracey threw us out.'

Kenny waved his hand dismissively. 'But it's a start,' he said with a laugh. 'They know who you are now, that Terry was your old man.'

'Yeah I suppose so.' Raymond shrugged. 'Not that it got me very far.'

As he leaned back in the chair, Kenny grinned. How he wished he could have been a fly on the wall to see their faces; it was bound to have been priceless. 'Keep at it,' he instructed. 'And remember,' he warned, jabbing a finger forward, his expression becoming serious. 'Be nice, especially to Tracey. She might come across like a piece of limp lettuce but those boys worship the ground she walks on. Get her on side and you've already won half the battle and before you know it you'll have wormed your way into their lives.'

Raymond sat up a little straighter, his eyebrows pinching together. 'I'm always nice,' he protested.

Kenny gave a knowing look. From experience, he knew that nice and Raymond were two words that didn't belong in the same sentence. There were plenty of other descriptions Kenny could use for Terry's son; arrogant, cocky, nutcase, even psychopath for instance would fit the bill, but most definitely not nice.

'Yeah all right.' Raymond shrugged before flashing a wide smile. 'I'll play nice but believe me when I say this, there is only so far I'm willing to go before I end up losing my rag and going garrity on them.'

Kenny's expression was one of pure glee as he laughed out loud. 'I don't doubt that in the slightest.' He grinned, rubbing his hands together before leaning in closer and lowering his voice a fraction. 'And what about the screw?' he asked, jerking his head in the direction of the prison officers. 'You had a word with him?'

'What do you think?' Lounging back on the chair, Raymond cracked his knuckles. 'Let's just say,' he said, twirling a locker key around his index finger, his eyes following Simon Peters as he walked the length of the visiting room, 'that he isn't going to be a problem. Whenever you want to go in for the kill, he'll turn a blind eye and if he tries getting lairy' – he smirked – 'just let me know and his home will go up in flames, preferably with his wife and kids still in it.' He winked.

As impressed as Kenny was, he couldn't help but shake his head. Raymond wasn't only a loose cannon but he was also sick in the head; he had to be if he was seriously contemplating burning down the screw's home, regardless of whether or not his family were still inside. That was the problem with Raymond though, Kenny conceded, he didn't have any morals, and certainly wouldn't have felt any kind of remorse if he was to put his threat into action. In fact, Kenny had a nasty feeling that Raymond would have got a kick out of watching the screw's family burn to death. The mere thought of being on the receiving end of Raymond's temper was enough to make Kenny inwardly shudder and he was thankful to have had the hindsight not to tear a strip into him. Who knew what the nutter was capable of, and as his gaze went to the key in Raymond's hand that he was still casually twirling around his index finger, he swallowed deeply. He wouldn't put it past Raymond to try and gauge his eye out with it; he certainly had the mentality to do so.

* * *

An hour later, once visiting time had finished, Cain waited in line to be searched before being escorted back to his cell.

'Hey Kenny,' he called out, making sure to keep his voice casual, no matter how much it rankled him to even give the man the time of day, let alone pretend that they were on friendly terms. 'How did your visit go?'

Turning his head, Kenny grinned, the ever present craftiness across his fat face almost enough to make Cain want to end him there and then. 'Good,' he called back, his hard gaze filtering across to Albert Nowak as he too stood in line awaiting to be escorted back to the cells, before settling on the prison guard Simon Peters. 'Really fucking good; you could even say that it was informative.'

Cain nodded, and as he was instructed to remove his clothes for a strip search, he pulled his T-shirt over his head without arguing for once or demanding to know why he'd been singled out. It didn't escape his notice that Kenny was never ordered to strip, not that any of them would want to see the fat fucker naked. The sight of Kenny's flabby belly was bound to be enough to put them off their dinners. 'So who was your visitor?' he asked as he kicked off his shoes and began unbuttoning his jeans. 'I've seen him here a few times; is he a relative of yours?'

Kenny's eyes hardened and as he flicked his gaze back to the prison officer, he squared his shoulders. 'That's my business,' he barked out, tapping his finger against the side of his nose. 'So keep that big hooter of yours out of it.'

Other than a slight twitch of his jaw, Cain's expression gave nothing away. 'That was one of my brothers,' he said, nodding back towards the visiting room in the hope that Kenny would open up and begin talking. He opened his mouth to continue his barrage of questions when Simon Peters held up his hand, his expression stern.

'Enough of the chatter, Daly,' Peters barked out. 'Get dressed. We haven't got all day to wait for you.'

Cain sighed and as he glanced across to Kenny, the sight of his smug grin was enough to confirm Cain's suspicions, that Kenny had somehow managed to get to the screw. He narrowed his eyes and as he begun to dress, he contemplated the situation. There was only one way Kenny could have intimadated a prison officer and he had a feeling the answers lay with Kenny's visitor. There could be no other explanation for it; how else could he have got the screw onside so easily?

More determined than ever to get to the bottom of the matter, Cain stared at the back of Kenny's head. His eyes were like two hard flints, his body like a coiled spring, a further testament to just how strong his desire to bring Kenny to his knees had become.

Once inside his cell, Cain sat on the bunk, and with his forearms resting on his knees he chewed on the inside of his cheek, his thoughts turning to that of his girlfriend and daughter. He'd promised Lucie that he would keep his head down and behave himself, and that after serving out the remainder of his prison sentence he would be home for good, that he would put a life of crime behind him and concentrate on becoming a family man. He rubbed his palm over his face and stared at a photograph of Lucie and Alisha pinned to the wall, knowing full well that his promises were empty and that there was every likelihood that on top of his conviction for armed robbery, another charge would be added to the long list of crimes that he'd committed over the years: murder.

Getting to his feet, Cain paced the length of his cell, his fists curling and uncurling with every step he took. He could just as easily tell Max that he wanted no part in Kenny's demise; it wasn't as though he owed Max anything other than their friendship of course and the fact that Max had taken him and Vincent under his wing and shown them the ropes the first time they had been banged up. Only deep down in his heart, Cain knew that he would do no such thing, that at no point would he make the phone call to his brother and tell him that he had changed his mind. His hatred of Kenny had become the equivalent of an itch, one that he couldn't quite reach. It ate away at him like a cancer, so much so that at times the only thing he could think about was ending Kenny's sorry excuse of a life and showing him the same mercy that he and Terry Tempest had shown to the women they had pimped out. After all, he was a father, and the mere thought that his Alisha, his little girl, could have one day ended up in their clutches and found herself in the same situation as that of their victims made his entire body shake with rage.

His mind made up, Cain tore down the photograph. 'I'm sorry babe,' he whispered as he tucked the image of his girlfriend and daughter underneath his mattress, out of sight. 'But I have to do this. I have to kill the bastard.'

13

Entering The Ship and Anchor public house, Max was oblivious to the buzz that his presence had created. Once upon a time he would have found their stares unnerving, and the muscles across his forearms would have become taut as if expecting some form of an attack on himself, not that any of them would have been brave enough to actually cause him any grief, let alone try to physically harm him; after all, he was a convicted killer. The crime he'd committed was not only legendary on the Dagenham council estate but was also still fresh in their minds, despite the fact he'd been a teenager when he'd carried out the brutal murder and that more than thirty-five years had passed since that time. It was the price he had to pay he supposed, a lingering reminder that he'd once taken a life, however noble his reasons for committing the murder may have been.

His expression hard, Max's stance was enough to alert anyone with half a brain cell to the fact something was amiss, and that trouble could very well be on the horizon. With purposeful strides he made his way to the bar with Ricky and Jamie falling into step beside him.

'Eddie,' Max said in a greeting, his gruff voice lacking any of its usual pleasantness.

Deep in conversation, Eddie turned his head and as he glanced between Max, Ricky and Jamie, he pulled himself up to his full height, the wrinkles across his forehead becoming even more pronounced. 'Max,' he said, his voice holding a hint of caution. 'What are you doing here?'

Max laughed. 'What kind of a greeting is that for your old mate?'

Hastily composing himself, Eddie flashed a tight smile. 'How are you doing?'

'Never been better,' Max answered, forcing a wide grin in return. It didn't escape his notice that he could hear a note of trepidation in Eddie's voice; not only that but he also appeared nervous, as if Max's appearance had somehow rattled him. 'You remember Terry's boys, don't you?' Max asked, gesturing towards Ricky and Jamie.

Eddie nodded, then shoving out his hand, he offered the brothers a stilted smile. 'Of course I do. I knew your old man well; he was a good bloke.'

Max lifted his eyebrows. The fact Eddie had taken over the running of the manor as soon as Terry and Kenny were out of the picture was lost on neither of them, least of all Ricky and Jamie, not that Max entirely blamed Eddie for stepping up and asserting his power. The opportunity had arisen, and he would have been a fool not to have grabbed it with both hands. Casually, Max leant against the bar, and motioning across to the optics, he dipped his hand into his pocket and pulled out his wallet. 'What can I get you?'

Eddie contemplated the question for a moment before nodding down at the glass in front of him. 'Brandy,' he said, his eyes automatically flicking towards the door as though he were on the lookout for someone. 'You're making a habit of this,' he said lightly, the smile he flashed his old friend not quite reaching his eyes. 'Turning up here twice in one week, that's got to be some sort of a record hasn't it.'

'I can't seem to stay away from the place,' Max retorted, the smile he gave in return mirroring Eddie's superficial one. 'Especially when some cunt has the audacity to try and take me down.'

Eddie lifted his chin in the air, the muscles across his back becoming rigid. 'I take it you're not any closer to finding out who was responsible then?' he probed.

'Nah I wouldn't say that. In fact, you could say that I'm close.' Max gave a wink, his hard gaze remaining firmly fixed on Eddie, scrutinising his demeanour for any signs that his gut instincts were right and that he could have been behind the arson attack. 'You better than anyone should know what I'm like; after all, we go way back, don't we? And it's not in my nature to back away from trouble; never have done and I sure as fuck don't intend to start now. I'm gunning for this bastard and if you were in my shoes, you would do the same. You'd hunt the no-good cunt down and not stop until you'd found the prick and battered the living daylights out of him.'

Beads of cold sweat broke out across Eddie's forehead and as he hastily wiped them away, he lifted the glass to his lips and drained the remainder of his brandy in one large gulp. 'All sounds a bit ominous,' he remarked, wiping the back of his hand over his lips. But anyway, the culprit could have been just about anyone; it could have been an accident, or maybe there could even be an innocent explanation,' he said, the words tumbling out of his mouth in a rush, 'a car malfunctioning perhaps or—'

'It was no accident,' Max interrupted, holding up his hand to cut Eddie off. 'The bastard left a voicemail telling me exactly what he intended to do, and you know yourself that there was more than one whisper doing the rounds confirming that someone had it in for me; that doesn't sound like an innocent explanation to me.'

'A voicemail.' The colour drained from Eddie's face and as he lifted the empty glass up to his lips, he quickly realised his mistake, shook his head then placed it back down on the bar again. 'You've never mentioned receiving a voicemail before now. Did you recognise his voice?'

Ignoring the question, Max gave his order, paid for the drinks then slipped his wallet back into his pocket. 'It's not like you to be on your own,' he said, changing the subject. 'No Charlie or Alfie today?'

Eddie shook his head and as his tongue snaked out, he licked nervously at his bottom lip. 'You know what it's like.' He attempted to smile. 'I have to force them out to work, otherwise the lazy little buggers would probably still be in bed gone lunchtime.'

Max laughed and as he motioned towards Ricky and Jamie, he lifted his eyebrows, feigning mock annoyance. 'I know the feeling mate.'

Relaxing slightly, Eddie gave a hearty chuckle. 'Kids these days, they don't know they're fucking born do they. When we were the same age we had to graft for our dough. We had no other choice on the matter. Nothing was handed down to us on a plate; we had to make a name for ourselves and fight off every other fucker out there trying to get to the top. And don't get me started on knife crime. It wasn't like that back in our day; we settled our differences with our fists; weapons were only ever used as a last resort.'

Max gave a nonchalant shrug. 'I wouldn't know, I was banged up and funnily enough, we weren't allowed to have weapons inside, not that that ever stopped us mind. You'd be surprised how imaginative you can be with a toothbrush or even a pencil. I've seen men have their throats slit with the most innocent of objects, things that you wouldn't even imagine could be turned into a weapon.'

'Yeah well.' Eddie took the glass Max offered out to him and, after swallowing down a large mouthful of the brandy, he noisily cleared his throat. 'That was all a long time ago mate. You did your time and you've done well for yourself since then. I hold my hands up to you; you've managed to turn your life around and that's no mean feat. There aren't many men who would have been able to do what you've done.'

'Maybe.' Taking a sip of his own drink Max nodded towards the door. 'So where are your brothers?'

Eddie narrowed his eyes, his back becoming ram rod straight and the muscles across his shoulder blades tense. 'Why the sudden interest in my brothers?' he asked.

For a few moments Max allowed the question to go unanswered, the atmosphere between the two men becoming heavier by the second. Finally, Max jerked his thumb towards Ricky and Jamie. 'They've just been told that Alfie's mate is their half-brother.'

'Who? Raymond Cole?' Eddie screwed up his face. 'Leave it out; he's a bonafide nutcase.' Standing back slightly, he gave Ricky and Jamie the once over. 'Come to think of it,' he said, scratching at his chin, 'you do look alike; I can see the resemblance. Fuck me, I didn't see this coming and as for Terry, well we all knew that he was a boy but not for one single second did I suspect he was Raymond's father. He kept that fucking quiet. I've never even seen them acknowledge one another, let alone have a father and son chat. Honestly,' he said, shaking his head. 'I didn't have a clue, not that it would have made much of a difference, my opinion of Cole would have still been the same regardless of who his father was.'

He glanced back across to the door. 'They should be here in a bit, my brothers I mean. I'm not so sure about Cole; he could be just about anywhere, more than likely up to no good knowing him and if you want my honest opinion, and no offence,' he said, turning to look at Ricky and Jamie as an afterthought. 'But he's got a screw loose.' He pointed to his head. 'Something's not right up here. If I didn't know any better, I'd put money on it that he'd been dropped on his nut as a kid. He's bad news if you ask me and the two of you are better off staying far away from him.'

'Finally,' Jamie piped up. 'Someone who actually agrees with me. I've been saying the same thing ever since we found out. He's not normal, and trust me, no offence taken, he's—'

'Yeah, I've heard the rumours about him,' Max butted in, his hard eyes silently warning Jamie to shut up and let him deal with the situation. 'He burnt his mother's house down, didn't he, or at least he tried to from my understanding? Sounds to me like he has a penchant for playing around with fire, for torching things that don't belong to him.'

Eddie paused and holding up his hands, he looked Max in the eyes. 'Believe me, I'm not his biggest fan but he was never formally charged with starting that fire.'

'Of course he wasn't,' Max retorted. 'Do you honestly believe that Terry would have allowed for that to happen? That he would have wanted the cat to be let out of the bag so to speak. You know as well as I do that he would have done everything in his power to keep the incident quiet, to stop all and sundry from learning that he was Raymond's father.'

'I suppose so,' Eddie sighed. As the door opened and Charlie walked through, his shoulders momentarily sagged. 'Over here,' he shouted out, beckoning for his brother to join them.

Max allowed himself to smile. It wasn't the brother he'd been hoping to see, but he was a patient man, he could wait. As his mobile phone began to ring, Max looked down at the device and seeing Vincent Daly's name flash up on the screen, his eyes ever so slightly narrowed. 'I need to take this,' he said, looking up, his expression becoming once again unreadable.

* * *

Thirty minutes later, after making his excuses to leave the pub, Max was sitting in his car with Vincent beside him in the passenger seat. 'Are you certain about this?' he asked for the third time in as many minutes as he tapped his fingers impatiently on the steering wheel. 'That you didn't maybe mishear or somehow get the wrong end of the stick?'

Vincent lifted his eyebrows. 'No, I made the whole thing up,' he said, shaking his head, incredulous. 'What do you take me for? Do you honestly think that this' – he gestured towards the casino they were parked outside – 'is exactly how I planned to spend my evening? Fuck me Max,' he said, rolling his eyes. 'Don't you think I've got better things to do with my time than stake out a poxy screw? I can't stand the bastards, you know that; they made my life a living hell when I was inside.'

Max held up his hands. 'I was only asking,' he groaned, his eyes remaining firmly fixed on the casino.

'Well stop asking stupid questions. If Cain reckons that the screw has been bought off, then that's good enough for me.' Shifting his weight to make himself more comfortable, Vincent pulled his cigarettes out of his pocket and lit up.

'And what about this bloke who visited Kenny,' Max asked. 'Who is he?'

For a few moments Vincent was quiet. 'I don't know,' he finally answered, taking a hard drag on the cigarette. 'But I've seen him somewhere before, I just can't think where. I dunno, he looked familiar.' He exhaled a cloud of smoke and, winding down the window, he threw the remainder of the cigarette out onto the pavement. 'One thing I do know is that it's bugging the life out of me.'

'Maybe he's just got one of those faces,' Max volunteered.

'Yeah maybe.' Vincent shrugged, still unconvinced.

Up ahead of them, the casino door opened, and spotting Simon Peters emerge, Max opened the car door and stepped outside. Within a matter of minutes he'd slammed his hand around Simon's throat and dragged him kicking and screaming into the alleyway adjoining the casino.

'We had a deal,' Max growled, his fist involuntarily curling into a tight ball as he shoved Simon roughly up against the wall. 'So why the fuck am I being told that your loyalties lie elsewhere?'

Simon's eyes almost bulged out of his head and as his terrified gaze went between Max and Vincent he began to whimper. 'Don't hurt me,' he cried, his eyes blinking in rapid succession as though the action would somehow ward off the attack. 'I didn't have any other choice.'

'Don't listen to this.' Vincent waved his hand dismissively. 'Smash the treacherous, little prick's face in. Or better still,' he said, opening his jacket to reveal a blade. 'Use this on him; from the look of things, he needs reminding of who exactly he's dealing with.'

'No, wait,' Simon screamed as Max held out his hand to take the weapon. 'I'm telling you the truth; he didn't give me any other choice.' Tears rolled down his cheeks, his rheumy blue eyes filled with anguish. 'He said that he would hurt my wife and kids if I didn't do as he said, he threatened to burn them alive.'

As he slightly released his grip from around Simon's throat, Max's eyes widened. 'What did you just say?' he asked, turning his head to lock eyes with Vincent.

'He said that he would hurt my family,' Simon continued to

wail, snot and tears mingling together to form rivulets that streaked his pale face.

Vincent threw up his arms and as he blew out his cheeks, he shook his head. 'It's got to be the same bloke,' he hissed privately in Max's ear. 'If it's not then it's one almighty fucking coincidence that they both like playing with fire.'

'Who said this?' Max roared once again, tightening his grip around Simon's neck. 'Who is he?'

'I don't know.' Collapsing against the wall, Simon gasped for air and rubbed at the indentations Max's fingers had left around his neck. 'How could I say no to him?' He steepled his hands and brought them up to his chest as if pleading with their better nature. 'He knows everything, even which school my kids go to; he showed me photographs of them in their school uniforms as evidence that he's been watching us, that he knows where I live.'

Shock resonated across Max's face. It was an unwritten rule that families, especially children, were off limits. They could beat the living daylights out of each other, shoot, stab, even torture one another if they so wished, but the minute children were brought into the equation it was a different ball game altogether. 'Come on,' he yelled. 'You must know who he is; give me a name.'

Simon swallowed deeply before shaking his head. 'He didn't give me one, I swear to you I'm telling the truth.'

'But you've seen him since then?' Vincent asked, his eyes hard as he studied Simon. 'Was he there today, at the nick, visiting Kenny Kempton?'

Simon paused, his mouth opening and closing, resembling that of a fish out of water.

'Was he there?' Vincent shouted, his hand reaching back inside his jacket as though he were about to pull out the knife. 'It's not a difficult question, a yes or no answer will suffice.'

'Yes.' Simon nodded furiously, his body trembling so much his knees were in grave danger of giving way.

Throwing Simon away from him, Max ran his hand through his hair. 'Fuck, fuck, fuck,' he muttered over and over again.

'You know what this means, don't you?' Vincent asked, lowering his voice. 'Whoever set out to destroy you is in cahoots with that ponce Kenny. Right from the start I warned you that something like this would happen.'

Max nodded; he knew exactly what it meant and as a direct result he was all but ready to commit murders, starting with the screw.

'So if he was there today,' Vincent said, turning his attention back to Simon, 'you can find out who he is. Surely there has to be some sort of record, who's visiting who?'

Simon shook his head. 'I don't have access to that kind of information, and it would be more than my job is worth to start asking questions; it would look suspicious,' he whined. 'There'd be an investigation, and I can't lose my job, I've got a mortgage to pay.' His eyes widened. 'I could be found guilty of taking bribes, of abetting criminals, it could mean imprisonment.' He began to cry, his chest heaving with each gut-wrenching sob. 'I can't go to prison; I can't do time.'

'Trust me, prison is the least of your worries.' Max's lips curled into a snarl as he shoved Simon back against the wall. 'What did he want from you? What was the deal?'

Sniffing loudly, Simon dragged the back of his hand under his nose, wiping away the snot and tears. 'The same thing you wanted,' he answered, sniffing again. 'He told me to turn a blind eye.'

'For what reason?' Vincent urged him.

Simon looked down at the floor and shrugged; the fact he couldn't look them in the eyes was lost on neither of them.

Giving Max a look of warning, Vincent bounded forward and,

grabbing Simon around the throat, he smashed his head against the wall with such force that a loud crack resonated through the air. 'Stop playing games with us,' he screamed in Simon's face, spraying him in spittle as he did so. 'And answer the fucking question. For what reason were you told to turn a blind eye?'

'He's planning to kill someone.' Simon's skin had turned ashen. 'One of the other prisoners. I don't know any more than that I swear to God I don't.' He paused, rubbed his hand across the back of head, then on seeing the streak of blood coating his palm, his blue eyes grew wider as if he'd just remembered a key piece of information. 'He said it's something to do with revenge, that Kempton had sussed out the plan and that the Judas was going to get what was coming to him.' He gave a helpless shrug. 'I swear to you,' he pleaded, 'that's all I know.'

Vincent's skin paled and as he turned his head to look at Max, his eyes were as wide as saucers. 'Cain,' he spluttered. 'He's planning to top Cain.'

* * *

At that precise moment in Belmarsh Prison, Cain's cell was being turned over. An anonymous tip off that narcotics were being stored was all it had taken for the screws armed with sniffer dogs to tear apart Cain's personal belongings.

As he screamed and shouted that he was being fitted up, it had taken six prison officers wearing riot equipment to restrain Cain and by the time the officers had searched through his clothes, letters, food items, pulled the mattress and bedding off the bed and inspected every nook and cranny of his cell, the only banned items they had located was the burner phone, his only source of contact with Vincent; in other words, Cain's lifeline to the outside world.

In his cell a few doors along, Kenny smirked, and lounging

back on his bed with his hands behind his head, he couldn't help but laugh out loud. They thought they were so clever, that he didn't have the nous to suss out Daly's connection to Hardcastle. Well they had another think coming if they thought they would be able to take him out unawares. He was no mug, and as such wouldn't be treated like one. He was a man who demanded respect and if anyone was going to take someone out then it would be him, and it was Hardcastle's mole Cain Daly that he had his sights set on.

Happier now that his tip off had given Cain a taster of what was to come, Kenny closed his eyes. Even Cain's continued screams and shouts weren't enough to stop Kenny from falling into a blissful sleep. In fact, Kenny would even go as far as to say that it was the best night's sleep he'd had in months, maybe even years.

* * *

Momentarily taking his eyes off the road, Max gave Vincent a sidelong glance. 'Is he still not answering?'

'What do you think?' Vincent growled back as he pressed redial for the umpteenth time since leaving the casino. 'Come on Cain,' he yelled, panic beginning to get the better of him. 'Answer your phone.'

Max flicked the indicator and as he pushed his foot down on the accelerator, he focused his attention back on the road. 'You don't know for definite that Cain is the target,' he said in an attempt to calm Vincent down. 'Look, this is Kenny we're talking about; you know what he's like, you'd only have to look at him the wrong way and he'd shit himself. He might be a sly fucker, but he isn't an idiot. He picks his battles wisely and we both know that compared to Kenny, Cain is in a different league. Kenny wouldn't have the bottle to go against him. Trust me, I know the sly cunt from old and without backup he's all mouth and no trousers, and who in their right mind would seriously want to back Kenny? He's small-time, a waste of space, a leach. Besides, didn't you say that he'd been getting lairy with the other cons, that he'd been acting the Billy big bollocks and throwing his weight around? He could be planning to take out just about anyone.'

Vincent shook his head. 'He managed to get backup when it came to torching the showroom, and if he's capable of orchestrating something of that magnitude then he's capable of anything.'

'That's different,' Max answered with a shake of his head. 'That's down to a personal beef between me and him. It's nothing to do with Cain.'

'And what, you think this isn't personal? Cain was planning to top him, remember. And you were there, you heard what the screw said, Kenny has sussed out the plan; how many other plans do you think there are to wipe him out?'

Max raised his eyebrows and, chewing on the inside of his cheek, he took a few moments to think the situation through. Considering this was Kenny they were talking about, he wouldn't be surprised if dozens of plans had been put into place to end his life. As it was, Max was amazed that Kenny had lasted this long inside without receiving death threats or at the very least, a dig or two from one or more of the inmates. Not only that, but from experience, Max knew that all it would take was one snide remark from Kenny or for Kenny to square up to the wrong person for all hell to break loose. After all, Kenny was a bully and it was in his nature to try and intimidate others, especially those he considered to be weaker than himself. Max had a feeling that in the two years Kenny had been banged up, he wouldn't have miraculously undergone a personality transplant, nor would he have suddenly become holier than thou, spouting love and peace to all of mankind. As for the prison itself, it was common knowledge that they could be volatile environments; tempers were often short and violence more often than not the only language prisoners understood. It was more than just a case of the cons asserting their power, it came down to survival. For some men, violence was all they had ever known, it was bred into them, a way of life, part and parcel of who they were.

Twenty minutes later, Max brought the car to a skidding halt outside Vincent's club and as the two men jumped out of the vehicle and bounded across the street, Vincent barked out his orders to the heavies on the door. 'Get my brothers here,' he ordered, his face set like thunder as he stormed inside the venue. 'Both of them.'

After entering the office and slamming the door firmly closed behind them, Vincent began to pace the floor, the phone still glued to his ear, his expression alternating between fear one moment and anger the next. 'If that fat cunt so much as touches a hair on my brother's head I'll kill him stone dead,' he seethed.

Knowing full well that despite his threat there was no way for Vincent to get to Kenny while he was incarcerated, Max sighed. 'Just keep trying him,' he urged. 'He's bound to answer sooner or later.'

'What do you think I've been doing?' he snarled as he glanced at his watch and took note of the time. As the answering service kicked in, indicating that Cain's phone was still switched off, Vincent stared down at the device for a long moment before flying into a fit of rage and repeatedly smashing the phone down on the desk.

Max shook his head and sitting forward in the chair, he looked from Vincent to the phone. 'What the fuck is wrong with you?' he barked out. 'That's hardly going to help matters, is it? How the fuck are you going to contact him now?'

'Not going to help,' Vincent screamed as he went on to haul the phone at the wall. On impact, the device shattered and as the broken pieces fell to the floor, Vincent immediately regretted his outburst. If he couldn't use the burner phone to contact Cain, the only other option left open to him was to contact the prison direct, to tell them that he was worried, that he'd been given some information, that Cain's life was in imminent danger. Or maybe he should call the police, and have them issue an Osman warning. Not that he was a fan of the filth; he distrusted them as much as he distrusted the screws, if not even more.

Slumping onto a chair, Vincent held his head in his hands. In all his life he'd never felt more helpless. 'He's my brother,' he said, looking up, his voice thick with emotion. 'How the fuck am I supposed to just stand by and do nothing? I've looked out for him since we were kids; I can't let him down, not now, not after everything we've been through.' Sheepishly he looked down at the floor. 'If it wasn't for me, he wouldn't even be inside. It was my idea to pull off that robbery. If anyone should have been sent down then it should have been me. Cain wasn't even interested; he didn't want to do the job, he even tried to talk me out of it. Right from the start he said it was a bad idea, that it was too risky.'

The despair in Vincent's voice was Max's undoing and getting to his feet, he bent down to retrieve the SIM card from the broken phone. 'Listen,' he said, straightening up and clasping Vincent by the shoulder. 'Cain can take care of himself; he's a hard fucker and it would take a lot more than Kenny to bring him down and you know it. Cain's got a temper on him and he certainly isn't some muppet. He's going to be all right; he knows the score.'

'You reckon?' Vincent asked, looking up, still unsure. Like Max, he'd spent a lot of years locked up and all it would take was for a makeshift blade to be thrust into Cain's gut and it could very well be game over. By the time the screws found him and had sought medical assistance, Cain could have bled to death; that was if anyone even came to his aid, seeing as Simon Peters had been instructed to turn a blind eye. How many more screws could have been given the same order? Getting to his feet, Vincent walked around the desk, opened the drawer and rummaged around for the spare burner phone he kept for emergencies.

'It's going to be okay,' Max reassured him as he handed over the SIM card. 'Cain isn't stupid. He can handle this. He'll be keeping a close eye on Kenny; he'll know his movements better than anyone and the very moment something feels off he'll be on his guard.'

Vincent nodded and switching the phone on, he took a seat and rested his forearms on the desk. 'Kenny has to go,' he said, pointing a stiff finger in Max's direction. 'No more sitting around doing fuck all. Enough is enough, and whether you like it or not I'm calling the shots on this; that sly fucker's time is up.'

Max sighed, admitting defeat. What was the point in keeping Kenny alive for any longer than was necessary anyway? It wasn't as though he was still searching for answers. In his mind there was no doubt that Kenny had been behind the arson attack and as much as it pained him to admit it, he had a pretty good inkling that Kenny had embroiled the Winters family to do his dirty work, that his old friend Eddie had betrayed him and was working alongside Kenny to bring him down. After all, his demise would have been the equivalent of killing two birds with one stone and with him out of the picture it would be easier for Eddie to maintain his stronghold on the manor.

'Okay,' he said, holding up his hands. 'We do it your way.' Even as he said the words, Max knew that he wouldn't have been able to change Vincent's mind even if he wanted to. Vincent could be as stubborn as a mule when the mood took him, not to mention a dangerous fucker when he needed to be. He nodded towards the replacement burner phone. 'When you finally get hold of Cain, tell him it's time to put the plan into action.'

For the first time in what seemed like hours, Vincent allowed himself to smile, albeit one that didn't quite reach his eyes. 'Now we're starting to get somewhere.'

14

'Don't make a scene,' Ricky warned his brother as Raymond Cole and Alfie Winters finally put in an appearance and entered the pub.

'Why would I make a scene?' Jamie shrugged.

Ricky rolled his eyes. 'Weren't you the one who said that you couldn't wait to grind your fist into Cole's face?'

'Oh that,' Jamie laughed. 'Nah, if I wanted to cause a scene I'd do a bit more than whack him.' He picked up an empty beer bottle and made to smash it against the bar. 'I'd at least leave him with a lasting reminder of our encounter, something he can show his kids and grandkids.' He winked.

Clamping his hand over the bottle clasped in Jamie's fist, Ricky shook his head. 'Leave it out bruv for fuck's sake. I'm seriously not in the mood to babysit you all evening.' He jerked his head behind him. 'For a start, the boozer's packed solid and believe me, he's not worth getting nicked over and definitely not worth serving time for.'

Jamie raised his eyebrows but lowered the bottle all the same. 'I don't like him,' he complained. 'And why is he cosying up to Nan so much? None of this is sitting right with me. You know what Nan's like; she'd be able to cause an argument in an empty room, she doesn't have a good word to say about anyone, so why the fuck hasn't she been able to see through that mad fucker?'

Ricky shrugged. 'No one likes him, and as for Nan, she loves a bit of drama; she'd do or say anything to score a point over Mum, and if Cole is giving her attention, she's going to lap it up.'

'Yeah I suppose so,' Jamie answered as he continued to watch Raymond out of the corner of his eye.

Moments later, Raymond sidled up beside them and, flashing a wide grin, he gestured to the optics. 'Seeing as we're family, can I buy you a drink?'

'That's debatable.' Jamie screwed up his face. 'Until I see the results of a DNA test we ain't family,' he mumbled under his breath.

Raymond smirked. 'That works both ways.'

The nerve at the side of Jamie's eye pulsated. 'Are you taking the piss? It's not our DNA that's in question. We already know who our dad is; you're the one who needs fucking testing.'

'Maybe, maybe not.' Raymond shrugged. 'Perhaps we should all get tested, just to make sure that there aren't any cuckoos in the nest.'

Jamie's eyes hardened and as he tried to get his head around what Raymond had just said, he balled his fist, more than ready to lash out, not that he needed much of an excuse when it came to Raymond. 'What the fuck are you trying to insinuate?'

'Me?' Flashing Alfie a sly grin, Raymond shook his head. 'Why would I need to insinuate anything, other than...' He paused for a moment to look Jamie up and down. 'Out of the three of us, it's you who looks different.' He reached up to touch his dark hair that was so like his father's. 'I'm a carbon copy of my old man, I'm not so sure the same can be said about you though. Oh, but hold on a minute,' he said, placing his finger on his chin as though thinking the situation over. 'Maybe you do look like your dad.' He grinned. 'Just a different one to mine and Ricky's. Maybe you're not even a Tempest. Maybe' – he smirked – 'you're the end result of a two-minute shag behind the back of some dingy boozer.'

'Oi.' Pushing himself away from the bar, Ricky stabbed his finger forward. 'Watch your mouth; that's bang out of order.'

Holding up his hands, Raymond took a step away. 'It was only an observation.' He shrugged. 'But even you have to admit that I could be on to something. Look at him,' he continued to goad. 'He doesn't look anything like Terry.'

Jamie's nostrils flared, and as rage washed over him, he resisted the urge to reach up and touch his own hair as if to clarify to himself that it wasn't a different shade of brown to that of Ricky and Terry's. 'You cunt,' he roared, making to lunge forward. Ricky, who had already anticipated his reaction, hauled him back. 'What the fuck are you trying to say?' he continued to scream as his feet kicked out at Raymond. 'That Terry wasn't my dad, that my mum is a slapper?'

'Your words not mine.' Raymond's smirk intensified. 'All I'm saying is that I know for a fact I'm no cuckoo; I'm not so sure the same can be said about you though. In fact, I have it on very good authority that my dad,' he said, making a point to emphasise the words, 'questioned whether or not you were his son.'

'If anyone was the result of some quick shag,' Jamie shouted as Ricky proceeded to drag him out of the pub before he had the chance to start throwing punches and laying into Raymond. 'Then it was you, not me.'

* * *

Outside in the car park, Ricky gave his brother a wary glance. 'Well, that escalated a lot quicker than I was expecting.'

Jamie was so livid that he was barely able to catch his breath, let alone think straight, and as he made to charge back inside the pub, Ricky held out his arms in an attempt to block his brother's path.

'Get out of my way,' Jamie snarled. 'I'm going to kill the mad fucker; I'm going to slit him from ear to fucking ear.'

'Enough.' Ricky's chest heaved, his breath coming out in short, sharp bursts. 'Just stop, okay.' Every inch of his body was on red alert, and holding up his hands, he took a tentative step closer, his eyes not wavering from his brother's face. 'As much as I know you want to swing for Cole, knocking him out isn't the answer.'

'Nah, but it would make me feel a whole lot better.' His face white with anger, Jamie tucked his head down, his feet fast as he attempted to swerve around his brother.

Swearing under his breath, Ricky's reached out and circled his arms around Jamie's waist, holding on for dear life, almost rugby tackling him to the floor in the process. 'I told you to stop.'

As he struggled to release himself from his brother's grasp, Jamie's fists flew out, punching whichever part of Ricky's body that he could lay his hands on, not that his efforts got him very far considering the tight grip Ricky had on him.

'Calm the fuck down,' Ricky pleaded.

'Calm down?' Jamie screamed. 'Calm fucking down? Were you actually there? Did it not register in your head what he just had the front to say to me, that the old man wasn't my dad. He accused me of being a cuckoo in the nest.'

Ricky nodded. 'I heard what the tosser said. Just ignore him.' Still breathing heavily, he struggled to maintain a grip on his brother. 'He's not worth it, you know what he's like, he'd do and say anything to cause aggro, it's all he ever does. He's toxic, sick in the head.'

His mind reeling, Raymond's words replayed over and over again in Jamie's head as though they were on a loop and ingraining themself into his mind. It was true his hair was a shade lighter than Terry's but they still looked alike, didn't they? And as for the word cuckoo, hadn't his nan mentioned something about a cuckoo? Yeah, that was it, she'd said that she wanted to have a long overdue chat with the cuckoo. Suddenly realising that he was the cuckoo she was referring to, Jamie felt sick to his stomach and with a final tug, he pulled himself out of Ricky's grasp, bent forward and began to retch.

'Tell me it's not true,' he begged of his brother, his eyes watering as he heaved, disguising the fact his world was crumbling down around him and that everything he'd ever known was a lie. 'Tell me that the old man was my dad.'

Running his hand through his hair, Ricky glanced back towards the pub. 'Of course it's not true,' he was quick to answer. 'Since when did you ever listen to a word Cole says?' He stepped forward and stabbed his finger into the side of Jamie's head. 'He's playing mind games, he's trying to get into here, to mess you up. He'll be getting a kick out of this, and you, like a stupid prick, fell for his lies, hook, line, and fucking sinker.'

'Then why did he pick me eh? Why not pick you? You were there, why didn't he accuse you of being the end result of some quick shag behind the back of a boozer?'

'Probably because you're a mouthy little bastard,' Ricky retorted before blowing out his cheeks. 'I warned you not to antagonise him, but you wouldn't listen, you never listen to a word anyone says, that's your problem, you're too headstrong.'

'So this is all my fault?' Jamie's mouth dropped open and as he straightened up, he wiped the back of his hand across his lips.

'Cheers for that bruv,' he spat. 'Not that I should have expected any different from you considering how you always blame me for everything. You've made it more than clear that you don't trust me; you even accused me of burning down the car lot as if I'm some kind of weirdo, a degenerate.'

Ricky gave an exasperated sigh. 'Give it a rest Jay. I've already apologised for that. I made a genuine mistake, and believe it or not, I was trying to help you out. How many more times do you want me to say that I'm sorry?'

'I need your idea of help like I need a hole in the head,' Jamie spat as he turned to walk away. 'I need to speak to Mum, that's if she even is my mum; for all I know, I could have been adopted. There you go, problem fucking solved; maybe we're not even brothers.'

'Leave it out,' Ricky called after him. 'Now you're just being stupid, of course we're brothers, stop being so dramatic.'

'How do you know?' Jamie shouted back. 'Were you there when I was conceived? Five minutes ago it would never have even entered my head to question my parentage, and now I don't know if I'm coming or going.'

'Do you really believe Dad would have been allowed to adopt?' Ricky gave an incredulous laugh and threw his arms up into the air. 'With his criminal record, he wouldn't have got past the first hurdle let alone be trusted to look after a kid. He'd been nicked so many times that he used to joke that he was on the old bill's Christmas card list. Think about it,' he said, pointing to his temple. 'He wouldn't exactly have been viewed as a suitable candidate would he.'

'Well how else do you explain it?' As he swallowed down the large lump in his throat, Jamie's eyes widened. 'What if Mum... what if she, you know?' He screwed up his face and pointed towards his brother's nether regions. 'She could have had...'

Ricky's expression hardened. 'Don't say it,' he warned, gritting his teeth and spitting out the words. 'Don't you dare fucking say it. Mum ain't like that, she would never have cheated on Dad. She was devoted to him; she worshipped the ground he walked on. He could never do any wrong in her eyes; even when he would let us down time and time again, she would make excuses for him.'

Jamie turned on his heel. 'I have to speak to her,' he said, beginning to walk away. 'I need to know if there's any truth to what that psycho said.'

Grasping his brother by the shoulders, Ricky forced Jamie to turn around and look at him. 'Deep down you know it isn't true. You and Dad look alike, we all look alike, even that lunatic back there.' He nodded towards the pub. 'Look at us, we're the image of one another.'

Jamie reached up to touch his hair. 'Apart from this,' he said, tugging on the light brown strands so hard that he almost ripped the roots from his head. 'Apart from fucking this.'

* * *

Raymond was laughing so hard that he was almost doubled over. 'Did you see his face?' he chuckled, wiping the tears from his eyes. 'At one point I thought the little pussy was going to start bawling his eyes out.'

'Yeah,' Alfie laughed. 'Serves the prick right. I've never liked him; him or his brother. The way they swan around, anyone would think they own the gaff. They really believe that they are something special. In fact, the way they carry on it's like we should all be scared of them or something.'

Raymond nodded, his face becoming serious. 'They're fuck all. If it wasn't for my dad's reputation, they'd be nobodies, and believe me, I'm not scared of the pricks. Jamie isn't even a Tempest, he's a no one, but the cunt still took my dad away from me, and he got his hands on his dough. That money should have been mine. I was his son, his real son, not him.'

Alfie frowned. 'So it's actually true then? I thought you'd only said all of that to wind him up.'

'Nah, it's true all right, Kenny told me everything. From day one my old man had his doubts. I mean,' he said, eyeing the door Ricky and Jamie had exited. 'You've only got to take one look at Jamie to see why my dad had his suspicions.' He reached up to touch his dark hair. 'This doesn't lie mate. And do you want to know what winds me up the most? What really riles me up?'

Alfie shook his head.

'They had everything handed to them on a plate: the scrap yard, the house, his car, they even got their hands on my old man's business pimping out the tarts, and you can't tell me that they aren't earning from it.'

'Fuck me.' Alfie paused for a moment and scratched his head. 'I thought they'd got rid of the brothels, what with the old bill crawling all over the houses and everything?'

'Of course they didn't,' Raymond snarled. 'They were a gold mine; do you really think they would have given that up? They might pretend to have washed their hands of everything associated with my dad but I know the truth; they're rolling in dough.'

'The cheeky bastards.'

'Yeah you can say that again,' Raymond said with a bitter laugh. 'And what did I get, eh?' he said, pointing towards himself. 'I got fuck all, that's what. I couldn't even tell anyone I was his son just in case it upset those two bastards. I wasn't even allowed to go to his funeral, and talking of funerals,' he said, tipping his beer bottle in Alfie's direction. 'That reminds me, we've still got some unfinished business to take care of... Dickie Dixon.' He tilted his head to the side and lifted his eyebrows. 'That big-mouthed fucker needs to be disposed of. For all we know Marc and Barry could have told him everything, and the last thing we need is for him to start talking, putting our names in the frame.'

'What was so funny?' Before Alfie could answer, Eddie Winters had sidled up beside them and as he looked between Alfie and Raymond, his expression was hard.

'Nothing.' Taking a sip of his drink, Alfie gave a nonchalant shrug.

'Well something's obviously tickled you; I could hear the two of you laughing from across the pub.'

'Like I said it was nothing, a joke that's all.'

Eddie narrowed his eyes. 'Well, are you going to share this joke? I could do with a belly laugh.'

Glancing towards Raymond, Alfie rolled his eyes. 'You would have had to have been there to get it.'

Not taking his eyes off his brother, Eddie nodded. 'So you're telling me it wasn't anything to do with the fact that Terry Tempest's boys left here screaming and shouting blue bloody murder then?'

Alfie snorted out a laugh and as he caught Raymond's eyes over the rim of his pint glass, he wiggled his eyebrows. 'Could have been.'

His shoulders tensing, Eddie stabbed his finger none too gently into the side of his brother's face. 'Are you for real?' he hissed. 'Have you actually got a death wish or something?'

'What?' Alfie protested.

'You heard what I said,' Eddie growled as his hard stare turned to Raymond. 'Have you got a death wish? You think it's funny to cause havoc, to stir up trouble?'

'They deserve it.' Leaning casually against the bar, Raymond waved his hand dismissively. 'What's it to do with you anyway?'

'What's it to do with me?' Eddie spat. 'I'll tell you exactly what it's got to do with me. Not only is he my brother,' he said, jerking his head towards Alfie. 'But Max Hardcastle happens to be a pal of mine, and as for Terry, I had a lot of respect for him, and that goes for his boys as well.'

'Leave it out,' Raymond laughed. 'You couldn't wait to get your hands on the manor. You jumped into Terry's grave so fast that I'm surprised you didn't knock yourself out on the way down. Where was your respect then eh?'

Eddie's face reddened and as his lips curled into a snarl, he pushed his face towards Raymond's. 'Remember who you're talking to, and as for you,' he said, turning back to look at his brother. 'You're pushing your luck. Hardcastle is already asking a few too many questions about that arson attack. He's got his suspicions. Why else do you think he keeps turning up here?' His hard stare went back to Raymond. 'If I find out you had anything to do with that fire then believe me, I won't hesitate when it comes to giving up your name.'

Raymond smirked. 'What, even if your precious brother was involved? You'd give up his name as well, would you?'

The colour drained from Eddie's face and as he straightened up, he grabbed Alfie by the scruff of his neck and pulled him close. 'This had better be some sick joke,' he implored, studying his brother's face. 'Because I won't be able to protect you. I've warned you time and time again that Hardcastle isn't the kind of man you mess with, he's got a rep, and believe me, he earned every last inch of his notoriety. He beat a man to death with his bare hands, and he was only a kid, so what the fuck do you think he is capable of now? He spent half his life banged up and I'm not talking about a youth detention centre I'm talking about big boys prison, the kind of environment that you wouldn't last two minutes in.'

'He doesn't need protecting.' Raymond sniggered. 'What is he, five? Next you'll be telling me that you still read him a bed time story.' He began to laugh and as he tipped his beer bottle towards Alfie again, a wicked gleam glinted in his eyes. 'He doesn't still try to tuck you into bed at night, or give you a bath does he? Because there's a name for men like that.'

Clenching his fists into tight balls, Eddie stifled the urge to crack his knuckles across Raymond's jaw. 'This is between me and my brother,' he snarled. 'So either keep that trap of yours shut or fuck off back to whichever hellhole you came from.' Turning back to face Alfie, Eddie shook his head, his eyes beseeching him to toe the line and rein in his behaviour. 'Carry on following this prick around and you'll end up signing your own death warrant. Have you got that? Do you understand what I'm telling you, or do I need to punch it into your skull for it to actually sink into that brain of yours that you're playing with fire? I've got my own wife and children to think about, and if you don't buck your ideas up, you'll give me no other choice except to wash my hands of you. You'll be on your own.'

Alfie gave a menacing grin. 'It's about time you fucked off. Every time I turn around you're in my face, barking out orders, telling me what to do, ordering me around. Unless it's escaped your notice, I'm not a little kid any more and I don't need another dad. The one I've already got is useless enough without adding a second one to the mix.'

At a loss for words, Eddie continued to shake his head, a combination of sadness, anger, but most of all disappointment, washing over him. He'd only been a youngster himself when he'd been left the task of raising his brothers, and as young as he'd been, he had done everything in his power to take care of them. He'd fed them, clothed them, put a roof over their heads and this was all the thanks he got for his trouble. Where had he gone so wrong? Charlie had turned out well; he had a head on his shoulders, and not only was he respectful, but he also grafted for his money, unlike Alfie who thrived on causing trouble. All you had to do was take one look at the company he kept to know that he was on the wrong path. With a significant age difference between them, he may not have been Charlie's or Alfie's biological father, but he'd been the only father figure they had ever known, the only one who had cared about their wellbeing, and along the way, Eddie had sacrificed a large chunk of his life. While his mates had been out partying, he'd spent his youth worrying about how he would be able to afford the rent, or how he would find the money to buy his brothers new shoes, not that he actually bought them. More often than not he would have stolen them, but the sentiment was still the same. The burden had fallen upon his shoulders and in the circumstances, he'd done well; the fact Charlie and Alfie were still alive was testament to that fact. 'You don't even realise what you've done, do you?' he said sadly. 'You're on the brink of starting a war,' he said, his voice rising as his temper began to get the better of him. 'Is that what you want?'

Alfie shrugged and placing his glass on the bar, he squared his shoulders and looked his brother in the eyes. 'I'm making a name for myself. What have you ever done, eh? It took you years to get your hands on this place, the manor.' He looked around the pub, his hard gaze falling upon the frayed carpet, the chrome tables that had been scratched so many times over the years they were beyond repair, and then the stained seat covers that had clearly seen better days. 'It wasn't even worth the wait,' he sneered. 'This place, like the rest of the manor, is a shit hole.'

As Alfie walked from the pub, Eddie called after him. 'Whichever game you think you're playing, you won't win. You won't stand a chance against Hardcastle, he's the real deal not some muppet you can take the piss out of.'

He didn't receive a reply, and what more was there to say that hadn't already been said? He could talk to his brother until he was blue in the face, but it wouldn't make any difference. Alfie had more than made his feelings known, that he harboured resentment towards his eldest brother, that for some unknown reason he despised him.

Nausea washed over Eddie and the tiny hairs on the back of his neck stood up on end. As much as they may have been equally matched when it came to their standing in the criminal fraternity, Max Hardcastle would always have the edge over him. In his youth, Max had been ruthless, afraid of no one, and as the years had passed he'd become even more dangerous, the type of man who could inflict fear without even breaking out in a sweat. Eddie sighed, and in the pit of his stomach, worry gnawed away at him. As much as he had told Alfie that he would wash his hands of him, deep down in his gut he knew that he would do no such thing. How could he? They were brothers, family, they shared the same blood. No, when it came down to it, he would fight tooth and nail to keep his brother safe, to keep him alive, even if that meant going up against Max himself. The mere thought of what was to come was enough to make him feel depressed.

15

Tracey was on a mission and after rummaging through her bedside table, she straightened up and looked around her at the chaos she had created. Think, she told herself, bloody think. Moving across to her wardrobe, she flung open the doors and in desperation, pulled out each of her handbags. She knew it had to be here somewhere. After contemplating whether or not to throw the item out, she had finally decided to put it away for safe keeping, just in case it came in useful one day. Well today was that day, only now she couldn't find what it was she was looking for.

From the inside pocket of one of her handbags, her fingers skimmed across a scrap of paper and tentatively holding her breath, she fished the object out. Triumph flooded through her and clasping the paper in her fist, she walked across to the bed and gingerly sat down. Ever so carefully she opened out the sheet of paper and stared down at the familiar scrawling writing. It was Kenny's prisoner number. Before she could talk herself out of it, she hastily retrieved her mobile phone and began to type out the words Belmarsh Prison.

Within a matter of minutes she'd requested a prison visit, and rather than the rigmarole she'd been fully expecting, the whole process had been a lot easier to set up than she'd ever imagined it would be. Throwing the phone down beside her, she chewed on her bottom lip, a part of her already regretting her decision to pay Kenny a visit. Her boys and Max were bound to go ballistic if they were to ever find out, not that she intended to actually tell them. Besides, what they didn't know couldn't hurt them, or so she tried to convince herself.

It was only the fact that she wanted answers from Kenny that had spurred her into action. After her chat with Kayla earlier that morning, she'd come to the realisation that it was time to move on and she could only do that once she had paid her husband's closest friend and business partner a visit. She had things she needed to say to him, things she needed to get off her chest and she knew she wouldn't be able to rest until she'd said them to Kenny's face. He needed to know exactly what she thought of him, that she despised him, that the mere thought of being in his presence made her skin crawl. In a roundabout way she supposed she wanted to hear him beg for her forgiveness, for him to tell her that he was sorry for destroying her life, and subsequently the lives of her sons and grandson.

No matter how much of a sham her marriage may have been, it should never have been Kenny's choice to take everything away from her. She should have been able to choose for herself, to make her own decision to walk away from Terry, from his womanising ways, and from the secrets he'd kept hidden away from her.

A loud knocking at the front door broke Tracey's reverie and getting to her feet, she slipped the crumpled piece of paper back into her handbag, then shoved the bag to the back of the wardrobe and after giving the bedroom the once over, checking that everything was as it should be and that she had left no incriminating evidence behind, she made her way down the stairs.

Flinging open the front door, Tracey took one look at Patricia's face and groaned out loud, not even bothering to conceal her annoyance.

'What do you want Pat?'

'Are they here?' Patricia slurred as she gripped on to the door frame for support.

Tracey wrinkled her nose. 'Have you been drinking?' She placed her hand over her nose, the alcoholic fumes that came off her mother-in-law almost enough to knock her out.

'I said, are they here?' Clutching Tracey's wrist, Patricia dug her fingers into the soft flesh, the desperation in her voice enough to startle Tracey. 'I need to speak to them; I need to warn them.'

'Who?' Tracey demanded as she prised Patricia's fingers away from her arm.

'The boys,' Patricia continued to slur between hiccups, her eyes straining to focus on her daughter-in-law. 'Are the boys here?'

'No, why would they be?' Tracey shouted, a sense of panic growing inside her. 'And why would you need to warn them? Warn them about what?'

Staggering across the threshold, Patricia held on to the banister rail in a bid to stop herself from falling flat on her face. 'I've done a wicked, awful thing,' she cried, tears welling up in her blue eyes. 'I'm so sorry,' she wept. 'So very sorry for what I've caused.'

'For fuck's sake Pat.' Slamming the front door closed, Tracey rounded on her mother-in-law. 'If you've done what I think you've done I will hammer the bloody life out of you. I warned you not to spew your wicked lies.' Her chest heaving, she grabbed Patricia by the shoulders and pulled her roughly around to face her. 'What have you done?' she screamed. 'If you broke my boy's heart, I swear to God I will end you.'

'Not me,' Patricia sobbed, shaking her head. 'I would never

harm those boys, I love them, they're all that I've got left of my Terry.'

Relief flooded through Tracey and releasing Patricia, she placed her hand upon her chest as if to steady her hammering heart. 'Then you'd best start talking and fast. What the bloody hell is going on?'

'It's Raymond.' Making her way unsteadily through to the lounge, Patricia flopped down onto the sofa before she collapsed. 'He's evil,' she whispered.

Tracey let out a bitter laugh. 'I wondered how long it would take before you turned on him,' she said, shaking her head, disbelief etched across her face. 'Just like you've turned on everyone else in your life.' As she pointed towards the hallway, her expression hardened. 'Come on, get out. I will not stand here and listen to you berate that poor boy.' Continuing to shake her head, she placed her hands on her hips. 'You just can't help yourself, can you Pat? You have to try and destroy every relationship you have. First of all, it was me; I was never good enough for your son, and you told me that at our very first meeting; you weren't even prepared to give me a chance or to try to get to know me. Then it was your grandsons. Nothing they ever did was right or met your approval. And as for Max, well we all know how you feel about him; you'd have him strung up if you had your way, and now Raymond. Who's going to be next, eh? Why don't you start on little Mason or Kayla while you're at it, find fault with them too?'

'You don't understand,' Pat wailed her eyelids beginning to droop. 'He's a wrong'un.'

'Yeah you've got that much right; I don't understand.' Tracey rolled her eyes then studying Patricia's drunken state, she sighed. How could she throw her out when she could barely walk in a straight line. As much as Patricia was the bane of her life, she was determined not to stoop down to her level. 'Just sleep it off Pat.'

Gathering the cushions and then the throw off the back of the sofa, she prepared a makeshift bed. 'I'll get you a glass of water and a bowl just in case,' she said, nodding down at the floor.

Patricia lay down, and as Tracey made to walk from the room, she grabbed hold of her hand, bringing her to a halt beside her. 'I never disliked you,' she said, looking up at her daughter-in-law. 'I was jealous that's all, jealous that Terry never wanted to be around me. Even when he was a little boy he treated me as though I were nothing more than an inconvenience to him. I was his mother, but he never needed me; in here, I know that,' she said, pointing to her chest, her voice so small that Tracey had to strain her ears to listen. 'He never loved me. I don't think he ever loved anyone, at least not in the way he should have done.'

Taken aback, Tracey stared at her mother-in-law as though she'd grown a second head. In all the years she had known her, Patricia had never uttered a kind word, let alone admitted to feeling jealous. Likewise, she had never given any indication that her and Terry's relationship was anything but rosy. In fact, the way Patricia carried on, anyone would think that her and Terry had been devoted to one another.

'Get some sleep,' Tracey said, her voice becoming gentle. 'And we'll talk in the morning.' Before she'd even left the room, Patricia's soft snores could be heard.

In the kitchen, Tracey slumped onto a chair, her mind reeling. It was only the fact that she knew her boys were with Max that stopped her from flying into a blind panic. Max would never let any harm come to them, and they had too much of their father in them to not be able to look after themselves. Her mind wandered to Raymond. From her first impressions of him he seemed like a nice young man. Polite, charming, perhaps a little too charming. She let out a long sigh, deciding not to take heed of Patricia's warning. Pat had always been a bitter woman, and it had been no lie when she'd told her sons that their grandmother would have been able to find fault with Jesus Christ himself. Satisfied that it had only been the drink talking, Tracey unlocked her phone and checked on her emails. The visit with Kenny couldn't come soon enough; her only wish was that she'd done it sooner. In fact, the quicker she gave him a piece of her mind, the quicker she would be able to leave the past behind her and look forward to the future.

Moments later, the front door burst open with such force that she wouldn't have been surprised if it had come off its hinges.

'What the bloody hell is going on?' Tracey demanded as she rushed through to the hallway. 'That's my door you're bashing about.'

Jamie's eyes were wild with anger, his face drained of all colour. 'Is it true Mum?' he snarled. 'That Terry wasn't my dad?'

There and then, Tracey's heart almost stopped beating and as she looked between her two sons, her mouth dropped open. 'I...' She snapped her lips closed, terror settling in her eyes. 'Jamie,' she said, her hand reaching out for her son. He looked so broken that all she wanted to do was pull him into her arms and never let him go. It made no difference to her that he was an adult; in her mind he was still her baby, her little boy, he always would be and to see him hurting so much was enough to break her heart.

'Answer the question, Mum,' Jamie shouted, shrugging her away from him. 'Is it true?'

'No of course it isn't true,' she cried, desperate for him to believe her. Snapping her gaze towards the lounge where Patricia was sleeping, Tracey was all but ready to race into the room and throttle her mother-in-law. 'Why on earth would you even ask me something like that?'

'Then what about this, eh?' Jamie tugged at his hair. 'How do you explain this?'

Shaking her head, Tracey screwed up her face. For the life of her she couldn't understand what he was asking her. 'Explain what?' she cried.

'This.' Jamie pointed to his brother. 'Dark hair,' he shouted. 'Dad had dark hair, even that nutter Raymond's hair is dark, but me...' He pulled on the light brown strands. 'Why is my hair brown?'

'How should I know?' Tracey answered. 'Genetics, I suppose.' She lifted her hand to smooth her fingers over her own locks. In her opinion, the colour wasn't much different from that of her youngest son's. 'You take after me I suppose.'

'Nah.' Jamie shook his head. 'There's more to this, there has to be. You're lying, you both are, you're keeping something from me.' He screwed up his face. 'Was I adopted, is that it? You just don't want to tell me.'

'Of course you weren't adopted,' Tracey snapped. 'Do you want me to show you my stretch marks to prove it? I gave birth to you; ten agonising hours I was in labour for. I remember that day like it was yesterday.'

'Then why have they all got the same hair? Dad's genes were strong, so why am I different, why the fuck am I different Mum?'

Tracey shook her head, and as a lone tear slipped down her cheek her hands instinctively reached out for her son again. 'Stop this, please. Terry was your dad; I swear to you, my darling. I wouldn't lie to you; I have no need to.'

'Your mum's right. Terry was your dad. You and him were identical, like two peas in a bleeding pod.'

Tracey, Ricky and Jamie turned their heads to look over their shoulders.

'But...' Jamie protested as Patricia entered the kitchen.

'No buts.' Patricia eased her body onto a chair and wearily clutched a hand to her throbbing head, the alcohol she'd consumed making her feel queasy. 'You're a Tempest darling if ever

I've seen one. And as for those blue eyes of yours, they came from my dad, your great grandad; it was the Irish in him, see,' she chuckled. 'Did you know you have Irish in you?'

Jamie shook his head.

'Well you do; he was a Cork man through and through my dad, a horse thief. That was the only reason he came over to England; it was either leave Ireland or stay there and end up swinging from the gallows and being the clever man that he was, he ran as if his life depended on it, which just so happened to be the case. It's from him that you get that temper of yours. He could be a right bugger when the mood took him, especially when he had a drink inside of him.' She smiled. 'So I hope that's cleared all of this up,' she said, spreading open her arms. 'You're your dad's son all right.'

Jamie rubbed at the back of his neck, his cheeks flushing pink. 'Are you sure?'

'Of course I am.' Patricia reached out to touch his hand. 'I wouldn't lie to you, sweetheart. I may not have been the best grandmother in the world to you or to your brother,' she said, turning to look at Ricky and giving him a gentle smile, 'but I would never lie to you, to either of you; you have my word on that.'

Amazed by the turn around in her mother-in-law, Tracey cleared her throat. 'What's brought all of this on, eh? Why would you even think such a thing?'

Locking eyes with his brother, Jamie shook his head. 'It was nothing,' he said, giving a shrug. 'It was just bugging me I suppose.'

The idea that Terry hadn't been his father wasn't something that Jamie would have plucked out of thin air and as Tracey pulled her youngest son into her embrace, the look she gave Patricia was scathing. 'We'll talk about this,' she mouthed behind her son's back.

Patricia nodded. In all honesty, she hadn't expected anything different.

* * *

Dickie Dixon was feeling troubled. He hadn't heard from his sons for more than three days. Under normal circumstances, he spoke to his boys on a daily basis and considering they worked for him at the used car lot, he would have expected to see at least one of them during the course of those days, if not both of them.

His ribs still aching from the pounding he had received from Max Hardcastle, Dickie walked around his desk and slowly eased himself into a chair, cursing out loud as a shot of pain tore through his chest muscles. Once the discomfort had settled somewhat, he pulled out his mobile phone and pressed redial. Biting down on his bottom lip, he prayed for his eldest son to answer. To his dismay, just as it had on his previous attempts, the call rang off.

Placing the device on the desk, Dickie rested his chin in his hands. Why the fuck were his sons ignoring his calls? They had to be ghosting him or whatever it was the kids called it these days. What other explanation could there be for them to be playing silly buggers and dodging his calls? He let out a long sigh, agitation edging its way down his spine. Surely they hadn't taken offence to the fact that he'd lied to them, that his altercation with Hardcastle had been one on one rather than what he'd claimed had taken place. Even the friends who'd stood beside him at the bar had backed him up and claimed that not only Max but also Terry Tempest's boys had laid into him, that he hadn't stood a chance against them. In the circumstances, he'd had to say something to limit the damage caused to his reputation; the last thing in the world he wanted was for his sons to think he'd gone soft, that his age was creeping up on him, or worse still, that he was heading for the knacker's yard.

Still, it made no sense for his boys to drop off the face of the earth. He knew them well enough to know that they would have been hell bent on having it out with Hardcastle, that there was enough bad blood between him and his adversary to instigate Barry and Marc wanting to seek revenge. After all, the hatred between the two men went beyond the close proximity of their car dealerships; they shared a mutual distrust, a mutual hatred that had been simmering away for years.

A sickening thought sprang to Dickie's mind; could it be possible that something untoward had taken place between Max Hardcastle and his sons? There was no doubt in Dickie's mind that his boys would have paid Hardcastle a visit; they would have wanted to have it out with him, they would have seen the attack on himself as a personal affront. In fact, the last time Dickie had seen his boys, they had been all but ready to commit murders; they had been baying for both Hardcastle's and the Tempest brothers' blood.

The headlights of a car shone through the office window and as Dickie got out of his seat there was a spring in his step. At last, his sons had finally put in an appearance. Opening the office door, he was all but ready to tear a strip off them for not turning up for work and would have done too if it wasn't for the full beam from the car headlights blinding his vision.

'Oi,' he called out as he brought his hand up to shield his eyes. 'What's your fucking game? Turn the lights off.'

Moments later, the lights went out and as Dickie's eyes strained to become accustomed to the darkness, he could just about make out the two hulking figures striding towards him.

As the men neared closer, the hairs on the back of Dickie's neck stood up on end and as his heart began to thunder inside his chest, he quickly came to realise that the muscular physiques didn't belong to his sons.

'What do you want?' he asked, careful to keep the tremor from his voice. 'We're closed. Come back tomorrow.'

He was met with silence. The men advanced towards him and before Dickie could even fathom out what was happening, they had easily overpowered him and shoved him back inside the portable office.

'I asked you a question.' As he bumped against the desk, Dickie clutched his arm across his ribs. 'What do you want?'

It was then that Dickie spotted the knives gleaming in the men's fists and as the taller of the two locked the office door behind them, Dickie's insides turned to liquid, the panic inside of him growing in intensity. As he cowered, Dickie had a sinking feeling that the situation wasn't going to end well, at least not for him anyway and he hastily sent up a silent prayer, wishing not for the first time that day that Barry and Marc would walk through the door.

Every inch of Alfie Winters' body was tense. He was so angry that the most innocent of remarks or a wrong look in his direction would be enough to send him over the edge, and the fact his brother Eddie had all but humiliated him in front of not only Raymond but the entire pub had just about been the icing on the cake.

The fury Alfie felt, coupled with the coke he had snorted by the bucket load on the drive over to Leigh-on-Sea was enough to make him feel so paranoid that he'd convinced himself Dickie Dixon was taking the piss out of him. That every time he opened his mouth to speak, no matter how innocent his words may have been, he was making a snide comment and looking down his nose at him, the same hooked nose Alfie was itching to smash into obliteration.

'What do you want from me?' There was a nasally whine to Dickie's voice as he glanced out of the office window. 'If it's the cars you're after, then take them, take the lot.' He motioned to a glass panelled box on the wall that contained the keys for the cars on the forecourt.

Raymond began to laugh as if it were the funniest thing he'd ever heard. 'Did you hear that?' he asked, nudging Alfie in his side. 'As if we would be seen dead driving around in one of those rust buckets.'

Alfie's hard eyes remained focused on Dickie, and as the older man frowned, the anger inside of Alfie rose a notch. He took a step forward, his lips curled into a snarl. 'Do we look desperate?' he spat.

Dickie swallowed deeply, his Adam's apple bobbing up and down with the motion.

'Answer me,' Alfie roared.

Clearly terrified, Dickie shook his head. 'My boys will be here soon.' He shot a glance back towards the window. 'So take what you want and leave while you have the chance, while you're still in one piece.'

For the first time since their arrival, Alfie flashed a maniacal grin. 'That won't be happening. Your boys won't be turning up to save the day.'

Dickie reeled back slightly and tilted his head to the side, his gaze darting towards the forecourt. As he spoke, his bottom lip trembled and his breath caught in the back of his throat. 'Why not?'

'You see,' Raymond said, as he made himself comfortable and lounged back on a chair, his long legs kicked out in front of him and crossed over at the ankles. 'This is the thing. You could even say it's a bit of a problem, a quandary so to speak, at least for us anyway.' Gesturing with the knife, he waved it casually between himself and Alfie. 'Your boys, they did a job for us, a big job. But the problem is, they had a bit too much of you in them, they had big mouths, they couldn't be trusted, a bit like yourself if you get my drift, and so we' – he motioned again between himself and Alfie – 'well, we had to get rid of them.'

Dickie gasped, his hand automatically fluttering up to his chest, his eyes wide and almost popping out if his head.

'And this is where we have a bit of problem.' Raymond got to his feet, his large frame filling the small office. 'I can't allow for you to talk, for you to open that big trap of yours and tell all and sundry my business, that it was me who organised for Hardcastle's showroom to be burnt to a crisp. He can't find out, at least not yet anyway. In time, he will be told that I had a hand in ruining him, but only once he's watched me destroy everything else in his life first.'

Dickie's skin turned ashen, and as a sharp, cramp-like pain ripped up his left arm and edged its way towards the centre of his chest, his legs almost gave way beneath him. 'No,' he cried, gasping for air. 'No, not my boys.'

'Yep, I'm afraid so.' Raymond shook his head sadly and made a slicing action across his throat, all the while grinning like a Cheshire cat. 'I would say that I'm sorry for your loss,' he said, spreading open his arms and beginning to laugh. 'But it would be a lie because I'm not. They were nothing but greedy bastards and deserved everything they had coming to them, not to mention they were as thick as shit. The way I see it, we did society a favour in getting rid of them. Let me put it this way, because I've got a feeling you're a bit more astute than your offspring, that you've got a bit of savvy about you. Now let's just say for example, someone was to offer you, oh I don't know,' he said, waving his hand in the air, 'say twenty grand, to burn down Hardcastle's car dealership, surely to fucking God the first thing you would want to do is ask one or two questions. At the very least, you would want to know what their motives are. I mean,' he said, leaning in closer, 'that would be the normal thing to do, wouldn't it? Now, me and Alfie over there, we did our homework. We knew exactly who we were dealing with, unlike your boys, who practically chewed my arm off to get their hands on that cash, no questions asked. Seriously' – he grinned with a shake of his head – 'they just blindly did everything we told them to do.' He tapped his temple. 'Like I said, no savvy, no common sense whatsoever.'

As he quivered from head to toe, Dickie's eyes bulged. 'No,' he cried. In a blind panic, he pushed himself away from the desk, his arms flailing around him as spittle gathered at the corners of his thin lips. Continuing to shake his head, his ruddy cheeks were pale, making the tiny red thread veins peppering his skin appear even more prominent. 'You're sick,' he shouted with as much strength as his failing body could muster. 'Sick in the head.'

'Yeah probably.' Raymond gave a nonchalant shrug. 'I've been called a lot worse in my lifetime.'

'And you.' Dickie turned to look at Alfie, his expression one of absolute disgust. 'You're as warped as he is. You won't get away with this; I'm a face, I've got a lot of clout. All it will take is just one phone call,' he said, his gaze darting to the telephone on the desk, 'and you'll be finished. You'll rue the day you messed with me and mine.'

Raymond raised his eyebrows towards Alfie, the hint of a smirk tugging at the corners of his lips. 'Are you going to allow him to talk to you like this?' he goaded. 'Like you're a piece of shit, like you're no better than scum. He reminds me of Eddie; he's another one that likes to put you down. All he ever does is have a pop at you, telling you that you're not good enough, that you won't amount to anything, that you've only got the mentality to be his lackey.'

Alfie snarled and as his fingers curled around the knife in his fist, he shook his head.

'What are you waiting for. Do him,' Raymond coaxed. 'Finish him off. Shut this big-mouthed fucker up once and for all.'

'My boys were worth ten of you,' Dickie screamed as he brought his hands up to his face in a last ditch attempt to save himself. 'They had a future, they—'

Before Dickie could finish the sentence, Alfie was upon him. Over and over again he thrust the knife in to Dickie's flesh, stabbing him with such ferocity that the blade almost broke clean in half.

Finally spent, Alfie dropped the knife to the floor with a loud clatter, his breath loud and harsh in the eerily quiet office. Covered from head to toe in Dickie's blood, he looked down at himself, his forehead furrowing as he turned his hands over and stared at the blood covering them, as though he couldn't quite work out where it had all come from.

Raymond clasped him on the shoulder, breaking his reverie. 'You did well,' he praised before kicking out at Dickie's corpse with his steel-toe-capped boot. 'I didn't think the fucker was ever going to shut up let alone kick the bucket.'

Still staring at the blood on his hands, the enormity of what he'd just done hit Alfie full on and as he brought his stained hand up to his mouth, the iron scent from Dickie's blood assaulted his nostrils. Lurching forward, he fumbled with the key in the lock, before finally shoving open the door and charging out of the portable cabin before promptly bending forward and vomiting up the contents of his stomach.

From behind him, Raymond chuckled. 'What the fuck is wrong

with you? If you can't handle seeing a bit of claret then how the fuck are you going to help me dismember the body? Here, do me a favour and get the chainsaw from out of the car boot.' He rubbed his hands together, his eyes glinting with amusement. 'What shall we start with first? His hands or his feet, or how about his head? We could even use it for a kickabout.'

It was a joke, albeit a sick joke, not that Alfie found it very funny and as he heaved even harder, the sound of Raymond's laughter continued to ring loudly in his ears.

16
_____

With a tall muscular body, Damon Daly was the image of his elder brothers and after learning about the attempt on Cain's life, he'd spent the past ten minutes screaming and shouting out obscenities before finally forcing himself to calm down. As he leant against the office door of Vincent's club, he crossed his arms over his broad chest, his fists clenched. 'Tell me what you want us to do.'

Vincent took a moment to think the question over and slouching back in the chair, he dragged the palm of his hand over his face. 'Our top priority is to warn Cain about Kenny's plans.' He glanced down at the burner phone sitting on his lap. Cain wasn't in the habit of switching his mobile phone off; in fact, the only times he'd ever known the device to be inactive was early in the morning when breakfast was being served or whenever his brother showered and didn't want to take the risk of the phone being discovered by the screws. 'I don't understand why his phone is still off,' he said, narrowing his eyes before looking back up. 'It's never switched off.'

Damon nodded. 'What about Lucie?' he asked.

'What about her?'

Pushing himself away from the door, Damon placed his hands on his hips. 'Well, has she heard from him? For all we know, her and Cain could have been on the blower for the best part of the day.'

Vincent shook his head, dismissing the notion. 'I don't want her involved in any of this. She's fragile enough as it is; she's not coping too well without Cain being around.' He frowned for a moment and looked back down at the phone. Lucie... there was something about their last meeting that was bothering him, and it wasn't just the stench of the cannabis that had stunk out the flat, nor was it the tears she had shed. He tried to think back, his mind going over everything that had been said between them; he was missing something, he knew he was, he had to be. Lucie hadn't been acting herself and it wasn't just the fact she'd had bailiffs on the doorstep demanding payment. Suddenly, he sat bolt upright, his eyes widening to the hilt. 'I knew that I'd seen him somewhere before,' he said, clicking his fingers together.

'Who?' Max asked with a frown.

'The geezer visiting Kenny.' Vincent jumped to his feet. 'It was him; I saw him. He passed me by on the stairs when I went to see Lucie. He'd come out of her flat.'

Max screwed up his face. 'What exactly are you trying to say? That she's in on it, that she wants to see Cain, the father of her child, topped?'

Vincent paused and giving a shake of his head, he looked in his brother's direction. 'No, she wouldn't do that, would she? She loves Cain, she idolises him.'

Damon shrugged. 'Fuck knows. Let's face it, Cain has been banged up for five years. Maybe she's getting her kicks elsewhere, maybe her and this bloke' – he brought his thumb and forefinger together to make a circle and then pushed the index finger of his

free hand through the hole several times – 'are shagging each
other.'

Vincent's lips curled in disgust, and he shook his head. 'She
wouldn't, would she?' he asked, his gaze going between Max,
Damon, and then his youngest brother Caleb.

Max lifted his shoulders. 'It does sound a bit suspicious,' he
admitted. 'And like Damon said, Cain has been away for a long
time. Who knows what she's been getting up to in his absence? She
wouldn't be the first wife or girlfriend to play away from home,
would she?'

'The dirty slag,' Caleb spat.

'Oi.' Vincent thrust his finger forward, his eyes hard. 'Whatever
you might think of her, she's still Cain's bird, so watch your mouth,'
he chastised.

Caleb lifted his eyebrows. 'I was only saying.'

'Well don't,' Vincent snapped back. 'Keep your opinions to
yourself in future.' Pulling his car keys out of his pocket, he
grasped them tightly in his fist. 'If I find out she's in any way, shape
or form involved in the attempt on Cain's life, I'll have her,' he
warned. 'I'll throttle the fucking life out of her.'

Caleb threw up his arms, his expression one of astonishment
as he looked around him. 'So it's all right for you to say something
about her,' he grumbled, 'but not anyone else.'

Giving his youngest brother a hard stare, Vincent fought the
urge to clip him around the back of the head. 'When it comes to a
threat on Cain's life, then that's a different matter entirely.'

As Max got to his feet, he pulled out his own car keys. 'So
what's the plan now then?' he asked.

'What do you think?' Vincent answered as he tossed the burner
phone in Damon's direction. 'We pay Lucie a visit. If nothing else
she'll be able to give us a name for this nutter, and you,' he said,
addressing Damon, 'keep trying to get a hold of Cain, but do not

under any circumstances mention Lucie. In fact, don't say anything at all other than I want a word with him.'

Raymond was making a habit of turning up at Lucie's flat unannounced; not that he actually wanted to see her per se, it was more to do with the fact that he had one over her old man that excited him, and that, coupled with the knowledge she did everything he asked of her no matter how abysmally he treated her, was a large part of the attraction. She didn't even complain when it came to him having it away on his toes the minute he'd finished screwing her, and let's face it, that should have been her biggest clue that he wasn't interested in having any kind of relationship with her. But that was the thing about Lucie, she was so easy to manipulate; a compliment here, or a kind word there, and she was like putty in his hands. And whenever that didn't work, all he had to do was mention Cain and she soon became pliable. If it wasn't so laughable it would be tragic; not that he actually gave a shit about Lucie or her feelings. As far as he was concerned, she was a means to end and nothing more than that.

Tapping his knuckles on the front door, he stood back slightly and silently observed his best mate. 'You all right?' he asked with a flick of his chin.

Alfie nodded, his face so pale that in Raymond's opinion, he was starting to look as though he was sickening for something. As it was, on the drive back from Leigh-on-Sea, Alfie had barely said more than two words, he'd just sat motionless, staring through the windscreen as though he were in some sort of trance.

Raymond attempted to smile. 'We'll get you cleaned up a bit, yeah?' He motioned to Dickie Dixon's blood that had dried to a rust colour and still stained Alfie's clothes and skin. 'I'll tell Lucie to sort us out some grub, you can have a bath, maybe have a smoke...' His voice trailed off as Lucie opened the front door and barging his way inside, he nodded towards Alfie. 'He needs to get cleaned up, and pronto.'

On seeing the blood, Lucie's mouth dropped open. 'No,' she said, panic registering across her face as she placed her hand's on Raymond's chest and using all of her strength, attempted to push him back towards the door. 'No, I can't have this Ray,' she pleaded when her attempts to shift his solid bulk proved to be fruitless. 'I can't have you bringing trouble to my door. I've got Alisha to think about, and then there's Cain...'

'Fuck Cain,' Raymond interrupted. 'You weren't thinking of him while I was fucking you. So do me a favour and drop the devoted girlfriend act. We both know that you couldn't give two shits about your old man; all I had to do was smile in your direction and you dropped your knickers for me.' His eyes hardened and his lips curled into a snarl, not caring one iota if he upset her. 'And fuck knows how many blokes came before me. Maybe the next time I'm at the nick I should have a word in his ear, tell him what you've been getting up to behind his back. I don't think he'd be too impressed when he finds out that I've fucked you every which way there is all over this flat while his little girl was sound asleep in the bedroom next door, do you?'

As he expected, tears sprang to Lucie's eyes and as she opened her mouth to answer, Raymond looked over his shoulder to where Alfie was standing. 'He needs to get cleaned up,' he said, lowering his voice, before turning back to face Lucie and flashing an amicable smile. 'So do me a favour and sort him out.'

Wiping away the tears from her eyes, Lucie turned her head to study Alfie. 'What happened?' she asked as she gave an involuntary shiver, her voice barely louder than a whisper. 'Did you hurt someone?'

Raymond sighed. 'Not me.' His voice holding a note of irritation, he held out his hands to show that they were clean, then jerked his thumb in Alfie's direction. 'We ran into a situation and things got out of control. No one can see him like this, least of all the old bill.'

Reluctantly, and against her better judgement, Lucie stepped aside. 'I'll wash his clothes and he can have a shower, but then you have to leave. I mean it Ray; I can't have this, not around Alisha.'

Raymond nodded, already bored with her whining. He'd heard it all before, countless times. Slinging his arm around Alfie's shoulders, he guided him towards the bathroom. 'Don't worry,' he growled, his hard gaze looking straight through her. 'We'll be out of your hair as soon as he's cleaned up.'

An hour later, Vincent pulled into the car park outside the block of flats where his brother had once lived. He turned off the ignition, rested his forearms on the steering wheel and looked up at his brother's flat, or rather Lucie's flat, seeing as the tenancy was in her name.

Max gave the block of flats a furtive glance. 'Are we getting out or what?' He made to open the car door when Vincent pulled back on his arm.

'I can't get my head around this,' he said. 'I mean this is Lucie we're talking about; she and Cain have been together for what feels like forever; they were still kids when they started knocking about. Why would she betray him? And then there's little Alisha to think about; her and Cain are like this.' He crossed two fingers together and gave a small smile before letting out a long sigh. 'Cain will be devastated; it's only the thought of coming home to his girls that is keeping him going.'

Max remained quiet, not knowing how best to answer. He'd never had what most people would call a long-term relationship. Oh, he'd had plenty of one-night stands, and some had even led to a second date and then a third, but that had been about the extent of his love life until he'd met Tracey. As soon as he'd clapped his eyes on her, he'd known there was something there, a connection, and that it was more than just the fact he was attracted to her. He actually wanted to be around her, and even more than that, he wanted to get to know her. He'd even made excuses just so that he could visit the area in the hope that he would catch a glimpse of her. Not that Tracey was aware of any of this. 'Are you going to tell him?'

Vincent swallowed before shaking his head. 'Not unless I have to.'

Max nodded. When he'd been inside, he'd seen first-hand the effects of a relationship breakdown, the circumstances all too similar, and the result hadn't been pretty. The man in question had gone on to instigate a three-day riot. In the end, the damage caused had been estimated in the region of near on one hundred thousand pounds and all because his missus hadn't been able to keep her legs closed.

'I need to get into the nick and see him.' Vincent gripped onto the steering wheel so hard his knuckles turned white, his face still turned upwards as he stared at the flat. 'I need to warn him about Kenny and—' Stopping mid-sentence, he slapped Max on the shoulder and nodded towards the entrance of the flats. 'That's him,' he growled, straightening up. 'That's the bastard.'

Max stared ahead of him, watching intently as two men exited the block. Immediately he recognised them, and dragging his hand across his jaw, he slowly shook his head. As much as it pained him to admit it, he'd been right all along. He was more surprised that Vincent hadn't recognised Raymond Cole as being Terry's son, that he hadn't been able to see the resemblance for himself seeing as Cole and Terry looked so alike.

'Do you recognise them?' Vincent asked.

Max nodded, the familiar sense of anger beginning to flow through his veins. 'Yeah,' he answered before clearing his throat. 'The taller of the two is Terry Tempest's son, Raymond Cole, and the second one is Alfie Winters.'

'Your pal's brother?'

'Yeah,' Max sighed. 'My so-called pal's brother.'

Vincent shook his head, his hand hovering over the door handle. 'So what the fuck do we do about this now?' he asked. 'Because the way I see it, we have one of two choices. We either charge over there and fuck them up here and now.' He glanced back towards the flats. 'Which will more than likely alert a dozen or more witnesses to the altercation, any one of who could call the old bill and get us nicked, or, and this is where things get interesting,' he said, giving a nod of his head, his eyes lighting up. 'We play this clever; we nab the no-good cunts when they're least expecting it and take them somewhere secluded, somewhere we won't be disturbed, somewhere like my club for example.'

Thinking the question through, Max allowed himself a small smile. 'Sounds to me like you've already got all of this sussed out.'

Vincent laughed. 'You know me Max, I don't leave anything to chance, and trust me, those two little cunts over there,' he said, pointing in the direction of Raymond and Alfie, 'more than deserve everything they have coming to them.'

17

Eddie Winters took one look at his youngest brother and screwed up his face. 'I'm seriously not in the mood for this,' he said, beginning to close the front door. 'You've already made your feelings known once tonight, and I'm not interested in going for round two.'

'No wait... please,' Alfie begged as he jammed his foot in the door in an attempt to stop Eddie from dismissing him.

The pleading in Alfie's voice made the hairs on the back of Eddie's neck stand to attention, and considering they had parted on bad terms, the last thing he had ever expected was to hear Alfie beg for his help. 'What's happened?' he said, flinging open the front door and hauling his brother across the threshold. 'Have you been hurt? Has someone threatened you?'

Shaking his head, Alfie stared down at his hands as though checking they were thoroughly clean, and that there were no lingering traces of Dickie Dixon's blood under his fingernails.

'Then what's the problem?' His eyes wide with fear, Eddie resisted the urge to shake Alfie. 'Talk to me,' he pleaded with him. 'If I can help you I will.'

'Eddie?'

Eddie turned his head and on seeing his wife Nancy standing in the doorway to the lounge, his heart sank. 'It's nothing,' he said, coming to stand in front of his brother and plastering a reassuring smile across his face. 'You know what he's like, he's had too much to drink and just needs to have a little chat that's all, more than likely girl trouble,' he whispered with a mock roll of his eyes.

Concern was etched across Nancy's face, and as she tried to peer around her husband to get a better glimpse of her brother-in-law, Eddie ushered her back into the lounge. 'Go on,' he said, flicking his head towards the living room. 'I won't be long, and I don't want the girls to see him like this. He's not acting like himself at the moment, and I don't want them to be frightened.'

Once his wife was out of earshot, Eddie spun back around to face his brother. 'You'd best start talking and fast,' he demanded, the smile quickly slipping from his face. 'Was it that nutter Cole? Has he done something?'

Alfie looked up. 'It was me,' he said, poking himself in the chest, his voice strained as he tried to swallow down the hard lump in his throat. 'It was all me, I...' He shook his head again as though he could barely believe what he'd done, what he was capable of. 'I killed someone.'

In that instant, Eddie's blood ran cold and as he took a large shuddering intake of breath, he collapsed back against the wall. 'No,' he said, shaking his head. 'Tell me this is some sick joke you and Cole have concocted, that it's a wind up.' Even as he said the words, Eddie knew it was no joke; just one look at his brother's pale, stricken face was enough to tell him that everything he had said was true. He closed his eyes and for several moments he breathed heavily through his nose. 'Who?' he asked, already dreading the answer, knowing full well that there would be come-backs. 'Was it Hardcastle, or one of the Tempest brothers?'

Alfie rocked back on his heels and screwing up his face he shook his head. 'No, of course not.'

Eddie let out a long breath. 'Then who was it?' he urged his brother. 'Who did you kill?'

Bringing his hands up to his face, Alfie massaged his temples, all the while shaking his head. 'I can't,' he cried.

Fast on his way to losing his patience, Eddie bounded forward and shoving his brother up against the front door, he pulled back his meaty fist. 'You've brought this trouble to my home so you had best start talking,' he growled. 'Because as I've already stated, I am seriously not in the mood for this.'

Alfie squeezed his eyes shut tight in preparation for the punch that he knew was coming. 'It was Dickie Dixon.'

Eddie narrowed his eyes and as he dropped his hand, he took a step away. 'Who the fuck is Dickie Dixon when he's at home?'

* * *

As Tracey sat at her kitchen table, she gulped down a mouthful of wine. Not for one single moment had she suspected that the nice young man Patricia had brought to her house could be so vindictive, so evil. From what she knew of Raymond now, Patricia's earlier choice of words, that Raymond was a wrong'un, were pretty much spot on. To her shame, Tracey had even defended Raymond when her sons had accused him of being a nasty piece of work. It just went to show that you should never judge a book by its cover, that anyone and everyone had the means of being deceitful, especially when they were trying to pull the wool over your eyes.

The grievance Raymond held against her sons and even Max for that matter was so unfounded that Tracey struggled to get her head around it all. Ricky and Jamie hadn't even known that Raymond was their brother and as for Max, he hadn't murdered

Terry, it had been Kenny who had orchestrated the execution, and it had been Kenny who had spewed his wicked, spiteful lies into both Raymond and Patricia's ears. Not content with ruining her and the boys lives, he also wanted to ruin Raymond's and Patricia's lives too.

'I believed him.' Patricia sniffed. 'I mean, he was Terry's best friend, why would I have doubted him? And when he told me that Terry suspected Jamie wasn't his son, well' – she gave a small shrug, knowing full well that her explanation wasn't going to cut it with her daughter-in-law – 'I fell for his lies.'

Tracey's expression hardened, her eyes flashing dangerously. 'And what about me?' she all but screamed. 'I was Terry's wife; it should have been me you believed, not Kenny. That man murdered your son, yet you stood by him, you even visited him in prison.'

'And now I feel like an old fool.' Patricia dabbed at her watery eyes. 'I even sent him what little money I had spare so that he could buy phone cards and luxuries.' She snapped her lips closed and noisily blew her nose. 'I just wanted my Terry back, that was all,' she said, reaching out for her cigarette packet. 'I wanted to feel close to him again and Kenny was the nearest thing to my son that I had left.'

Tracey's jaw dropped. 'You had your grandsons,' she shouted in disbelief. 'You couldn't get any closer to Terry than that. It's Terry's blood that runs through their veins.'

Patricia looked down at her hands. Mascara was smeared beneath her eyes and the peroxide blonde beehive she had painstakingly backcombed to within an inch of its life resembled a bird's nest on top of her head. 'So what happens now?' she said, looking up. 'Are you going to warn Ricky and Jamie that Raymond is gunning for them?'

'I'm going to do better than that,' Tracey snarled. Realising that she'd said too much, she began to backpedal. 'Of course I'm going to tell them; what sort of mother would I be if I didn't warn them to be on their guard?'

Patricia nodded, and lighting her cigarette, she inhaled a lungful of smoke. 'What your man said' – she averted her gaze, looking everywhere but at her daughter-in-law – 'he hit the nail on the head, I suppose. I tried to be a good mother to Terry, but you know what he was like, he did what he wanted regardless of the consequences or who he hurt in the process.'

'Max had nothing to do with Terry's death.'

For a few moments, Patricia was quiet, then lifting her head, she looked Tracey in the eyes. 'Maybe you're right,' she conceded with a shrug. 'But I have to believe it was him, otherwise…'

'Otherwise you would have been spending time with Terry's actual murderer?' Tracey finished off the sentence. 'That you had gone as far as to even send him money.'

'Oh God.' Patricia held her head in her hands. 'How could I have been so stupid?' she cried.

Tracey didn't answer; what was she supposed to even say? Patricia had always been a law unto herself; she believed what she wanted to believe rather than look at the facts, and Patricia had been given the facts. Tracey knew for certain that her mother-in-law had attended court every day during Kenny's trial, just as she herself had. Hesitantly, she reached out her arm and taking Patricia's hand in hers, she gave it a gentle squeeze. 'This' – she gestured between them – 'ends today, is that understood? Because I will not allow my sons to be subjected to any more of your hate.' She looked up at the ceiling and took a deep breath, almost as though she were trying to talk herself out of what was going to come from her mouth next. 'Accept that Max didn't kill Terry and there will be a place for you in this family, or,' she said, giving a shrug, 'continue to spew your hatred and lies and I swear before God that I will wipe my hands of you.'

Patricia sniffed back her tears. The fact she had been offered an olive branch was more than she could have ever hoped for or even expected for that matter. 'And what about the boys? Will they accept me back into the family?'

Tracey gave a light laugh and as she released Patricia's hand, she picked up the wine glass and chugged back the contents. 'You're their grandmother, their blood,' she said, refilling their glasses. 'What do you think?'

* * *

Sitting in the dark with only the streetlight from directly outside his house illuminating the lounge, Eddie watched the rise and fall of his youngest brother's chest as he slept on the sofa.

Each and every noise from outside the house had him jumping up from his seat to peer through the net curtains. A large part of Eddie half expected Max to burst through the door at any given moment. The other part of him, or at least the more rational side of him, knew that Max would do no such thing, that their friendship would be enough to stop Max from kicking the door off its hinges.

As he resumed his position beside the window, Eddie briefly closed his eyes. He could barely get his head around the things Alfie had admitted to him; how he and Raymond Cole had enlisted Barry and Marc Dixon to destroy Max's car dealership, how they had then gone on to murder the brothers and their father Dickie Dixon. The mere thought that his brother had been responsible for taking a life made him feel sick to his stomach. Admittedly, he himself was no angel, but he had never harmed anyone who hadn't deserved it, let alone killed anyone, and by all accounts, the Dixons hadn't deserved their brutal, bloody ending. They had done nothing to harm or threaten his brother's life; their only crime as far as Eddie could tell was that they had loose lips and couldn't be trusted to keep quiet.

Kicking the blanket away from him, Alfie sat up and rubbed at his eyes before turning his head to look past his brother towards the window.

'There's been no sign of him,' Eddie sighed. 'But it's only a matter of time until he figures everything out. I warned you not to mess with Hardcastle, but you wouldn't listen to me.'

Alfie remained quiet and sitting forward, he rested his forearms on his knees. 'I'm sorry,' he finally answered.

Getting to his feet, Eddie looked down at his brother. 'Get some sleep and we'll talk in the morning. I need to think.'

As he wearily made his way up the stairs to his bedroom, Eddie had a sinking feeling that he wouldn't sleep no matter how much he might want to; how could he when every time he heard a car door slam shut his stomach would lurch and the tiny hairs on the back of his neck would prickle? Despite what he'd told Alfie, Max Hardcastle was coming for them, and he knew that as well as he knew his own name.

18

Tracey was a bundle of nerves, and as much as she had tried to talk herself out of it, it was the fact she had some choice words to say to Kenny that spurred her on.

Having arrived at Belmarsh Prison far earlier than she'd needed to be there, Tracey sat in her car watching as the minutes ticked by on her watch. Finally, she could put the moment off no longer and stepping out of the Audi, she locked up then made her way towards the visitors' centre. Taking her direction from the other visitors who were queueing up, Tracey waited in line to give over her identification. She half expected to be turned away; perhaps Kenny would have refused the visit, or maybe the prison staff could have somehow worked out that her intentions weren't pure. After all, Kenny had murdered her husband; shouldn't she have actually been barred from visiting him?

To her surprise, Tracey was waved through security and as she made her way towards the prison itself, she lowered her head, her high heels clip clopping across the paved path. A part of her fully expected to be called back at any given moment and told that a mistake had been made before being escorted off the property as though she were the criminal.

* * *

Tracey wasn't the only person at Belmarsh Prison. At the front of the queue, Vincent had arrived even earlier than Tracey had. His stomach was tied up in knots and he was so eager to get into the visitors' room that he could barely keep himself still.

Pacing backwards and forwards, he glanced up at the clock on the wall. 'Come on,' he hissed under his breath.

It hadn't been an easy decision to make, but in the end, Vincent had come to the conclusion that he had to be straight with Cain. That not only did he need to warn him about Kenny and the threat on his life, but he also had to break the bad news and tell him everything there was to know concerning Lucie.

He placed his hand on the door that led to the visitors' room and stared through the glass panel, his gaze searching for his brother.

'How much longer do we have to wait before we can go in?' he barked out to a prison officer.

The officer slowly lifted her head to look up at the clock. 'Five minutes.'

Vincent gritted his teeth. Five fucking minutes. He resumed pacing the floor, rehearsing in his mind what he was about to tell Cain. No matter which way he said it, he knew that he was about to break his brother's heart. He could only hope and pray that Cain wouldn't take the news as badly as he had a feeling he would. And even more than that, he hoped that his brother wouldn't kick off and end up being carted off to the block, not that he would entirely blame him if he did.

* * *

Twenty minutes later, Tracey finally made her way into the visiting area and after taking a seat on the chair she had been allocated, she nervously glanced around her.

On either side of her she could hear excited chatter and closing her eyes, Tracey tuned them out. She had to stay strong, had to keep focused on the words she intended to say.

'Tracey.'

Tracey snapped her eyes open, and as Kenny took a seat opposite her, she reeled back in the chair, the carefully thought-out speech she had prepared wiped from her mind.

'Well, this is a nice surprise, I must say.' Kenny grinned. 'I couldn't quite believe what I was hearing when I was told who was visiting me, and I thought to myself, nah that's got to be a mistake, but here you are as large as life.' He spread open his arms, the same sickening smile still plastered across his face. 'It's good to see you darling.'

Gooseflesh covered Tracey's skin and as her heartbeat began to quicken, it took everything in her power not to jump up from the seat and race out of the room. How could he smile at her as though nothing had ever happened? He'd wrecked her and her sons' lives. Surely somewhere in the bottomless pit he called a heart he must have known what he'd done to them?

'And how are the boys doing? No doubt they're getting up to all sorts of mischief.'

At the mention of her sons, something snapped inside of Tracey. Kenny had no right to enquire after Ricky and Jamie, he'd lost that privilege the very moment he'd decided to kill their father. 'Don't,' she warned, 'speak of my sons. I do not want to hear their names come out of your mouth.'

Kenny's smile froze and lounging back in the chair, he

narrowed his eyes. 'Oh, I see.' He shook his head, the malicious-ness in his eyes rushing to the fore. 'And there was me thinking this was going to be a friendly visit, that you were concerned for my welfare after that bastard Hardcastle had me fitted up for murder.'

Tracey's jaw dropped. 'You weren't fitted up; you murdered Terry, and you pimped out those poor women.'

Kenny laughed. 'And you did well out of it, just you remember that,' he said, tapping the side of his nose. 'Terry gave you every-thing you could have ever wished for, and where do you think the money came from to build that extension on the kitchen? I'll tell you exactly where it came from, the tarts, that's where.' He crossed his arms over his chest. 'Not that it had anything to do with me,' he said craftily. 'Right from the off I told Terry that I didn't want any part of it, but he wouldn't listen to a word I said. Why else do you think he brought in the Murphy family? They were his business partners, not mine.'

Tracey's mouth suddenly became dry. She felt sick to her stom-ach. She'd been so proud of her state-of-the-art kitchen, and to know it had been bought from the immoral earnings of the women she had helped to rescue was enough for her to want to tear it down with her bare hands. 'I don't believe you,' she cried.

Kenny shrugged. 'Believe what you want to believe darling.' He made to get up from the chair, signalling the end of their visit, when a commotion across the other side of the room stopped him dead in his tracks.

* * *

Holding his breath, Vincent awaited his brother's response. Over the course of the past few minutes Cain had become so deathly still, and his skin so pale, that Vincent was actually becoming concerned for his health.

'I know this isn't what you wanted to hear,' he said as gently as he could. 'But I thought you had a right to know.'

It was in that moment that Cain jumped to his feet, his eyes flashing dangerously. 'I'm going to kill him,' he roared. 'I'm going to tear him limb from limb.'

Aware that his brother's outburst had caught the attention of the prison officers, Vincent charged out of his seat, his arms outstretched as he made his way around the small table that separated them. 'Cain,' he said, his voice low as he made to pull his brother into his embrace in a bid to calm him down.

Shrugging his brother away from him, Cain yanked on the chair, almost pulling it free from the bolts that pinned it to the floor. 'I'm going to fucking kill him.'

Within a matter of moments, it was all over and as Cain was hauled from the room, he continued to scream and holler. 'Find him,' he continued to shout, his voice raw with emotion. 'Find the bastard and kill him.'

Left standing alone now that his visit was clearly over, Vincent dug his hands into his pockets. It went without saying that he *would* kill Raymond Cole; he owed his brother that much. He looked around him, more than aware that Cain's angry shouts had caused both prisoners and visitors alike to stop their conversations and stare in his direction. His gaze fell upon Kenny, or to be more precise, Kenny's visitor. In that instant, Vincent's eyes widened to their fullest. 'No,' he wanted to yell. No, this couldn't be happening. Why the hell was Tracey Tempest visiting Kenny?

* * *

As she watched the altercation unfold, a bolt of fear shot down the length of Tracey's spine. She may have only met him the once, but she would recognise him anywhere. It was Vincent Daly, Max's friend who owned the Soho club. A sickening thought sprang to her mind and as she turned back to look at Kenny, her breath caught in the back of her throat.

It could be no coincidence that Kenny and the man Vincent was visiting were in the same prison. Was Vincent the one who was in partnership with Kenny, and all the while he'd been hiding in plain sight like a snake in the grass?

Feeling lightheaded, she jumped out of her seat. She needed to breathe some fresh air into her lungs, and more than anything, she needed to get out of the prison. She felt suffocated, as if the walls were closing in on her. Without saying another word to Kenny, she ran from the room as fast as her high heels would allow her to. She needed to speak to Max and fast, she had to warn him that his life was in danger. Not content with destroying his businesses, she had a sinking feeling in the pit of her stomach that they were planning to kill him too.

19

After leaving the prison then being stuck in traffic for over thirty minutes, Tracey was beside herself with worry. Over and over again she had called Max's phone and he wasn't picking up. Fear engulfed her. Had he come to harm? Could he already be dead? As much as she knew she was being irrational, the fear inside of her was all too real; it consumed her very being.

Chewing on her bottom lip, she approached the turn off to where her youngest son lived and without giving the matter a second's thought, she flicked the indicator.

Minutes later, she brought the car to a screeching halt, jumped out and after rummaging around in her handbag, she found the spare key to Jamie's flat. Letting herself in through the communal door, she rushed up the stairs to the top floor. By the time she had reached the front door, she was panting for breath, not that her brain registered this fact, she was so hell bent on warning Max that everything else paled into significance.

'Jamie,' she called out as she let herself in. She rushed through the flat, glancing into the lounge and kitchen as she made her towards her son's bedroom. 'Jamie,' she continued to pant as she pushed open the door.

The sight before her was enough to make Tracey's cheeks turn crimson and as she brought her hand up to her lips, she gasped.

'For fuck's sake Mum,' Jamie shouted, his shock mirroring that of his mother's as he pulled the duvet over both himself and the blonde woman beside him in an attempt to hide their nakedness. 'Get out.'

Backing out of the room, Tracey averted her gaze. In the kitchen, she came to stand in front of the sink; she had never felt so embarrassed, and as her cheeks continued to burn she wished that the floor would open up and swallow her whole.

Bare footed, Jamie padded into the kitchen and as he pulled a T-shirt over his head, his hair was dishevelled and his cheeks almost as red as his mother's. He glanced behind him then pulled his fingers through his hair, as if trying to flatten it back into place. 'What the fuck Mum?' he cried. 'You could have at least let me know that you were going to turn up.'

Barely able to look her son in the eyes, Tracey cleared her throat. 'I think it would be best if I leave—' A movement from behind Jamie stopped Tracey mid-sentence and as she turned her head, her jaw dropped. 'Georgiana,' she gasped. 'What are you doing here?'

Georgiana Cazacu gave a shy smile. With long blonde hair and bright blue eyes, she was so tiny that she was almost dwarfed by Jamie's tall frame.

'I thought that you went home, that you went back to Romania?' Tracey asked as she looked Georgiana over. Far from being the terrified girl, her, Max, Ricky and Jamie had helped escape from the prostitution ring, Georgiana had blossomed into a beautiful young woman, not that she hadn't been beautiful before because she had, only now she looked happy and full of life, if her beaming smile was anything to go by.

'I did,' Georgiana answered in broken English, 'but' – she reached out for Jamie's hand and looked up at him as though unsure if she was pronouncing the words correctly – 'I come back for Jamie.'

Tracey lifted her eyebrows. 'Well, this is a shock,' she said, pulling out a chair and sinking on to the seat.

'Not as much as the shock I've just had,' Jamie grumbled, his cheeks still a bright shade of pink as he rubbed at the nape of his neck.

Tracey covered her face with her hands. 'I am so sorry,' she cried before looking back at Georgiana. 'If I'd have known you were here, I would never have turned up unannounced. And as for you,' she said to Jamie. 'You're a dark horse; why didn't say anything?'

Jamie shrugged and pulling out a seat for Georgiana, he pulled out a second seat for himself and sat down. 'I didn't want everyone to interfere and, seeing as Georgie,' he said, flashing Georgiana a wide smile, 'was, well you know,' he said, referring to the fact Georgiana had been trafficked into the country by Terry with the intention of pimping her out. 'I just wanted to keep it quiet, at least for a while anyway; we're still getting to know one another.'

Still unable to fully look her son in the eyes, Tracey shook her head. Going by what she'd just witnessed, they knew each other well enough. Not that she should have been surprised; she'd seen for herself that there was a spark between them, the way they had looked at one another had been testament to that. 'And is this why you've been so secretive lately? Why you've always got your head in your phone?'

Giving a sheepish grin, Jamie turned to look at Georgiana. 'Yeah.'

Tracey couldn't help but smile. Her boy was in love, she knew that much. 'You could have at least told your brother; it would have been one way to put an end to the arguments.'

Jamie shrugged again. 'It's none of his business what I get up to. Anyway,' he said, changing the subject, 'what are you doing here Mum?'

Tracey took a deep breath. 'I went to see Kenny,' she said, bracing herself for her son's reaction.

Jamie's eyes narrowed. 'Why the fuck would you do that? After what he did,' he said, his voice rising, 'to Dad, to Georgie, to the other women.'

Holding up her hand in a bid to quieten him down, Tracey sighed. 'I had to see him, I had things to say that could only be said face to face. But while I was there, I saw someone. Max introduced him to me once at a jazz club in Soho, Vincent Daly. Well, I think it was him who burnt down the car lot; he's in cahoots with Kenny, and that's not everything, they're planning to kill Max. I heard them. Not only do they want to destroy his businesses, but they also want to end his life.'

Jamie's eyes widened and, giving a nervous laugh, he shook his head. 'You're wrong Mum.'

Tracey puffed out her cheeks in annoyance. 'I am not wrong, I heard it with my own ears. We have to warn Max.' She pulled out her mobile phone. 'I've been trying to call him, to warn him, but he isn't picking up.'

Still shaking his head, Jamie placed his hand over Tracey's, forcing her to lower the phone. 'Mum,' he said as though he were speaking to a child, 'you're wrong.' He paused for a moment as if debating within himself just how much information he should give away. Finally, he spoke, his eyes never leaving his mother's face. 'It's Max and Vincent who are in partnership; they're planning to have Kenny taken out.'

Tracey gasped and as her eyes widened, she looked down at the phone in her hand. 'No,' she cried. 'No, Max would never do that.'

Jamie lifted his eyebrows, the look across his face telling Tracey everything she needed to know. It was true, and as realisation finally took hold, she slouched back in her seat, her free hand clamped across her mouth. After the situation with the cars, Max had sworn to her that he would never lie to her again. She was starting to wonder if she even knew him at all. Oh, she knew the person he portrayed himself to be – a gentleman, a man of honour – but could it be that she had never known the real Max Hardcastle, the murderer, the man who had schemed and plotted another man's death?

Sickened to her stomach, Tracey got to her feet and after kissing both Jamie and Georgiana goodbye, she left the flat with as much dignity as she could physically muster. By the time she climbed into the car, she was so angry at herself for allowing yet another man to steal her heart and ultimately crush it, that all she wanted to do was scream in frustration.

* * *

As he sat at traffic lights, Max was so angry that it took everything inside of him not to smash his fists down on the steering wheel. Having just come off the phone to Vincent, he'd jumped into his car and driven at breakneck speed towards Dagenham.

Arriving at Tracey's house, he stormed down the path then banged his fist on the front door. Moments later, Tracey was in front of him, and barging his way inside, Max slammed the door shut behind him.

'What the fuck have you done?' he roared at her. 'You went to see Kenny; you went to the fucking nick.'

Tracey lifted her chin in the air. 'That's right, I did,' she snarled back at him. 'And from the sound of it, it was a good job that I did otherwise I would never have found out the truth. When were you actually going to tell me that you were planning to kill Kenny?'

In an attempt to calm himself down, Max grasped the kitchen chair for support and bowing his head, he breathed heavily through his nostrils, avoiding her question. 'Do you know what you've done?' he said, looking up, his face a mask of anger. 'There shouldn't have been any contact, at least, nothing that would link you, me or the boys back to that bastard while he was banged up, no paper trails and certainly no fucking visits that would end up incriminating any of us. You've fucked everything up,' he shouted. 'Everything.'

Tracey placed her hands on her hips. 'Isn't it enough,' she implored, 'that he'll spend the rest of his life locked up without you having to take his life?'

'No,' Max answered, his voice becoming eerily calm. 'The only thing he deserves is to die, knowing that it was me who ordered it,' he spat. 'It's because of him I spent the best part of my life banged up. Him and Terry stabbed me in the back, they betrayed me, they grassed me up.'

Her mouth falling open, Tracey took a step away. 'This was never about the women was it? It was never about saving them from a life of trafficking,' she said, shaking her head in dismay. 'All you wanted was revenge for what he'd done to you.'

Wiping his hand across his jaw, Max looked away.

'Was it?' Tracey yelled.

Momentarily closing his eyes, Max sighed. 'Of course it was about the women,' he answered. 'My mum was forced to sell her body; do you really think that I would just stand by and let that happen to other innocent women?'

Still shaking her head, Tracey screwed up her face. 'But most of all this was about you and how hard done by you were. This is your retribution.'

When Max didn't answer, Tracey let out a bitter laugh. 'Get out,' she hissed.

Max didn't move and lifting his eyebrows, he stared at her in disbelief.

'I said get out.'

'You're actually going to throw me out?' Max's grey eyes were hard.

For the briefest of moments, Tracey faltered. 'That's right, I am. Get out of my house.'

Max gave an incredulous laugh and shaking his head, he held up his hands. 'I'm going,' he said, striding towards the door. 'I don't need to listen to this.'

Once he was in his car, Max gave the house one final glance before pulling out his phone and scrolling down to Vincent's contact details. All along, Vincent had warned him that sooner or later Kenny would cause him problems, that he wouldn't do his time quietly, that there would be comebacks, but being the stupid, stubborn fool that he was, he'd ignored the warnings, and now look at the upshot. Not only had his business been destroyed, but Cain's life was also in danger and if that wasn't bad enough, he'd also lost the only woman he had ever wanted to actually settle down with. He pressed dial and brought the device up to his ear. 'This ends today,' he growled into the phone. He didn't wait for Vincent to reply and ending the call, he started the ignition then sped away from the kerb.

20

For the first time since he had owned the Soho club, Vincent had instructed his staff that the venue would be closed for the night. Not that this meant he wouldn't be there, because he would, only for what they had planned out, he didn't want any witnesses, at least none who would state that they had seen Raymond Cole or Alfie Winters on the premises.

'Are you sure about this?' Vincent asked Max as he watched him pull on his jacket. 'You do realise that there's going to be comebacks. The minute you nab Alfie Winters there'll be a war on the cards.'

Max paused, his expression hard. 'Are you having doubts?'

'Not on your fucking life,' Vincent bit back. He held up his hands. 'I'm just giving you the chance of an out if you want one.'

'What do you think?' Max retorted. 'Those bastards have done everything in their power to destroy me. Do you really think that I'm just going to stand by and do nothing?'

Vincent shook his head. He knew Max well enough to know that it wasn't in his nature to allow people to mug him off.

They made their way through the club to where Vincent's

younger brothers and Ricky and Jamie were waiting for them in the foyer.

'Are those cameras switched off?' Vincent asked as he flicked his head towards the camera pointing down on the reception area.

'Every single one disconnected,' Caleb answered.

'Right then,' Max said. 'We'll start at The Ship and Anchor, and I'll take these two with me,' he said, gesturing towards Ricky and Jamie.

Nodding, Vincent slipped his hand into his pocket and pulled out his car keys. 'And keep your eyes peeled,' he instructed. 'The last thing we want is for Cole and Winters to give us the slip.'

* * *

Once they were seated in his car, Max started the ignition and as he watched Vincent pull out onto the road up ahead of him, he turned his head.

'How's your mum?' he asked. 'I was going to call her but after...' He swallowed then tapped his fingers against the steering wheel. 'Well let's just say that I didn't think she'd pick up.'

Ricky and Jamie shared a surreptitious glance.

'She's okay,' Jamie volunteered. 'The last I heard from her she was going to go and see Kayla.' He nodded towards his brother. 'They'll more than likely be on their second bottle of wine by now,' he said as a joke.

'Good.' Turning back in his seat, Max flicked the indicator and pulled out onto the road, his movements stiff. For a few moments he was quiet before giving an agitated sigh. 'How the fuck did your mum come up with the idea that Vincent was planning to kill me?'

'You know what she's like,' Ricky answered.

'I know that she's too feisty for her own good.'

'Yeah, well, at least she didn't try to swing for you,' Jamie said, meeting Max's eyes in the rear-view mirror. 'So you couldn't have pissed her off that much.'

'Yeah, there is that.' Max smiled. He cleared his throat, the smile slipping from his face. 'Raymond,' he said, glancing across to Ricky. 'You do realise that he's going down, that this isn't a game.'

'Yeah, and?'

Max turned his attention back to the road. 'Whether you like it or not, he is your brother.'

'He ain't no brother of mine,' Jamie quipped from the back seat.

Max glanced back to Ricky. 'Is the feeling mutual?'

Ricky paused.

Gripping on to the steering wheel, Max sighed. 'Because if there is even a tiny part of you that doesn't want this then you need to get out. I can't have any last-minute ditch attempts to save him. It's not going to happen, do you understand what I'm telling you?'

'Bruv.' Sitting forward, Jamie stared at the back of his brother's head. 'He isn't our brother, not really. Dad shagged his mum, that's about the crux of it. We're never going to sit around the table eating Sunday lunch together or go out for a drink, or even spend Christmas together. He's no one to us.'

Ricky nodded. 'Yeah, he's right,' he said, jerking his head behind him.

'So you don't want an out?' Max asked, taking his eyes off the road.

'Nah.' Shifting his weight to make himself more comfortable, Ricky shook his head. 'Do whatever the fuck you want to him, he's no one to me.'

As much as Max didn't want to hear it, there was a slight note of trepidation in Ricky's voice and out of the two brothers it was Ricky who was worrying him the most. When the shit hit the fan, which it would, he had a sinking feeling that Ricky would be the one to hold back, that despite his agreement to end Cole he would try to step in and save his half-brother's life.

Tracey was drowning her sorrows and as she sat on her eldest son's sofa with her legs tucked underneath her, she sipped at a glass of wine. She still couldn't believe that she'd actually thrown Max out of the house, and more to the point that she'd done so in Kenny's honour. Why should she care if Kenny lived or died? He certainly hadn't given two hoots when he'd murdered Terry.

'Be honest with me; was I in the wrong?' she asked. 'I mean, would it really be so bad if Kenny died?'

Kayla paused and giving a large sigh, she dragged her index finger up and down the wine glass, smearing the beads of condensation into oblivion. 'I'm probably the wrong person to ask,' she finally answered. 'But what I do know is that I've watched my husband suffer. Ricky beat himself up, wondering if he could have done more to save Terry's life. And as for my little boy, he was traumatised by what he witnessed, he still is to a certain degree.'

'So I was in the wrong?' Tracey's forehead furrowed. 'You think that I should have turned a blind eye.'

Getting to her feet to answer the knock at the front door, the glass of wine still in her hand, Kayla gave a gentle smile. 'You did what you thought was right, and if Max doesn't understand that then...' She lifted her shoulders, leaving the rest of the sentence to go unsaid.

Tracey nodded and staring down at the glass in her hand, she sighed. She felt as though she had the weight of the world on her shoulders and, if anything, her visit with Kenny had left her feeling even more depressed rather than giving her the fresh start she'd hoped for.

The sound of the front door opening followed by the unmistakable noise of a glass smashing broke Tracey's reverie and scrambling up from the sofa, she placed her own glass on the coffee table. 'Are you okay darling?' she called out to her daughter-in-law.

Seconds later, a terrified Kayla, followed by Raymond, who held a knife to her throat, entered the lounge.

'Oh, this just gets better and better,' Raymond laughed on seeing Tracey as he roughly shoved Kayla into the room. 'Now I can really fuck up both of your sons.'

21

Despite his concerns, Eddie had decided the best way to deal with the situation was to carry on as usual. Why do anything to make Max even more suspicious of them? After all, a break from their routine would be the first indication that something was amiss, that they were hiding something.

Picking up his brandy glass, he watched his youngest brother out of the corner of his eye. To his dismay, Alfie's sombre mood hadn't lasted long and he was in fact back to his usual chip-on-the-shoulder self. Whether that was a good sign or a bad sign, Eddie had no idea, the only thing he did know was that his brother now had a taste for blood. He'd taken a life, and Eddie had a nasty suspicion that given half the chance he would kill again.

'What's he so happy about?' As he sidled up beside his elder brother, Charlie jerked his thumb in Alfie's direction. 'Makes a change to see him actually smile for once.'

'Fuck knows,' Eddie answered as he took a swig of his drink. 'But at least that nutter Cole hasn't shown his face in here tonight.'

Charlie was thoughtful for a moment. 'He's going to bring Alfie down; you know that don't you? He's bad news.'

Eddie nodded. In his mind, Raymond Cole had already led Alfie astray and nothing he or Charlie said was ever going to change that fact.

* * *

Pulling up outside the pub, Max rolled down the car window and as Vincent walked towards him, he studied his surroundings.

'So what's the plan?' Vincent asked as he glanced over his shoulder to the pub. 'We can't just bowl in there mob-handed; it would draw too much attention to us.'

Max turned to look at Ricky. 'Go and have a butcher's,' he said. 'And see if they are inside.'

Ricky jumped out of the car and as Max watched him go, Jamie sat forward and rested his forearms on the front seats. 'You're going to have to watch him,' he said quietly. 'When it comes down to it, he's going to falter. Cole was my dad's son, and Ricky won't be able to kill him.'

Max already knew this; he'd heard for himself the hesitation in Ricky's voice. 'Then do me a favour; when it comes to it, get him out of the way.'

'Yeah, I will do,' Jamie agreed.

Moments later, Ricky walked back towards them. 'Alfie Winters is in there,' he said, jumping back into the car.

'And what about Cole?' Jamie asked.

Ricky shook his head. 'Nah, he wasn't there.'

'Right then,' Max said, rubbing his hands together. 'We sit and wait for the bastard and the minute he steps outside, we grab him.'

'And what if there are any witnesses? They could phone the old bill.'

Max gave a small laugh and as he turned to look at Jamie, he lifted his eyebrows. 'Do you really think anyone would call the filth? I'm infamous around here, and that lot in there,' he said, stabbing his finger in the direction of the pub, 'know exactly what I'm capable of; the majority of them still give me a wide berth. Trust me, they'll turn a blind eye. One of the first rules when it comes to surviving around here is to keep your nose out of other people's business.'

* * *

By the end of the evening, Eddie swayed slightly on his feet. Thankfully there had been no sign of either Raymond Cole or Max Hardcastle, a result as far as he was concerned.

Chugging back the remainder of his brandy, he called out to his brothers, 'Are we ready for the off?'

Both Charlie and Alfie nodded and setting their own glasses on the bar, they walked unsteadily towards the door.

'It was good to have you out with us tonight,' Eddie slurred as he slung his arm around Alfie's shoulders. 'It was just like old times when we used to go out for a drink without that lunatic Cole being around.'

'Yeah,' Charlie agreed. 'Where is he anyway?'

Alfie smirked. 'He had some business to deal with.'

'Ooh business,' Charlie chuckled as he bumped into Eddie. 'What with all that money he's supposedly coming into.'

Alfie's expression hardened. 'He is.'

'Yeah right.' Charlie rolled his eyes. 'And pigs might fly.' He shook his head as he studied his brother. 'You're gullible, that's your trouble, because if Cole thinks he's going to get his hands on Terry Tempest's money, then he's got another think coming.'

They pushed open the doors and stepped outside into the car park.

'Who fancies a kebab?' Eddie asked as he pulled up the collar of his coat.

'Yeah.' Charlie rubbed his hand over his stomach. 'That would go down a—'

Before he could finish the sentence, a swarm of bodies rushed into them and as fists began to fly Charlie was so stunned by the blow to the back of his head that he was seeing double.

'What's going on?' Eddie yelled as he was physically held back despite his best efforts to break free.

'Do yourself a favour and shut the fuck up,' Max growled. 'This is between me and him,' he said, motioning towards Alfie.

A combination of both fear and anger registered across Eddie's face and as his youngest brother was dragged kicking and screaming towards the awaiting car, he punched out in a desperate attempt to reach him. His voice hoarse, he continued to scream. 'You wanted a war?' he roared, stabbing a stiff finger in Max's direction. 'Then you've got one, do you hear me? Touch one hair on my brother's head and I swear to God, I will end you; I will fuck you up so fucking bad that you'll be finished.'

Max's face was white with anger. 'Then so fucking be it,' he answered before climbing into his car and starting the ignition. 'Because he brought all of this on himself; no one forced him to try and destroy me.'

'The fucker,' Jamie hissed from the back seat as he swiped away a trickle of blood from his lip. 'The bastard caught me.'

Turning to look over his shoulder, Ricky laughed. 'Stop being such a wuss, there's hardly anything there. Mason could have done more damage than that and he's five.'

'Yeah, well.' Jamie inspected the blood on his finger before wiping his hand down the side of his jeans. 'The fucker still managed to get me.'

Ricky turned back to face the windscreen and pulling out his mobile phone, a message flashed up on the screen. It was from Kayla and without even opening the text, he slipped the device back into his pocket. 'What about Cole?' he asked.

Max gave a half laugh and as he turned the steering wheel, the muscles across his forearms were taut. 'Don't worry,' he said, looking up at the rear-view mirror to check they weren't being followed. 'We'll find him, and trust me, once I've finished with him, he'll be squealing like a fucking pig.'

* * *

Eddie was so distraught that he held his head in his hands and sobbed like a baby. He couldn't believe what had just taken place; it had all happened so fast that he hadn't even seen the men approach, nor had he ever felt so helpless.

Getting to his feet, Charlie rubbed at the back of his head, his face pale and his eyes wide. 'They're going to kill him,' he choked out.

The fear inside of Eddie intensified and as his heartrate began to quicken, he took out his mobile phone. In desperation, he stabbed at the keys then brought the device up to his ear. Just as he'd expected it would, the call rang off. It had been a long shot he knew but he'd had to try. He needed to talk to Max. Just maybe he'd be able to smooth the situation over; he'd even beg if he had to. In fact, he'd do anything if it meant saving his brother's life.

* * *

Tracey's eyes were wide and as she tucked Kayla in beside her, she warily eyed the knife in Raymond's hand. 'You don't want to do something silly,' she pleaded with him. 'This isn't the answer.'

Raymond chuckled. 'And what is the answer, eh?'

Swallowing deeply, Tracey tore her eyes away from the knife to look at Raymond's face. 'We're family now…'

'Family,' Raymond roared. 'You ain't my family; my dad was the only family I ever had and even he didn't want me. No.' His eyes flashed dangerously. 'The only family he wanted was his precious sons,' he mocked. 'Well I'm going to fuck them up, starting with you two. They took my dad away from me; it's all because of them that my dad didn't want me.'

The madness in Raymond's eyes was enough to terrify Tracey and as Kayla's body trembled beside her, she tried again. 'You don't have to do this.'

'Shut the fuck up,' Raymond screamed as he lunged towards them.

'Okay, okay,' Tracey cried as she squeezed her eyes shut and braced herself for his onslaught. 'We'll keep quiet, I promise, just please don't hurt us.'

Satisfied, Raymond began to pace the floor. In his free hand he held Kayla's mobile phone and as his fingers flew over the keys, he typed out another message to Ricky, all the while giving a maniacal chuckle. 'Imagine his face,' he laughed, 'when he realises that it was me who killed his whore of a mother and wife.'

Beside her, Kayla began to cry and as Tracey pulled her even closer, her daughter-in-law whispered in her ear. 'Mason,' she sobbed. 'My baby is upstairs.'

Tracey's blood ran cold and as her eyes automatically went to the ceiling, her ears strained to listen for any movement coming from her grandson's bedroom. Please no, she silently prayed. Please don't let Mason wake up.

22

Strapped to a chair in the middle of the club's basement, Alfie Winters had become subdued. It was only the scowl plastered across his face that gave any kind of a hint to the fact he took great displeasure in being held captive.

Max rolled up his sleeves and as he stalked towards Alfie, his expression was one of loathing. 'Where's Cole?' he asked through clenched teeth.

Alfie looked up, his eyes flashing with malice. 'How the fuck should I know?'

It wasn't the answer Max wanted and as his fist shot out, he caught Alfie on the jaw. 'I'll ask you again,' he said, his voice rising. 'Where is Cole?'

As he opened and closed his mouth as though accessing the damage caused, Alfie remained quiet, his eyes narrowed into slits as he warily watched Max stalk around him.

Max's fist shot out again, this time catching Alfie just above his abdomen. 'I am really beginning to lose my patience,' he snarled. 'And trust me, you don't want that. Where is he?'

Gasping for breath, Alfie shook his head, the hint of a smirk still playing out across his lips. 'Fuck you.'

It was the worst thing Alfie could have said and as Max began laying into him, his fists flew out in rapid succession. The grunts that escaped from Alfie's lips were loud and harrowing, not that those who stood by watching the spectacle were willing to lift a finger to help him out.

After several minutes had passed, Max gripped Alfie by the jaw and yanked his head up so that he could look at him. Already Alfie's face was beginning to swell, one eye swollen shut, the other so bloodshot that the entire eye was red. 'Where is he?'

Alfie's lips opened, his teeth coated in blood, his equally blood shot eye turning to look in the direction of Ricky.

The hairs on the back of Max's neck prickled and as he too turned to look at Ricky, his face paled. 'Where's Kayla?'

Ricky's eyes widened, the panic that began to engulf him clearly visible. 'She's at home with Mum,' he answered, the words tumbling out of his mouth in a rush.

Max snapped his head back to Alfie, his grip on his jaw tightening. 'Is that where he is?' he screamed in his face.

Alfie closed his eyes, or at least he closed his good eye.

It was all the confirmation Max needed and as he threw Alfie away from him, he jerked his head towards Vincent. 'He's all fucking yours,' he snarled as he charged out of the basement with Ricky and Jamie hot on his heels.

* * *

As they tore through the club, Ricky pulled out his mobile phone. Hastily he brought up his text messages. 'The cunt,' he roared as a wave of nausea washed over him. 'He's got Mum and Kayla.' He shoved the phone into Jamie's hands. 'I'm going to kill him.'

Max didn't answer. He was so preoccupied with unlocking the car and calculating how long it would take for them to get from London to Dagenham that he could think of nothing else; if truth be told, he didn't want to think of anything else; the alternative of what could happen before they arrived was too much to even bear thinking about.

Standing on her daughter-in-law's doorstep, Patricia lifted the letter box and peered through the opening before allowing it to fall back down with a clatter and tapping her knuckles on the PVC door. When she received no answer, she chewed on the inside of her cheek and glanced towards the upstairs windows. Coming to the conclusion that no one was home, she made her way down the path. At the gate, she turned to look in the direction of her eldest grandson's home, just a short five-minute walk away. Bugger it, she decided as she set off towards Ricky's home. Seeing as she had some bridges to build, she may as well make a start and pay Kayla and her great-grandson a visit.

A few minutes later, Patricia turned into Ricky's road and patting her blonde beehive into place, she smiled, a spring in her step. Perhaps she should have brought Mason some sweets. Coming to a halt, she looked behind her to where the local shops were situated. No, she decided as she carried on walking, it was getting late and Mason was bound to be in bed asleep. She would give him some money instead; she had some loose change some-where at the bottom of her handbag.

* * *

At the sound of knocking on the front door, Kayla's eyes widened, her back becoming ramrod straight and grasping Tracey's hand tighter, she turned her fearful gaze to Raymond.

'Who's that?' Raymond hissed. With the knife still pointing towards the women, he edged towards the lounge door and shot a glance down the hallway. 'Who the fuck is it?' he growled as he stepped back into the lounge.

'I don't know,' Kayla cried, her body inadvertently shaking.

The knocking on the front door became louder and as the letterbox lifted, Patricia's voice filtered through to the lounge.

'Kayla,' Patricia called out. 'Are you in, darling?'

Raymond screwed up his face, and as his lips curled into a snarl he waved the knife in the air. 'Get rid of her.' He cocked his head to one side, a smirk creasing his face. 'No, better still.' He backed out of the lounge. 'Don't move,' he warned. 'Otherwise, I'll kill you.'

The front door opened and seeing this as their chance to escape, Tracey shouted at the top of her lungs, 'Run Pat, he's got a...' On hearing Patricia scream, followed by the slamming of the front door, the words died in Tracey's throat. Desperately, she looked around her for a weapon and remembering the baseball bat her son kept behind the television, she darted across the room and pulled it out from its hiding place.

Shock resonated across Patricia's face and as she was shoved into the room, she clutched at her arm; blood seeped through her fingers. 'He stabbed me,' she gasped, her voice a lot higher than usual. 'He's fucking stabbed me.'

Tracey took one look at the blood coating her mother-in-law's hand and lifted the bat in the air. 'Stay away from us,' she warned, breathing heavily. 'Believe me, I'm not scared to use this.'

Raymond began to laugh, a huge belly laugh that almost had him doubled over, and wiping the tears from his eyes, he moved towards them, the knife in his fist glistening underneath the light. 'Do you really think you can take me down?'

'No, but I will.' From behind him, Ricky's gruff voice was loud and as his fist shot out, all it took was one punch to knock Raymond off his feet. 'That's my wife and my mum you're threatening,' he continued to roar as he pummelled his fists into Raymond's face, head and torso before kicking out with his heavy boots. The sound of bone splintering spurred Ricky on, and it was only the screams that came from his wife that finally made him pause for breath.

'Stop,' Kayla sobbed, pulling on his arm. 'Please darling, stop, you're scaring me.'

Ricky ran his hand through his hair and breathed heavily. Pulling his wife into his arms, he was barely aware of Jamie dragging their half-brother out of the house. He didn't even know if Raymond was dead or alive, not that he cared either way. As far as he was concerned, Raymond was the epitome of evil and the quicker they got shot of him the better, they could even dump his body in a ditch for all he was bothered; it was nothing less than the bastard deserved.

Tears slipped down Tracey's cheeks and as she brought her hands up to her face, she took a large shuddering intake of breath. They had been so close to being harmed, perhaps even murdered, and all because Raymond had wanted revenge. The only person Raymond should have taken his rage out on was his father. Terry was the one who should have been made accountable for his actions, he was the one who'd denied Raymond a family.

As for little Mason, the mere thought of what could have happened to her grandson if he'd have woken and taken it upon himself to investigate the screams and shouts coming from the lounge, didn't bear thinking about. There was no doubt in Tracey's mind that Raymond would have hurt him too.

Strong arms engulfed her. She didn't need to open her eyes to know that it was Max; she would know his embrace anywhere. The scent of his citrus aftershave filled her nostrils; it was somewhat comforting and made her feel safe.

'I'm so sorry, darling,' he whispered into her hair. 'I wasn't up front with you and I should have been.'

Tracey could hear the emotion in Max's voice and as she opened her eyes, she looked up at him. 'No, I'm the one who's sorry,' she choked out, fresh tears welling in her eyes, 'I should never have thrown you out of the house, I should never have put Kenny first. That man doesn't deserve my sympathy; he tore my sons lives apart.'

'Are you hurt?' Holding her at arms-length, Max looked her over, his hands roaming over her shoulders and arms, checking for any injuries.

Tracey shook her head. 'He didn't touch me.' She glanced across to Patricia and winced as she took in the blood that stained her mother-in-law's coat sleeve. 'Pat bore the brunt of his anger; she might need a couple of stitches.'

Max nodded and closing his eyes, he pulled Tracey back into his arms. 'You might drive me up the wall sometimes, but I fucking love you and when I thought that you were in danger, that you could have been...' He shook his head, unable to say the words out loud.

'I'm safe.' Despite the seriousness of the situation, Tracey couldn't help but smile and as she rested her head against Max's chest, she breathed him in, safe in the knowledge that he loved her and that would never let her come to harm. 'And as much as you might drive me nuts at times, I love you too.'

* * *

In Belmarsh Prison, Kenny leant against the door frame of his cell. A smirk creased his face as he silently observed Cain Daly's cell just a few doors down from his. Hidden behind his back, he held a makeshift weapon, the blade sharp and more than capable of causing some serious damage, which was just as well considering he didn't intend to leave Daly's cell until the bastard's life had been extinguished.

His smirk grew as he watched the bent screw Simon Peters make his way along the landing. They locked eyes and Kenny gave a slight nod of his head.

Simon Peters reciprocated the nod and using this as his cue, Kenny pushed himself away from the door; he'd barely walked more than two paces when a figure crashed into him.

Kenny's eyes widened and as he stumbled forward, he hastily managed to regain his balance, his fist instinctively clenching into a tight ball.

Considering his slight frame, the man was strong, far stronger than Kenny had ever given him credit for.

'Fuck off,' Kenny barked out.

Albert Nowak's expression was one of pure hatred and as he lifted the metal can that still held lingering traces of rotting tuna, his hard eyes bore into Kenny's. 'My daughter,' he spat with such conviction that spittle sprayed over Kenny's face. 'She was innocent until you ruined her, until you forced her to sell her body.'

In that instant, shock resonated across Kenny's face. He opened his mouth to answer when Albert, using the sharp lid of the can, dug it deep into Kenny's neck then proceeded to slice through the flesh and muscle.

Kenny dropped the makeshift weapon he'd been concealing, his hands automatically reaching up to clutch at the wound, not that the action was ever going to do much to help him; the damage had already been done. Thick, hot spurts of blood gushed from the gaping slit in his neck, and as Kenny's eyes bulged, his lips opened in a silent scream as his life's blood continued to coat the walls and floor in a fine red mist.

For his part, Simon Peters did as he'd been instructed and as Kenny lay dying in a pool of his own blood, he turned a blind eye, promptly spun around and wandered along the landing as though he didn't have a care in the world.

EPILOGUE

In a restaurant in South Woodford, Tracey cast her gaze across the table, her eager eyes inspecting the starched white linen table cloth, the pristine glistening glasses, and then finally the golden candelabra adorned with crystal droplets that took centre stage. Everything had to be perfect; she'd been planning the evening for so long that she was determined the occasion would be a night to remember.

'Nanny.'

Tracey turned her head and as her grandson hurtled towards her, she hugged his small frame tight.

'Look at this.' As she entered the restaurant, Kayla's eyes widened. 'It looks wonderful.' She embraced Tracey then looked around her. 'Are we the first to arrive?'

Tracey nodded and giving the table one final glance, she looked expectantly towards the door. Where was everyone? She'd specifically instructed her sons to arrive at seven, and they were already ten minutes late.

Following her mother-in-law's gaze, Kayla gave a gentle smile. 'They'll be here, don't worry.'

'Oh I know that.' Tracey flapped her hand dismissively, although she had to admit she was feeling nervous. It was the what ifs, she supposed. What if their car broke down, or what if they ended up having to work late. She reached out for a glass of wine and took a long sip, more to settle her nerves than anything else.

'I'll bloody throttle him if he lets me down.'

Kayla laughed out loud. 'Not a chance.' She winked. 'That man adores you.'

Tracey's cheeks flushed pink. Oh, she knew that he loved her, he told her often enough, but there was always that doubt, the what ifs again. Pushing the thought from her mind, she concentrated on settling Mason at the table when the door opened.

'Trust you,' Patricia grumbled, 'to pick a restaurant out in the sticks. Twenty quid it cost me to get here in a taxi.'

Rolling her eyes, Tracey turned to face her mother-in-law. 'Kayla did offer to drive you, remember.'

Patricia stuck her chin in the air. 'I wasn't ready to leave at that time.' She patted her beehive. 'I had to get myself dolled up, didn't I?'

Tracey couldn't help but laugh, and as she glanced at her watch she chewed on her bottom lip. Where the bloody hell were her boys?

* * *

In a pub just up the road from the restaurant, Max downed a glass of brandy.

'Fucking hell,' Jamie laughed. 'It must be bad.'

Max rolled his eyes and as he ordered another round of drinks, he pushed his hand into his pocket, his fingers skimming across the small velvet box there.

Like his brother had before him, Ricky sniggered. 'He's even worse than I was.'

'All right.' Holding up his hands to quieten them down, Max turned his attention to Jamie. 'You wait until it's your turn,' he said with a wink.

Jamie's skin paled. 'That ain't likely,' he retorted.

Both Ricky and Max laughed. Despite what Jamie said, it was clear to see that he was head over heels and it was only a matter of time until he got down on one knee and popped the question.

Not that Max had ever expected to find himself in the same situation. It was only sheer luck that he was still alive. If Kenny Kempton and Raymond Cole had had their way, he could very well have found himself six feet under and it wasn't from the want of them trying either. A bloody war had been on the cards, and the ending could have been so very different. As it was, lives had been erased; Kempton's and Cole's anyway. Alfie Winters had been spared his life, much to the relief of his brother Eddie. Cain was another who'd had a miraculous escape and if it hadn't been for a father seeking revenge for his daughter's death, then he too could have been a victim of Kenny's wrath.

'Come on, are we going to get a move on? Mum will be going garrity if we're late.'

Max nodded, knowing full well that it would be his guts Tracey would go for. They were celebrating the opening of his new car dealership in South Woodford; the area was affluent and he had no doubt that it would be a success.

He patted his pocket, making sure that the box was still there before glancing at his watch. They were fifteen minutes late and if it wasn't for the fact he'd needed to ask Ricky and Jamie an important question, they would have been on time, not that he expected Tracey to fully forgive him; she could be funny like that, and it was just one of the many things he loved about her.

* * *

As the restaurant door opened and Max and her sons walked though, Tracey heaved a sigh of relief. 'Where the bloody hell have you been?' she berated them.

'At the car lot,' Jamie answered. 'Where do you think we've been?'

Tracey raised her eyebrows. 'Knowing you three, the pub.'

They took their seats, and as their food was being ordered, Max felt around in his pocket and pulled out the box. Beside him, Tracey was oblivious and as she chatted away to Kayla and Georgiana, Max cleared his throat before gently nudging her in the side.

He gave a sheepish grin. 'You know what I'm like,' he said. 'I don't go in for big speeches or making an exhibition of myself. I've made mistakes in the past, plenty of them,' he said with a wry grin. 'We both have. But I want us to move forward, and this, me and you, what we have.' He gestured between them. 'I've never been more sure.'

The hairs on the back of Tracey's neck stood up on end, and she narrowed her eyes, unsure of what he was trying to say to her. Had he decided that he preferred being single, that he didn't want to settle down, that he was calling it a day on their relationship?

'But...' Placing the box in the palm of his hand, Max opened the lid to reveal a ring consisting of three diamonds: one large oval shaped diamond nestled between two smaller diamonds. 'I love you and I know in here,' he said, placing his hand above his heart, 'that you are the only woman for me, the only woman I want to spend the rest of my life with. Will you marry me?'

Tracey gasped and as her hand fluttered up to her face, she stared down at the ring.

'Go on Mum, say yes,' Jamie called out.

Tracey looked up, surprise etched across her face. 'You knew?'

'Of course they did.' Max grinned. 'I even asked for their permission.'

Tears of joy sprang to Tracey's eyes and nodding, she wrapped her arms around Max's neck. 'Of course I will,' she whispered in his ear. 'Yes.'

As he slipped the ring onto her finger amid a large cheer that went up around them, Max pulled her close. 'I'm going to make sure that you're the happiest woman alive.'

'Oh, I know you will.' Tracey grinned back. 'You already do.'

ACKNOWLEDGMENTS

A huge thank you to Boldwood Books for your continued support and belief in me.

Thank you to Joana Castro, Thanu Ranawaka Hewagey, Sammee Hart, Liz Tyler, and Sarah Warman, for your support and encouragement.

A huge thank you to the members of the NotRights book group; your support means so much to me.

Thank you to Lucie Burke for allowing me to use your name.

And finally a huge thank you to my family for listening to the endless plots and plot twists, as each novel takes shape.

MORE FROM KERRY KAYA

We hope you enjoyed reading *Revenge*. If you did, please leave a review.

If you'd like to gift a copy, this book is also available as an ebook, digital audio download and audiobook CD.

Sign up to Kerry Kaya's mailing list for news, competitions and updates on future books.

http://bit.ly/KerryKayaNewsletter

Why not explore Kerry Kaya's Carter Brothers Series?

ABOUT THE AUTHOR

Kerry Kaya is the hugely popular author of Essex-based gritty gangland thrillers with strong family dynamics. She grew up on one of the largest council estates in the UK, where she sets her novels. She also works full-time in a busy maternity department for the NHS.

Follow Kerry on social media:

 twitter.com/KerryKayaWriter
 instagram.com/kerry_kaya_writer
 facebook.com/kerry.bryant.58

PEAKY READERS

GANG LOYALTIES. DARK SECRETS.
BLOODY REVENGE.

A READER COMMUNITY FOR
GANGLAND CRIME THRILLER FANS!

DISCOVER PAGE-TURNING NOVELS
FROM YOUR FAVOURITE AUTHORS
AND MEET NEW FRIENDS.

**JOIN OUR BOOK CLUB
FACEBOOK GROUP**

BIT.LY/PEAKYREADERSFB

**SIGN UP TO OUR
NEWSLETTER**

BIT.LY/PEAKYREADERSNEWS

Boldwood

Boldwood Books is an award-winning fiction publishing company seeking out the best stories from around the world.

Find out more at www.boldwoodbooks.com

Join our reader community for brilliant books, competitions and offers!

Follow us
@BoldwoodBooks
@BookandTonic

Sign up to our weekly deals newsletter

https://bit.ly/BoldwoodBNewsletter

Printed in Great Britain
by Amazon